Rogelia's House of Magic

Also by Jamie Martinez Wood

NONFICTION

Latino Writers and Journalists (A to Z of Latino Americans)

The Enchanted Diary: A Teen's Guide to Magick and Life

The Wicca Herbal: Recipes, Magick, and Abundance

Como Te Llamas, Baby?: The Hispanic Baby Name Book

The Teen Spell Book: Magick for Young Witches

The Wicca Cookbook: Recipes, Ritual, and Lore

Rogelia's House of Magic

Jamie
Martinez Wood

DELACORTE PRESS

Copyright © 2008 by Jamie Martinez Wood

All rights reserved. Published in the United States by Delacorte Press, an imprint of Random House Children's Books, a division of Random House, Inc., New York. Originally published in hardcover by Delacorte Press in 2008.

Delacorte Press is a registered trademark and the colophon is a trademark of Random House, Inc.

Visit us on the Web! www.randomhouse.com/teens

Educators and librarians, for a variety of teaching tools, visit us at www.randomhouse.com/teachers

The Library of Congress has cataloged the hardcover edition of this work as follows:
Martinez Wood, Jamie.
Rogelia's house of magic / Jamie Martinez Wood.
p. cm.
Summary: Marina and Fern, eager to learn magic just for fun, convince Xochitl to ask her grandmother, a curandera, to teach them, and as her apprentices the three learn about casting spells, healing, and life.
ISBN: 978-0-385-73477-6 (hardcover)—
ISBN: 978-0-385-90476-6 (Gibraltar lib. ed.) [1. Magic—Fiction. 2. Healers—Fiction. 3. Extrasensory perception—Fiction. 4. Faith—Fiction. 5. Self-reliance—Fiction. 6. Hispanic Americans—Fiction. 7. California—Fiction.]
I. Title.
PZ7.M367185 Rog 2008
[Fic]—dc22   2007051588

ISBN 978-0-385-73478-3 (tr. pbk.)

Printed in the United States of America
10 9 8 7 6 5 4 3 2 1
First Trade Paperback Edition

To the women who inspired the character
of Rogelia—Nana Della and Nana Mame,
my mentors always. *Besos.*

ACKNOWLEDGMENTS

Special thanks to my editor, Claudia Gabel, for her enthusiasm, insight, guidance, and patience. Her wise direction helped make *Rogelia's House of Magic* the best it can be. My gratitude also goes out to my agent, Julie Castiglia, for believing in me from the beginning. Greece, here we come!

Kevin Wood, Julia Budd-Bredek, Alethia Kasben, Dana Wardrop, Stella Ramirez-Gollnick, Lynne Blackman, Stephanie Keefer, Charyn Gant, Carmen Gonzales, and Helena Pasquarelli offered consistent and amazing assistance and support. Thanks to Anna, Sarah, Eden, Jessica, and Kayla; to Daryl and Nila of Four Crows for the rabbit tale; Kim Koplin for her Bolsa Chica information; Elena Avila for her *curanderismo;* and Rocio Watson for her story. Great big fat hugs and wet kisses to Gina Illes for all the walks and talks that helped make Rojo's Mojo and my girls, Fern, Marina, and Xochitl, real and accessible to a world beyond my own head and heart.

Besos y abrazos para mi Cielo y Diego.

One

Marina Peralta stared out the passenger-side front window of her mother's Infiniti SUV as it pulled into the driveway of a canary yellow A-frame where her best friend, Fernanda Fuego, lived. Between the wild mix of luscious flowers in the front yard and the bright colors trimming the house, it seemed like the Fuego family used nearly every color Crayola ever invented to decorate. Marina looked longingly at the powder blue and white house next door, with its relatively boring agapanthus-filled garden. She remembered how she used to peer out its upstairs window at the eclectic neighborhood.

"I miss living here sometimes," Marina said wistfully. She twirled the ends of her long brown hair and stared reflectively at the porch swing where she and Fern had gobbled down ice cream cones nearly every summer night.

"How could you miss living in the barrio?" Marina's mother asked as she lay on the horn, causing Marina to flinch. "I worked hard to get us out of this neighborhood, and I don't want you spending any more time here than you have to."

Five years ago, Marina's mother, Rebecca, had become an instant success as a real estate agent. She uprooted the family, consisting of Marina; her younger sisters, Monica and Samantha; and their stepfather, Steve Michelson, to an upper-middle-class section of Orange Olive at the base of the prestigious Peralta Hills. For the most part, Marina liked her new neighborhood—every yard was immaculate, there was a pool in her backyard, and a gorgeous gate marked the entrance of the subdivision—but it was also kind of sterile and a little too perfect. She missed the cozy feel of her old neighborhood.

Marina twiddled the drawstrings of her khaki miniskirt and frowned at the seagull appliqué on her Hollister tank top to keep from saying anything. She didn't dare give the answer she wanted to give. The retort at the tip of her tongue would have started an argument, but at that moment, Fernanda came bounding out of her house.

"I'm ready!" Fernanda called as she ran down the bright red porch steps and across the lawn. Her curly shoulder-length auburn hair flopped playfully over her Plimsouls T-shirt, a tribute to her love of 1980s psychedelic and punk bands. She opened the car door, held on to her paisley wraparound skirt, and slid into the backseat. Immediately she kicked off her Birkenstock sandals. "Hey, Marina. Good afternoon, Mrs. Peralta."

"Hey, Fern. We've got to pick up something before we go to my house," Marina said.

"What do you need to pick up?" Fern asked, leaning forward from the backseat.

Marina twisted around and tugged one of Fern's untamed ringlets. "A chart."

Fern swatted her hand away and Marina chuckled under her breath before settling back into her seat. She had started pulling Fern's tangle of corkscrew, cinnamon-colored curls when they were in grade school. It was the one thing Marina could do to get talkative Fern to shut up. Now that they were both fifteen, Marina just did it to annoy her.

"What kind of chart?" Fern asked.

"An astrological chart," Marina's mother answered as they cruised down the streets of Orange County, California, looking for a specialty store among the historic brick storefronts. "And I need you to run in and get it for me, Marina."

"Mom!" Marina protested.

"I need to pick up the special invitation paper for your Grandpy's birthday party, and this will save me time," Marina's mother said.

Marina glared out the window, frustration clouding her big brown eyes. She hated it when her mom sent her on errands, especially when it came to goofy ones like fetching an astrology chart. What if she said something stupid and embarrassed herself? Marina twisted her hair at the nape of her neck and got one of her many silver rings caught in a knot of her unbrushed mane. Impervious to the pain, she yanked her finger free along with several long light brown strands.

"It makes me so mad every time I pass through here," Marina's mother said suddenly as she navigated a roundabout known as the Orange Circle. At the center was a circular park with a fountain, benches, and tall cypress trees. The Orange Circle was intersected by two streets, Glassell and Chapman.

"Not again," Marina moaned. She had heard her mother's rant about their family's glory days way too often. Her mother took every possible opportunity to gloat about being Spanish and yet despised anything that connected her to Mexican roots, especially the barrio. Marina didn't quite understand the difference.

Marina's mother ignored her daughter and looked in the rearview mirror at Fern. "Our Spanish ancestors, José Antonio Yorba and Juan Pablo Peralta, built a very successful ranching business with the land grant they received from the king of Spain."

"Over two hundred years ago," Marina grumbled.

"They lost all of it when California became a state," Marina's mother continued. "Then those damn gringo lawyers Chapman and Glassell stole our land."

"Here we are," Marina said in a forced lighthearted tone, pointing at a store with floor-to-ceiling windows and a large wooden sign with the words MOONLIGHT MIDWIFERY painted in dark blue calligraphy next to a crescent moon.

Marina's mother pulled into a space in front of the shop.

"Oooh, look at the crystals hanging from the trees! Come on, let's go." Fern was chomping at the bit. She dug her toes into her Birks and opened the car door.

Marina groaned softly. While she adored Fern's wild and unpredictable nature, Fern often got the two of them into trouble that Marina had to bail them out of with a combination of cleverness and false bravado. Marina liked adventures, too, as long as her mother didn't find out about them.

"I'll be back in twenty minutes," Marina's mother said. "I want you outside waiting for me."

"Okay," Marina replied as she quickly hopped out of the car.

The wind whistled through the overgrown ficus trees, whose roots buckled the brick sidewalks. Across the street a faded antique-shop window offered an ancient metal tricycle, a claw-foot tub with flowers blooming in it, and a washboard with several coats of peeling paint.

Wind chimes jingled as Fern opened the shop's front door. "This place is so cool!" she shrieked.

"You don't have to shout." Marina clutched the silver chimes to stop them ringing.

A small, yapping white poodle sniffed their shoes. Fern reached down to pet the dog's matted dreadlocks.

"Don't!" Marina pulled Fern up by the arm. "Molly's blind and deaf, with a real attitude. She'll bite you. Come on, let's go inside."

Fern frowned at the dog with regret and practically skipped inside. Marina prayed that her friend wouldn't do anything stupid or embarrassing—or both.

Large windows covered by several sun catchers served as walls for the New Age store. Etheric, angelic music filled the air. To their left, clear shelves were stacked high with tarot, divination, and meditation cards; bath salts; statues of fairies and angels; and self-help books. A circle of five or so djembe drums painted in pastel colors lined the floor in front of baskets filled with different-shaped brass bells. Tons of sparkling, jewel-toned shawls were draped over a hat tree next to a rack of relaxation CDs.

A woman with long, straight, graying brown hair stepped through a doorway covered by a colorful tapestry. She had a long nose pierced with a ring and wore a flowing ankle-length purple dress. "May I help you?" she asked.

"I'm here to pick up an astrological chart for my mom, Rebecca Peralta," Marina replied.

"I'll just be a few minutes." The woman retreated to the back of the store.

Fern began browsing through a rack of elaborately drawn fairy cards. She spun the rack to goggle at the drawings of forests, lakes, and waterfalls enchanted by a variety of elves, imps, fairies, and other elemental creatures.

Marina turned to Fern. "So we finally hired a new maid."

"Will you still have to clean your own room?" Fern inquired, picking out a card of a mermaid.

"Of course," Marina said sourly. "I'll have to scour my bathroom grout with a toothbrush to keep my cell phone. Want to hear something totally wild?"

Fern nodded as she put back the card and turned to examine the hundreds of essential oils displayed in a glass case. She pulled the door open by the attached drop crystal and selected a sample bottle of frankincense oil. She sniffed the deep resin scent and trembled with delight.

"The new maid recently came here from Mexico with her twin granddaughters," Marina said. "There was an accident on the way and one of her granddaughters was killed, but the other survived. I guess she's our age. Her name is Xochitl."

Fern glanced at Marina with concern in her eyes. "Xochitl is pronounced 'So-chee,' not 'So-chit-ley.' The 't' is silent."

"I never can pronounce Spanish correctly," Marina said distractedly. Despite the fact that her mother's family was Mexican American, the only time she ever heard anyone in her family speak Spanish was at her great-grandfather's

ninety-fourth birthday party. And when she had tried to understand what the old people were saying, her mother had
ushered her off to another room.

Fern placed the oil back in the case. "Her sister died?
That's so sad."

"I know. The maid's name is Rogelia Garcia. She's going
to stay in the room next to the garage during the week. I think
Xochitl may be living with her some of the time, since her dad
works some late nights. He works with my stepfather."

"You mean the room *in* the garage?" Fern asked with a sly
smirk. She picked up the lavender oil and took a whiff of the
camphorlike flowery smell before putting it down and closing
the case door.

"Now that they've converted it from a three-car garage to
a two-car garage, the extra space is like a big room. Mom even
put curtains on the windows. Besides, the garage is attached
to the hall, so it's kind of part of the house."

"I hate to tell you, but it's still a garage." Fern picked up a
crystal and held it to the window. The crystal caught the light
and sent rainbows dancing across the room.

Marina sighed. Fern could be such a smart-ass.

"Anyway, you should see all the stuff Rogelia has in her
room. There's the tooth of some animal, a dead butterfly, candles, crosses, crystals, and bundles of herbs hanging from the
ceiling. And she's got one of these." Marina pointed to a picture of a red heart with flames shooting out the top.

"That's a Sacred Heart," Fern replied. When Marina gave
her a questioning glance, Fern smiled, took a deep breath, and
recited in one amazingly fast string of words, "O Sacred
Heart of Jesus who said, 'Ask and you shall receive,' I beg that
by the ardent flames of love that kindle your heart you hear

my prayer, grant the graces I ask, and pour your blessings and mercy over me that I may be made worthy of your divine Sacred Heart. Amen."

Marina laughed. "What was that?"

"A Catholic prayer. Unlike you, heathen that you are, I still go to church." Fern tossed her head with a pompous air, sending her curls flapping in all directions.

"That's pretty harsh," Marina commented. "The church ostracized Mom when she divorced my first dad and married my stepfather when I was only six. What was I supposed to do? Go to church by myself?" Marina shuddered. "Besides, the Catholic Church freaks me out. They're so superstitious and rigid."

"Really? I love the ritual of it. The incense, the saints, the chanting. All those candles burning." Fern moved to a shelf and ran her finger along the spines of several books. Marina followed her.

"So what does the Sacred Heart have to do with all that other stuff I saw in Rogelia's room?" Marina persisted. Rogelia intrigued her, and she wanted to get to the bottom of this mystery.

"The Sacred Heart is a Catholic thing, but combined with the herbs and an animal tooth, I don't know. We'll definitely have to get to know this Rogelia a bit more," Fern suggested.

"That's exactly what I was thinking," Marina answered.

"Hey, check this out." Fern held up a spell book for teens, entitled *Magik for Teens*. She opened it carefully and scanned the pages. "Look, here's a spell to lessen homework."

"I thought you were a devout Catholic," Marina said, raising her eyebrows.

"I said I like the ritual part. They can keep their guilt and sacrifice. Come on, let's do a spell." Fern danced the book in front of Marina's face.

The sound of footsteps on the creaking wood floors caused Marina to spin around. The store owner stood there, observing her and Fern with beady eyes.

"Some people say giving a teen a spell book is like giving them keys to a car without teaching them how to drive." The woman watched them gravely for a moment longer; then apparently she decided they passed some test, and her mouth crinkled into a smile. Marina noticed a small blue crescent-moon tattoo on the woman's neck behind her earlobe and thought she was pretty when she smiled.

"Well, why don't you teach us some stuff, then?" Fern blurted out.

Marina stared at her in total amazement. Fern rarely thought before she spoke, but Marina was used to that, even if she didn't understand how Fern could be so straightforward at all times. Marina cared way too much about other people's opinions. Her moods and self-esteem fluctuated based on others' compliments or insults.

"I'm not the kind of teacher you need," the woman answered. "If you are interested in magic, you should find a mentor, someone who can be available for all your questions. Perhaps a *curandera*."

"What's a *curandera*?" Marina asked Fern in a low whisper.

"A folk healer," Fern whispered back. She put her hands on her hips and turned to the store owner. "Will she teach me how to do spells?"

Marina rolled her eyes.

"That's what a *curandera* does. You can call them spells, remedies, prayers, whatever you like," the woman said. "If the *curandera* chooses to accept you as an apprentice . . ." She paused and rubbed her long nose, continuing to stare at Marina and Fern with her intense gaze. "Learning magic is not something you enter into lightly. The *curandera* teaches you as much about life as she does about magic or whatever she calls it. To the *curandera,* the supernatural is not as far-fetched as the word 'magic' typically appears."

Molly the Rastafarian Poodle came screeching around the corner and skidded into the store owner's ankle. The dog was yapping her fool head off to announce the arrival of two customers, an older man and woman. The man had a ponytail and the woman wore several crystal necklaces.

"Do you know anyone who can teach us?" Fern asked briskly.

Marina's mouth fell open. She looked slightly horrified at Fern's audacity, then nervously dug through her purse for her cell phone to check the time. They should pay for the chart and go wait for her mom at the curb, Marina thought. Otherwise her mother would blast the horn until she and Fern got in the car. Then there would be at least a five-minute tirade about keeping her waiting.

"No, I'm sorry, I don't." The woman handed Marina the chart. "I'll be right back," she said, and she walked away to help the new customers.

"Buy the book, Marina," Fern pleaded. "I know you have the money. I was with you when you bought that pair of Sevens yesterday."

"Fern, I don't want it," Marina protested. She looked around to see if anyone was watching them argue. That would be humiliating.

Fern pushed the book into Marina's hands. "Come on, I'll pay you back." Fern flashed her sweetest smile.

"You always say that and you never do," Marina said tartly. She knew she was going to lose this battle. She gave in to Fern way more often than she cared to admit.

"I promise I will this time." Fern flipped open the book to the table of contents. "Wow, there's even a spell in here to boost your confidence." When Fern smiled again, Marina was caught like a fish on a hook.

The woman returned to the counter. "Well?" she asked.

Marina gave her both the chart and the *Magik for Teens* spell book. "We'll take the book, too."

Two

Xochitl Garcia lay asleep on a small bed in a tiny room next to the only other piece of furniture—a secondhand lime green dresser. In her dream, the bright blue sky shone down upon her and her twin sister, Graciela. They strolled along the cobbled streets of their hometown, Santa Anita, a little village outside of Guadalajara, Mexico. Both girls were long-legged with waist-length raven black hair, dark complexions, and thick eyelashes trimming coal black almond-shaped eyes. The only difference in their appearance was the mole on Xochitl's right cheek.

Actually, the dream was more of a memory, a memory of a terrible evening that Xochitl would never forget. Only a few short months ago, Xochitl and Graciela, along with their nana, Rogelia, left Guadalajara to join their father, Sebastian, in California. Driven by Xochitl's irresistible desire to attend an American college, her father had secured work as a floor manager at an electronics plant in California, similar to his employment at a *maquiladora* in Mexico. Sebastian Garcia left at the first of the year to investigate the area; the girls and their nana followed. Mamá would come with the younger siblings, Tano, José, Amelia, and Pepito, in a few more months. Xochitl had been eager to review the right college-track programs at the Orange County high schools. But things rarely work out exactly as planned.

In her dream memory, Xochitl recalled a wrinkled old woman sitting in front of a blanket that displayed colorfully woven cotton bracelets. "Buy one of my wishing bracelets," she said. With a mischievous sparkle in her eyes, the crone held one up for inspection. "Whatever you wish for will come true when the bracelet falls off."

"Just like magic." Graciela winked.

Xochitl laughed at her sister's enthusiasm. Graciela loved anything mysterious.

Graciela's long black hair fell over her face as she leaned down to pay the woman for two bright bracelets. Afterward, she asked Xochitl to put out her hand and tied a green and yellow bracelet around Xochitl's wrist. "For a safe journey," she said.

Xochitl tied a pink and blue bracelet around Graciela's wrist. "For a chance to go to an American college."

The dream fast-forwarded to the Tijuana airport, where Xochitl, Graciela, and Nana Rogelia got inside a delivery truck from her father's company. Most often the truck was used to transport electronic parts from the factory in Santa Ana to the factories in Mexico, but tonight it would be taking Xochitl into a whole new world.

"This will only take a couple of hours," Nana promised Xochitl and Graciela, "and then we'll be with your *papá*."

Xochitl felt excited but nervous to be going. Finally she was following her dream to go to an American college. Graciela gripped her hand reassuringly. Although she was only ten minutes older, Graciela always acted like the big sister.

In the next flash—she saw the bright lights of an on-coming van swerving into their lane. The driver of the company truck turned sharply to the left and ran over thousands of pebbles on the far left side of the road that bordered a small cliff. The driver tried to regain his position in his lane, but another fast-approaching car zoomed straight for them. He swerved back to the left and hit a bump in the road. Everyone screamed. The truck teetered on its right wheels, fell on its left side, rolled over, and plummeted into the ditch.

⌘ ⌘ ⌘

Cold fear shot through Xochitl like a bullet. She sat bolt upright in bed, dripping with sweat. Startled, she looked around the sparsely decorated room. The dream faded and reality came flooding back. She grasped the wishing bracelet on her left wrist just to make sure it was still there.

Xochitl fell back onto her bed, rolled on her tummy, and buried her face deep in her pillow. Outside her house in the Wilshire Square barrio, she could hear children laughing, women gossiping about whoever wasn't within earshot, and a

Mexican *novela* blaring from someone's television. She tried to let the noise drown out her thoughts of the accident, but it was impossible.

Xochitl jumped off the bed and wandered out of her bedroom to the living room. She didn't want to remember. It was too painful. It felt like the accident had happened yesterday, and then again, it felt like it could have happened a lifetime ago. She twisted the bracelet back and forth.

Xochitl paced in front of the shrine dedicated to La Virgen de Guadalupe, known as Our Lady of Guadalupe in English, that her father had placed prominently in the living room. She paused to glance up at the statue of the Madonna with her loving, downcast eyes. But when she received no comfort from La Virgen de Guadalupe, she bolted out the front door, hopped onto a decrepit, rusty bike that her dad had bought her at a garage sale, and pedaled as fast as her legs could carry her.

Xochitl's raven black hair whipped in the wind behind her, beating her back like a flail. She lifted her dark brown face to the late-morning sun, hoping the warm rays could pierce the coldness she felt inside. Faster and faster Xochitl rode, her breathing short and shallow. She had no idea where she was going. Wherever she ended up, Xochitl hoped that when she got there, she wouldn't be able to recall her frantic search through the creosote for her sister. She wanted to will the images away.

❊ ❊ ❊

She could still hear her own screaming when the side door burst open on impact and Graciela fell out. In her mind's eye she saw herself landing hard on her hands and knees, her skin breaking on contact with the rocky cliff and oozing blood. Clutching her legs close to her body, she rolled across thousands of shardlike stones. Scrambling over the desert floor, ripping long gashes in her knees, she found Graciela with her eyes wide open, staring unseeing into the dark night-time sky.

❀ ❀ ❀

Clutching the handlebars of her bike, Xochitl looked around as if waking up from a nightmare. She was now on a high bank of the Santa Ana River. Being here was like being in Mexico. A familiar land scorched by the sun—occasionally spotted with succulents, creeping jimsonweed, and cordgrass. Still, it was a little freaky that every time she got on a bike and rode without thinking, she ended up at this river.

As Xochitl wiped her watery eyes, she thought bitterly how if she had stayed in Mexico, Graciela might still be alive. Xochitl got off the bike, propped it up on its kickstand, and marched through tall cattails down to the river's edge. Yellow-bellied American goldfinches chirped happily in the fields of anise. A turkey vulture circled above her head with its sleek black body and ugly red face. Xochitl reached down and brushed the top of a mugwort bush. She could name most of the healing plants here—yerba buena, mountain misery, white sage—from the lessons Nana had given her and Graciela back home. She touched the tip of an aloe branch. After the accident Nana had mended Xochitl's wounds with this plant's sticky goo. But Nana couldn't do anything to save Graciela's life.

As the most trusted *curandera* in the entire state of Jalisco, Nana had treated every disease imaginable with her crazy singing and the plants she grew in her garden. Xochitl had seen people carried in on a stretcher walk out on their own after only an hour with Nana. The townsfolk called on Nana for problems of the soul and heart as well as the body. Graciela and Xochitl had been her best students, learning how to respect the life force in all things, trust in the miraculous, and believe in the power of tuning in to silence. But ever since Nana had failed to save Graciela, Xochitl didn't believe in Nana's miracles anymore.

The wind sent ripples over the river. The water was low, really low. It was barely ankle deep, and yet it was as wide as a football field. Nana said there was a dam in the San Bernardino Mountains, and this river once caused murderous floods almost every year. The river god told her this truth. Even in dry riverbeds, the river spirits still lived there. Despite her doubts about magic and mystery, Xochitl wanted to believe that the spirit of the river—the spirit of everyone or everything, for that matter—lived on after its form on earth disappeared.

If that was so, could she speak with Graciela right here, right now? Xochitl wondered. She had seen Nana speak with their dead relatives on *Dia de los Muertos*. Even during séances for people she barely knew, Nana had answered questions with information that was totally impossible for her to have known. Xochitl had seen it all. She had just never participated. And although she wasn't sure she was up to the task of speaking to someone who had died, she was desperate to talk with her sister.

First Xochitl closed her eyes and concentrated on the memory of her sister's round, dark brown face with its slightly upturned nose. Next she tried to hear Graciela's giddy voice in the wind that blew gently against her skin. The Santa Ana

River carried the sea air from the Pacific Ocean a few miles west. The sweet desert smell mixed with a faint salty scent, reminding her of family vacations to Puerto Vallarta and late-night walks on the beach with Graciela. Xochitl opened her eyes and looked around expectantly for any sign from her sister.

Xochitl chanted Graciela's name over and over again in her mind, the only part of the séance she remembered. But the minutes dragged on, and Graciela did not appear.

Xochitl shook herself free of the trance, frustrated, and instantly the wind stopped blowing, as if on command. Xochitl was so disappointed that Graciela hadn't responded to her that she prayed La Llorona the Weeping Woman would come. La Llorona, a legendary ghost woman, cries for her lost children along rivers and is rumored to steal other children. At fifteen, Xochitl probably didn't count as a child anymore. Maybe La Llorona would take her anyway. But where did she want to go? Where was home? This strange land they had moved to, or Mexico, where her choices were so limited?

Just then, Xochitl heard the laughter of two boys riding bikes along the river trail. She closed her eyes and thought of being as light as a feather in her sister's old, soft down pillow. She could feel her body becoming paper thin, and when she opened her eyes, she saw that her hands and feet were slowly fading away. By the time the boys whizzed past, Xochitl had become invisible and they didn't see her at all.

Both Xochitl and Graciela had learned this trick from their nana. While Xochitl would use her invisibility to retreat deep into herself when she was afraid or overwhelmed, Graciela had used it to play pranks on unsuspecting neighbors and deserving enemies. Although the twins had looked the same, their personalities had been quite different. Graciela had been the only one who could coax Xochitl out of her co-coon of shyness.

Xochitl waited until the boys had turned a bend that followed the winding Santa Ana River. She then concentrated on the density of her bones and the feel of the warm sun on her skin and watched her body materialize. She hopped on her bike. As she pedaled for the Peralta house, where Nana would be staying, Xochitl began to wonder. If Graciela would not speak to her from beyond, how would she ever find a place of happiness again?

Three

The night after Fern and Marina bought *Magik for Teens,* the full moon sent bluish light over the pool in the backyard of Marina's house. Fern admired the long, mysterious shadows the moonlight created and thought it was an ideal time to cast their first spell. Fern's parents were throwing another party at their house. Their Colombian parties were likely to last until the sun rose, and her mom and dad did not want her to attend. They seemed to have the idea that Fern might try some of the sangría, because she usually did. So Fern was spending the night at Marina's house.

Marina and Fern sat on the floor of Marina's bedroom, hunched over the spell book. Fern had studied it all day and had become completely enraptured by the connection magic had with nature. As a self-proclaimed environmentalist, this was a definite plus, in her opinion. Each of the four directions—north, south, east, and west—was associated with a color and an element, such as fire or air. Who knew?

The book said magic was strongest when you practiced the spell or ritual in a sacred space by honoring the four directions. Fern insisted they scour Marina's house for materials to represent the directions and their elements. They found long multicolored birthday candles and some Play-Doh, last used by Marina's five-year-old sister Samantha. They plastered the Play-Doh to the candles' bottoms to create bases for the candles to stand straight. Fern set the four multicolored candles within a circle of popcorn kernels, since corn is considered sacred.

The ceremonial circle contrasted with Marina's professionally decorated room, which featured a white four-poster bed, cotton-candy pink walls, nasty olive green and pink wallpaper, and heavy forest green curtains that were peppered with tiny pink flowers and tied back with ivory lace. Marina's mother did not let her daughter put so much as a tiny picture on her walls.

Fern was extremely grateful that her mother wasn't so strict. Fern had plastered a Colombian flag to her bedroom wall and painted a mural of a waterfall, a rain forest canopy, flowers of every color, and tons of animals, inspired by her recent trip to Sierra Nevada de Santa Marta, Colombia, where she had met all of her father's five siblings: Uncle Jacinto, the priest, whose vocation made her paternal grandmother Fuego happy beyond words; the twin bachelors, Mateo and Mario; Carlos, the barista; and her impetuous, sometimes secretive aunt Ibis.

"I don't know how you can stand sleeping in here," Fern said, bewildered. "It's like a hotel room."

"I know, it sucks," Marina agreed. "But what am I supposed

to do? The last time I pinned up a poster of Orlando Bloom, my mom ripped it down. 'Member?"

"Legolas or Will Turner," Fern sighed dreamily. "I'd take him with or without the ears."

"You're boy-crazed," Marina joked.

"And proud of it," Fern laughed.

In addition to being an environmentalist, Fern was a romantic. She believed in passionate Romeo-and-Juliet affairs, in which nothing ever came between two people's love for each other. So far she hadn't found anyone worthy of her total devotion, so she contented herself with tons of fantasy crushes on hot celebrities. She was a free spirit, which to her mattered more than being stuck to someone boring or dull.

Fern returned her attention to their candles and smiled. "Okay, let's get this started."

"Are you sure this is safe?" Marina said warily. "My mom will kill me if I get wax on anything."

"Relax, girl. I'm a natural at this."

"Just don't burn the house down, all right?"

"Where is your faith?" Fern asked. "Oh yeah, I forgot. You're a heathen."

Marina rolled her eyes and pouted. "Whatever."

Fern struck the match and the smell of sulfur filled the room. She held the flaming match to the wick of the yellow candle, which stood closest to the window and the moon's ascent into the eastern sky. She ignited a red candle in the south, a blue candle in the west, and a green candle on the northern point. She shook the match, extinguishing the flame, which had come close to her fingertips.

She struck another match and watched the flame dance

with deep appreciation before she held it to an incense stick propped in a ceramic fairy incense holder. Smoke swirled in spirals, emanating the deep, earthy scent of sandalwood.

"There are seventy-five spells here. How are we supposed to choose?" Marina said in a hesitant voice.

"You worry too much." Fern ran her fingers along the flowery images in the book. "Something will come to us," she said confidently. The grandfather clock down the hall rang out ten times.

"Be quiet," Marina whispered. "I don't want anyone to hear us."

Fern tore her eyes from the book and stared at the closed bedroom door to be sure it was shut. The back of the door was covered with a Nickelback poster, a couple of collages on eight-by-ten-inch poster paper, first-place soccer merit awards, academic certificates, and to-do lists—the only mark of personal expression in Marina's bedroom, with the exception of her Roxy sweatshirts, designer jeans, and an assortment of Abercrombie T-shirts littering the floor.

Fern looked out the window. The moonlight glowed tenderly on her face. She watched the clouds and the trees swaying softly. "Did you know today, Monday, is named for the moon, like moonday?"

"I had no idea," Marina said.

"We're getting close to the summer solstice."

"What's that?" Marina asked. She plucked the pencil from Fern's reddish brown mane and used the eraser to flip through the book.

"First day of summer is the longest day of the year. It's June twenty-first this year," Fern answered.

Marina pointed to the book with the pencil, her

multicolored, iridescent bangle bracelets clinking together. "The book says to cast spells of self-empowerment for this day."

"Great, so let's cast a spell for a magical power!" Fern clapped her hands in glee.

"I don't know." Marina twisted a strand of her silken brown hair around her forefinger. A sure sign of anxiety.

"Come on. Where's your sense of adventure?" Fern consulted the book, scanning it for instructions. "Look, we'll make a god's eye. All we need is yarn, glue, scissors, and Popsicle sticks. How can anything go wrong when we're following the rules?"

"Well, okay. My mom should have all that in Samantha's craft drawer," Marina agreed.

"Good, and we'll get some snacks while we're at it," Fern said. Whatever Marina might say negatively about her mother, she usually kept the pantry chock-full of food. Fern hopped up to her knees and pulled up the sleeves of her over-shirt, which featured an Alphonse Mucha–style girl holding a sign that read PEACE, LOVE, AND ROCK 'N' ROLL. She placed her hands palms down about a foot over the candles.

"What are you doing?" Marina asked.

"Making sure the fire doesn't spread while we're gone." Fern shook her flamelike hair. "As a fire sign, if there's one thing I can do, it's talk to fire elementals."

Fern held her hands over the fire. She flicked her fingers through the flame to see if she coud stand the heat, then held her hands steady. Fern tried to concentrate on telling the fire to keep confined while they scoped out the goods in the kitchen. She didn't really know what she was doing, but she liked the danger of it. The heat sent uncomfortable prickles racing across her palms. Part of her wanted to stop, but something made her keep her hands exactly where they were. That fire was really getting hot, though.

"Okay, Fern, that's enough," Marina said testily.

Fern smiled slyly and lowered her hands closer to the candles. She poked and prodded the flames once again, mostly for the effect, and because it hurt less than holding her hands still over the fire.

"Knock it off," Marina demanded.

"It's a test of strength to see if I can get the fire to do what I want," Fern replied calmly. "I saw a couple of guys from the neighborhood, Ruben Gomez and Salvadore Ramirez, trying it last night. Well, until Mrs. Ramirez caught them. It's kinda fun. Wanna try it?"

Marina snatched Fern's hands from the fire. "No thanks, Miss Pyro."

Fern shrugged and jumped to her feet. Her hands hurt a little, but she didn't want Marina to know. Actually, she ached to rub her hands on her skirt, but it was the cutest vintage 1960s number she got on a trip to San Francisco's Haight-Ashbury district, and she didn't want to smudge soot on it.

Marina bent over and blew out the candles.

"Why did you do that?" Fern asked.

"They're only birthday candles," Marina said impatiently, flipping back her hair. "They'll burn down before we get to the kitchen."

"Oh yeah. Oh well, come on, let's eat." Fern marched out the door and almost collided with a small, dark-skinned woman. "I'm sorry."

"No problema," the woman said with a smile. She carried two steaming mugs and wore a housedress with a blue shawl

draped over her shoulders. A single gray braid fell to the small of her back. Her deep-set brownish black eyes crinkled into slants when she smiled. Except for the laugh lines, her face was like smooth, tanned leather.

The woman reminded Fern of her aunt Ibis. In whispers of mixed disdain and awe, Fern's family had told her that Ibis was a seer and that she cured people in the ice-capped mountains where she lived. Now that Fern thought about it, Ibis wore a necklace of bright turquoise and emerald with a charm of the Virgin Mary very similar to the one this woman was wearing.

"Fern, this is our new maid, Rogelia." Marina quickly stepped into the hall and closed her bedroom door behind her. Rogelia peeked over Marina's shoulder and looked back at Fern with an inscrutable expression. Marina took a deep breath as she cautiously said, "Rogelia, this me amiguh, Fernanda."

"Fern," Fern corrected her with a warm smile. She could have corrected Marina's butchered Spanglish but let it pass. Inwardly, Fern giggled. Rogelia might be small, and as the maid, she had no authority to demand that Marina and Fern go back to bed, but she had a self-assured, commanding quality about her. She wasn't mousy like some of the maids who had worked for the Peraltas before. And Marina was so obviously in awe of Rogelia and wanted to get off on the right foot with her. Fern decided to play along. *"Mucho gusto, Doña Rogelia. Espero que usted goce su permanece aquí."*

Besides, Fern loved the soft rolling sounds of the Spanish language, the first language she had learned. It had more descriptive words for her feelings. It was satisfying to speak Spanish with someone in Marina's house for once.

"Gracias." Rogelia smiled and nodded to both girls before heading off to her bedroom in the garage.

"What did you say to her?" Marina asked curiously.

"I told her that it was nice to meet her and I hope she enjoys it here," Fern answered. It kind of annoyed Fern how much Marina's family bragged about the Spanish side of being Mexican, but they didn't speak the language. She couldn't get over how the Peraltas rejected their culture. Fern was glad she still had family in Colombia; they were proud of their nationality, and so was she. "Why don't you learn Spanish already?"

Marina gave Fern a steely glare. Then she raised her eyebrows in haughty disdain and with a toss of her golden-brown hair headed down the hallway, past the bedrooms where her sisters, Monica and Samantha, slept, to the kitchen. "You know perfectly well I took one year of Spanish."

"Then you quit," Fern reminded her.

"Yeah, well, Mr. Sandoval smoked." Marina flicked her hand backward like she was batting away a fly. "He smelled disgusting." She turned on the kitchen light.

Tiles imported from Portugal lay in intricate patterns on the walls of the kitchen, china and crystal gleamed inside polished teak cabinetry with designer cutouts, and an ornate glass lamp hung above the large butcher-block island. Fern almost laughed each time she saw another example of professional decorating in the Peralta house. It was as if having a polished look straight out of *Martha Stewart Living* magazine meant you were a person of value. It was surreal in an emotionless, mechanical sort of way.

Fern's home was a chaotic celebration of life. Plants grew wildly everywhere. Each room was painted a different color and splattered with pictures or artifacts of the places they had visited. Fern lived with her older sister, Pilar, when their parents traveled. Sometimes they took her with them. Fern had been to Spain, the mother country; Colombia (of course); Mexico, because it's a neighboring Latin country; and Greece, due to her mother's obsession with Greek mythology. Fern loved to travel and considered it quite the bonus to speak two languages.

"So you quit Spanish because the teacher smoked?" Fern asked as she looked around at the spotless stainless-steel appliances, without a single smudge. Not a dish lay out on the counter, not a thing was out of place.

Marina turned on her heel, coming almost nose to nose with Fern, who backed away. "Well, the truth is, I didn't like having to ask questions with everybody else," she said. "My mom or Grandpy should've taught me Spanish at home."

"You need to get over that someday." Fern put her hand on Marina's shoulder.

"It was embarrassing." Marina turned away. She bent down to a drawer and pulled out a few spools of yarn, scissors, a fistful of Popsicle sticks, and glue. "I mean, obviously I can get by without speaking Spanish, but still, it wouldn't suck to be able to tell the gardener I need a little space when I'm lying out at the pool."

Fern thought she should bop Marina for her arrogance, but she decided to drop it for now. "Why don't you let me teach you?"

Marina paused for a fraction of a second. However, when she spoke there was an edge to her voice, "You know, I don't even get how to conjugate verbs. And what makes a noun male or female?" Marina yanked open the fridge and grabbed a bowl of orange slices, which she handed to Fern. "And what's up with the *usted*? Why should there be a whole verb family for your elders?"

Marina strode across the kitchen and flipped on the

pantry light. The shelves were lined with food. She grabbed caramel popcorn with macadamia nuts (Fern's and her favorite snack) and two cans of Hansen's cherry vanilla creme soda. "I don't see why I have to show respect to someone like my mom if she doesn't respect me."

Fern didn't reply. What could she say? Respect for her elders had been drilled into Fern every day since her birth, like the importance of breathing. It wasn't something she could explain. Besides, something had caught Fern's eye: a Mexican *talavera* tile stuck to one of the shelves with a picture of the earth and the saying LOVE YOUR MOTHER.

Fern sighed pensively. "I wish everyone loved Mother Earth the way I do." Fern couldn't wait to register as part of the Green Party. She attended every local rally, supporting causes like stopping deforestation in South America, protesting illegal exhumation of local Indian skeletons, and planting indigenous herbs as a steward on the Bolsa Chica wetlands. It was her dream to be arrested for forming a human chain around a beached whale or for handcuffing herself to a bulldozer threatening to turn up the remains of an ancient civilization.

"That's not what the tile means," Marina said, pushing aside cans of soup in a desperate attempt to find something. "She's not so much into me loving Mother Earth as she is into drilling the idea into my head: love your mother. No matter what she does. No matter what she says. Love your mother. Let me repeat: love your mother. I'd say it's a Latina thing, but it could be cuz she's crazy."

A full minute later the door at the end of the hall opened, and Rogelia shuffled to the kitchen carrying two empty mugs. She placed the dishes in the dishwasher.

"Rogelia, do you know where the chocolate chips are?" Marina asked.

Rogelia walked to the pantry and grabbed the bag of chocolate chips, seemingly out of thin air, from a shelf directly in front of Marina. She handed the bag to her with a terse smile.

"How could I have not seen that?" Marina asked, dumb-struck.

Rogelia turned to face Fern. In a serious voice she said, "Fernanda, you are right to protect nature. It is very impor-tant that you never lose that passion." Rogelia nodded sternly, gave a wink, then shuffled back to her room. Marina and Fern looked at each other in shocked silence.

"How did she know I said anything about nature?" Fern asked. "She was still in her room."

"I have no idea," Marina said as she led the way back down the hall. "But it was totally bizarre."

"Maybe Rogelia can read minds," Fern said in a flabber-gasted whisper as she followed Marina into her bedroom.

four

Xochitl peeked through the crack of her nana's open bedroom door, which was connected to the Peraltas' house by the hall. Xochitl found if she looked though the doorway just right, she could catch a glimpse of Marina's bedroom door. She watched Fern and Marina disappear into their room. Then she silently closed the door with a sigh.

"*Las muchachas son muy amigables,*" Nana said.

"I'm sure they are very friendly, Nana." Xochitl sighed, resting her forehead on the door.

"*Marina y Fern que te serán buenas amigas,*" Nana pressed on.

Xochitl turned around and stared at Nana in exasperation. She clenched her teeth and squared her jaw. "I don't need friends."

Xochitl walked across the bedroom, batting at one of the many bunches of chamomile hanging upside down from the ceiling. Small white flowers with tiny yellow centers fluttered to the ground. Xochitl sat on the bed and gazed at the displays of her nana's impervious faith: wooden crosses, a statue of St. Jude, the flaming Sacred Heart, and images of Mary, both as the mother of Jesus and as La Virgen de Guadalupe with her hands in prayer. Several candles burned on the window ledge. Copal incense billowed out from a thurible.

How did she do it? Xochitl wanted to know. How did Nana hold on to her faith, her saints, in a time like this?

"Everyone needs friends, *mi'jita,*" Nana said as she knelt at her altar. "Who else is going to tell you when you have spinach stuck between your teeth?"

"That is so gross, Nana."

"It's true." Nana moved a crystal cluster to the back of the altar and pulled forward a dead monarch butterfly whose wings had closed. "*Ven aqui.* Come here, *mi amor,*" she said sweetly, but there was no denying the resolution in her dark brown eyes.

Xochitl shook her head. Nana was a good yet predictable woman. Xochitl could tell she was itching to give one of her little pep talks. Xochitl was not in the mood. She turned her head away, but everywhere she looked reminded her of Mexico and Graciela, and how lonely she was without her. Her eyes fell upon a vibrant rainbow-colored Huichol weaving her uncle Guillermo had made and Nana had somehow managed to hold on to despite the accident. Xochitl lowered her eyes and smoothed out the quilt. Why did her nana bring that thing?

"*Ai Díos,* must you resist everything?" Nana moaned as she stood up, her old knees crackling like a log full of sap in a fire.

She padded over to the bed, sat down next to Xochitl, and held out her hand, holding the orange-and-black butterfly.

Xochitl shuddered. "Is that the butterfly you found, after the, the . . ." Her voice trailed off. She couldn't bring herself to say it.

"After the accident, yes." Nana placed her arm around Xochitl's shoulders. "Do you remember what butterfly medicine represents?"

Xochitl shook her head. She didn't really care for any of Nana's teachings anymore. What good was it to be a *curandera* and have magical powers if you couldn't stop bad things from happening, like a family member dying right in front of you? Nana placed the butterfly in Xochitl's hand. "In the teachings of our people, butterflies represent transformation. When I was younger than you, my grandmother took me out to the fields to watch the chrysalis transform into this beautiful winged creature. This animal totem will help you make the transition from sadness to happiness."

"Can't you just whip up some remedy to bring Graciela back?" Xochitl begged. She folded her long legs beneath her.

"You know I can't do that," Nana said gently. "I work with nature, not against it."

Nana picked up a wide, flat-handled boar's-hair brush and tenderly pulled it through Xochitl's waist-length hair. Xochitl's shoulders tensed and her fingers flinched, nearly crushing the butterfly. This nightly ritual was something she used to do with Graciela. They had taken turns brushing long strokes through each other's hair. She didn't want Nana to do it now, but she couldn't seem to stop her.

Xochitl looked over at the bedside table, where dried lupine flowers from the accident scene lay next to a picture of her and Graciela standing in the river that ran behind their town.

"What about making a special concoction to make Graciela's spirit visit?" Xochitl asked.

"We can only invite spirits to come. There is no magic that can pluck Graciela from wherever she is and make her do our will," Nana said as she swept the brush through Xochitl's hair again.

"I tried to speak with Graciela at the Santa Ana River earlier today, but nothing happened," Xochitl admitted.

"Graciela will come to you when the time is right," Nana said wisely.

"When?" Xochitl croaked over the lump in her throat. The tears had swelled in her eyes.

"*¿Quien sabe?*" Nana answered. "Who knows?"

Xochitl's shoulders slouched in defeat while Nana kept brushing. Xochitl closed her eyes and remembered how Graciela had plaited her hair into two long braids before they got into the truck that would take them to their father and America, the Land of the Free.

"I know it is hard, but you can't stay sad forever. Graciela wouldn't want that. You must be strong for her," Nana persisted.

"I can't," Xochitl mumbled.

"Yes, you can. It's in your blood. When the Spanish conquered the Aztec people—your people, our people—the Aztecs kept their faith. Through the Spanish Virgin Mary and Aztec Tonanztin, a prophecy was given that the power of the people would return. From the combination of these two Great Mothers, La Virgen de Guadalupe brought hope when she first appeared with the miraculous fragrant red Castilian roses at her feet."

Nana patted Xochitl so hard on the back of the shoulder that Xochitl lurched forward. " *'Xochitlcheztal'* means 'where the flowers bloom' in the Aztec language. Your name is special and has deep meaning."

"I know, I know." Xochitl dismissed her nana with an impatient wave of her hand.

"Don't ever forget the long line of wise women you come from, Xochitl. We passed the lessons of *curanderismo* for generations. I learned from my grandmother. My grandmother was taught by her grandmother, who was taught by her grandmother, and so on, all the way to the ancient Aztec healers." Nana smiled widely, revealing a missing tooth toward the back of her mouth.

"You're always telling me stories like that," Xochitl countered.

"And I'll tell you as many times as I like until my teeth fall out," Nana retorted.

"They already are," Xochitl pointed out. "You'd better be careful before you only have gums to chew with."

Nana turned Xochitl so that they faced each other. Nana searched Xochitl's face and held her granddaughter's wavering gaze.

"I'm not interested in ancient history, Nana. I just want my sister back," Xochitl said sadly.

"I know, *mi'jita*." Nana squeezed Xochitl's hand. "I wish Graciela were here, too. But . . . *al vivo la hogaza y al muerto, la mortaja*. We must live by the living, not by the dead."

Not another dicho, Xochitl thought wearily. She wished she could shout at Nana and tell her to stop lecturing. But she didn't dare. Nana was kind but tough, and would not tolerate any disrespect.

"You have been given life, you must live. To do that

properly, you must engage." Nana patted Xochitl's chest like she was trying to wake up her heart, but Xochitl could only sigh. "Now quiet down, I am going to pray for you to find friends."

"Nana," Xochitl protested. She pulled Nana's arm to keep her from performing her ritual, but her grandmother easily broke her grip and marched to the altar.

Nana pulled out another votive candle, placed it in the center of the altar, and lit it. Xochitl watched the bright flame flicker. The *curandera* sprinkled more of the pale yellow copal resin onto the burning charcoal. The heavy, musky scent of deep magic filled the room. The air felt charged with electricity, like during a storm.

Up until three months ago, Xochitl believed in Nana's powers and her ability to defend, protect, and heal. But the loss of Graciela put a dark shadow over everything Nana had taught Xochitl. Even so, when Nana began to meditate, Xochitl closed her eyes and concentrated hard on becoming weightless. Within seconds, her skin felt flushed and her body felt like it was floating. Xochitl wasn't sure what to do now that she was invisible, but as long as she stayed this way, at least Nana wouldn't be able to see the look of doubt on her face.

Five

Marina leaned back against the footboard of her queen-sized four-poster bed and stared at the circle of candles and popcorn. She had to admire Fern's ingenuity. It really looked like a ritual was going to take place.

"What do we do first?" Marina nibbled nervously on the cuticle of her index finger.

Fern pulled Marina's finger out of her mouth. "Stop that."

"Well, what if the store owner in Moonlight Midwifery was wrong, and casting spells isn't at all the same as prayer? What if a bolt of lightning strikes us from above?" Marina glanced at the ceiling as if she expected shards of electric light to burst through any minute.

Fern burst out laughing. "You've got to be kidding! How did you get so much guilt?"

"The Catholic religion," Marina said resolutely.

"But you're not Catholic," Fern said.

"I know that," Marina retorted. "But I'm the first generation in my family to not be raised in '*the* religion,' as Grandpy would say. I think I got Catholic guilt through osmosis."

Fern stared at Marina in disbelief. "So does your brain ever turn off? I mean, how do you come up with these ideas?"

"Do you think it's possible to pass guilt like some defective gene?" Marina insisted as she toyed with the hem of her kelly green Pink sweats.

"Maybe in your case," Fern said. "Not to mention a case of insanity and runaway anxiety. When will you ever learn to trust me?"

"When you say something sensible." Marina poked Fern on the shoulder. "How is any of this going to work? We don't know what we're doing."

Sitting cross-legged, Fern teetered side to side. "I've got it all figured out. I'll cast a circle and lead the meditation. Then we raise a Cone of Power, call in the quarters, welcome Spirit, and do the spell. That's probably when we make the god's eyes. Then we eat," she added lovingly, patting the bag of caramel popcorn. "Lastly, we lower the Cone of Power, give thanks, say farewell to the quarters, and erase the circle."

"How do you know so much?" Marina was awestruck at the command Fern had over this project. She herself was never that dedicated or passionate about . . . anything.

"What do you think I was doing all day? I studied the book," Fern replied as she struck a match to relight the candles.

There was no stopping Fern now. *And anyway*, thought

Marina, *it's high time I did something without worrying about every inch of it.*

Fern stood up. With a straight arm and extended index and middle fingers, she slowly turned, drawing the circle around the room. "I now cast this circle for magic. Let this space become a world between heaven and earth."

Marina closed her eyes. She felt a jolt in her stomach, and her heart leapt to her throat. Chills chased each other up her arms.

"Imagine your body is the trunk of a tree with branches reaching to the sky and roots pushing down through the earth," Fern read, speaking in a trancelike monotone.

Marina wondered if it mattered what kind of tree. She thought of the massive five-hundred-year-old oak tree in Irvine Park. When they were kids, she and Fern had hugged the tree from opposite sides and hadn't even come close to touching each other's fingertips. The more she concentrated on being an oak tree, which seemed solid and strong to her, the more she could feel her feet stretch into roots that grew and grew through the layers of earth. Her arms became waving branches that extended through the heavens to wrap around a single star of an intricate constellation. She liked being a tree. It made her feel like no one could push her around.

"Okay," Fern whispered. "It's time to welcome the four quarters."

"What's a quarter?" Marina asked dreamily.

"Quarters represent the directions; you know, like east, west. And you need to face each direction as you welcome it."

After they took turns welcoming the four directions, Father Sky, and Mother Earth, Marina grabbed two Popsicle sticks. "I feel all tingly."

"I know," Fern agreed. "Okay, the book says to make an equilateral cross with the Popsicle sticks and glue them together at the center." After completing the first task, they cut several long strands of yarn. Following the directions, Fern showed Marina how to weave the yarn over the top of the first stick, then under the next stick. "Now we concentrate on receiving a magical power while we work," Fern said. "It's like when Native Americans say prayers as they make dream catchers."

Marina wove together shades of blue until she had completed a perfect diamond-shaped god's eye.

"Next we need to bury them in the earth and bless them by saying, 'Sun above, whose gift of light is given to me, I ask for your blessings of a magical power. This I make true, three times three, times three,' " Fern announced.

"Why three?" Marina asked.

"Three must be a magic number. You know, like 'third time's a charm'?"

"Maybe we should make three god's eyes?" Marina suggested.

"Okay," Fern agreed.

When they finished, Marina slipped into her sandals to go outside. Fern was barefoot, as usual. They collected the three god's eyes and their food, then stole down the hallway and through the immaculate kitchen. As they traipsed through the den, Marina stared at the oval sepia picture of her maternal grandmother and wondered what that mysterious woman would have thought of this ritual. Marina had never known her nana, who had died one month before Marina was born. Everyone in the family said Marina's birth was a blessing, which for someone like Marina translated into a lot of pressure to be successful and accomplished.

In this sepia photograph, Nana was four, and she looked like an angel with her tranquil expression and velvety smooth face. Marina had come to think of her nana as a legend, more surreal and imaginary than a real person. The exact same picture of Nana was on display at Marina's home, and in the homes of her aunt Carmen and Grandpy. Her mother spoke in reverential tones about Nana and her prestigious Spanish bloodline. On the other hand, no one ever spoke of Grandpy's poor family from Mexico.

Marina tore her eyes from her nana's photograph and quietly opened one of the French doors to the backyard. Behind the lush foliage and large rocks bordering the pool, she and Fern found a patch of dirt in a spot farthest from the house. The full moon had traveled past the zenith, the highest point in the sky, and crept silently toward the western horizon. The moonlight illuminated Fern and Marina as they dug into the earth.

"We should have brought shovels," Marina whined as she surveyed a broken fingernail with regret. "And look how dirty our feet are getting. I just had a pedicure!"

"You are such a princess, Marina," Fern said. "Would you concentrate, please? If you don't, it won't work."

"Fine," Marina mumbled, taking one last glance at her toes.

They placed their creations side by side in the hole. Marina marveled at their handiwork. Together they chanted three times: "Sun above, whose gift of light is given to me, I ask for your blessings of a magical power. This I make true, three times three, times three."

Satisfied, they covered the three god's eyes with dirt and patted it down. Fern tore into the popcorn and crunched loudly. Marina cracked open a soda and gulped it down. She belched loudly and smiled when Fern made a face.

"That's revolting," Fern reproached.

I'm no princess, Marina thought rebelliously as she gave an untroubled shrug. "So when do you think we'll get our powers?" she asked eagerly.

Fern leaned back and stared up at the indigo sky speckled with stars. "Dunno. I guess it depends on whether or not the stars are listening."

Marina looked up to the heavens. She concentrated with all her might on the brightest star she could find. Combined with the stars around it, it looked like the tip of a goat's tail. Marina focused all her energy on that star. With a steady gaze, she sent her wish for a magical power, and the star seemed to wink back at her. "I think they are," Marina said.

"Hope so." Fern yawned. "Come on. Let's go to bed. Magic makes you tired."

Marina nodded to the star as if she was confirming their contract. "Okay," she said to Fern and the star simultaneously. Marina placed a couple of twigs over the dirt mound that concealed their creations. She got up, shook the dirt off her sweats, and led the way back into the house.

Marina checked the stairwell to her mother and stepfather's bedroom suite to be sure they were both snoring and hadn't woken. All was safe. She and Fern crept down the hallway to Marina's bedroom. After changing into her nightgown, Marina crawled into her bed and snuggled under the covers.

"Good night, Fern," she whispered.

"Night," Fern said as she settled onto the trundle bed next to Marina.

Soon they fell fast asleep, completely forgetting to close the portal to the world of magic.

An hour or so later, Marina tossed and turned, lost in a place between consciousness and deep REM sleep. She moaned, quietly at first, but within minutes she began to hyperventilate.

Fern woke up and blinked several times, looking around groggily. "Marina?" she whispered.

"There are imps in the orange trees," Marina mumbled in a raspy voice. She tossed her head back and forth, as if she was spotting these magical creatures in a dense wood before her.

"What?" Fern asked, rubbing the sleep from her eyes.

"They were put there on purpose," Marina continued. Her voice became clearer, not so hoarse. "They agreed to come to this dark place. They say I can help. I don't think I can. I like orange trees, though. Yes, I do." She began to talk faster. "My favorite orange crates were the ones from Sunkist, where I used to work. Glad I don't have to pack them anymore. I used to get caught in the spiderwebs." Marina tried to sit up, her eyes still closed.

"Marina, are you okay?" Fern sat up in bed, concern creasing her forehead.

"They lost the land, but the markings are still on Thomas Guide maps." Marina kept talking to no one in particular. "You can still find a few orange groves here and there." Then her voice became lighter, more girlish. *"Me gusta oler las flores del naranjo,"* she said.

"You like the smell of orange blossoms?" Fern repeated, bewildered. "Hey, when did you start sleep-talking in Spanish?"

"Hace mucho frio aquí," Marina began to shiver.

"What are you talking about? It's not cold. It's probably seventy-five degrees," Fern said in a worried voice. "Wake up, Marina, this isn't funny anymore." She reached out and touched Marina's right shoulder.

Marina jerked Fern's hand off, panicking. "*¿Donde está el sol?*"

"The sun set hours ago. Marina, you're scaring me. Stop this." Fern jumped onto Marina's bed and straddled her friend. She grabbed Marina by the shoulders and shook her hard. "Marina, wake up!"

Marina started trembling violently. Her hand fluttered to her forehead. Panic gripped her heart. She screamed, "Stop them, please! Stop them! Here they come again! Ahhh!"

Rogelia burst into the room with her shawl slung haphazardly over her shoulders. Xochitl entered the room at her nana's heels.

"She's babbling in Spanish and doesn't even speak the language!" Fern yelled.

With closed eyes, Marina mumbled incoherently while she rocked back and forth. A cold terror filled her entire body. Rogelia shook Marina by the shoulders. "Wake up, Marina. Come back to us." She turned to Xochitl. Marina shook her head and began to whimper. "Xochitl, get the chamomile and the rattle. And water!"

Xochitl gave her nana a skeptical look before darting out of the room.

Rogelia caressed Marina's forehead and hair. "*Está bien.* You're going to be okay."

Voices clashed in Marina's head, like people were yelling at her, vying for her attention. She shook all over. Her toes felt like icicles.

Xochitl quickly returned to the bedroom with a handful of chamomile, a rattle, and a bowl of water, which she gave to Rogelia.

Rogelia placed the bowl under Marina's bed. She shook the rattle over Marina, broke off dried chamomile flowers, and rubbed them behind Marina's ears, on her temples, and across her forehead. Rogelia sang incomprehensible yet soothing words as she gently stroked Marina's hair. She worked on Marina for five tense minutes.

The tingly heat emanating from Rogelia's hand sent warmth spreading throughout Marina. Finally, Marina's breathing returned to normal. Her trembling gradually subsided. She took a shaky breath. She was going to be okay. She tentatively opened her eyes and looked around. She was safe in her room, and thankfully nobody was talking in her head.

What the hell was that?

"Thank you," Marina whispered, and pulled her pink and green comforter up to her chest.

"You'll be all right now." Rogelia stroked Marina's hair. "Go to sleep. *Buena suerte.* Have good dreams."

Rogelia and Xochitl left the room and closed the door behind them.

"What happened?" Marina asked Fern, her head throbbing a little.

"You spoke in Spanish," Fern said incredulously.

"I did?" Marina could only vaguely remember voices in her head. Voices that were not her own. Was she going crazy?

"Yeah. It was weird. You got all panicky," Fern said. "Then Rogelia and her granddaughter came in and Rogelia did some kick-ass witch-doctor stuff on you. God, it was *awesome!*"

"Right, awesome," Marina said weakly.

Fern plopped back down on the trundle bed. "We *definitely* need to get to know those two."

Marina stared at her closed door. Although she knew Fern was attracted to Rogelia because of her spiritual powers, Marina suddenly realized that she herself was interested in her family maid for an entirely different reason. When Rogelia caressed her head, Marina felt a pang in her heart for the grandmother she never had. The only problem was her mother. Rebecca Peralta didn't really approve of socializing with the hired help. But maybe it was finally time for Marina to worry less about her mother's ideals and figure out her own.

Six

Two days later, just after lunch on Wednesday, Fern gripped the steering wheel of Pilar Fuego's beat-up Volvo, twisting the loose leather covering back and forth. She and her sister were parked in the virtually empty lot in front of Glassell High School, waiting to begin her third test drive. Fern could pretend she was in a race car if it wasn't for the smashed pretzels and empty juice boxes littering the floor of her older sister's station wagon. Pilar's seven- and eight-year-old boys, Danny and Miguel, treated their mom's old but dependable ride like their personal trash can.

The ice cream truck tootled down Flower Street to Fern's left, blaring "La Cucaracha" over the crackling loudspeaker.

Children raced after the truck joyfully, waving their dollar bills. Fern plucked at the sleeves of her Social Distortion cap-sleeved T-shirt, giving her arms plenty of room to move freely, and adjusted her purple-tinted sunglasses low on the bridge of her nose; then she turned up the volume of KROQ, the local alternative rock station.

"Fernandita, you shouldn't drive with this many distractions." Pilar turned the music off and pushed her wavy brown hair off her angular, almost regal face. "Let's make this quick. I've got to pick up Danny and Miguel at the soccer field in an hour and run to Sports Galaxy after I drop you off at Marina's."

"Don't get one of those lame T-shirts with 'Soccer Mom' plastered over the boobs in glitter," Fern said.

"I would never," Pilar said, looking offended. At twenty-seven, and pretty as well as hip, Pilar was not ready to advertise her mommy status across her chest. She pointed to the dashboard. "Okay, I know we've been over this, but repetition is the key to learning. We're in park. Pull this stick thingy forward and down to drive and the indicator will move to 'D'. Slowly—I mean, *slowly*—take your foot off the brake pedal and press down lightly on the gas pedal."

Fern pulled the gearshift forward and down, and the car started to roll forward. "Is that the official word? 'Thingy'?"

"No, it's actually a thingamabob," Pilar said sarcastically. "But since you're only fifteen I thought I'd use a simple term. Brake!" She pointed to the cement foundation of a lamppost directly in their path.

Fern stomped both feet on the brake and they jerked to a stop. "Stop yelling. And I'm fifteen and a half. You know every month counts." Fern turned the wheel away from the cement barrier, took her foot off the brake, and carefully pushed on the gas. They inched along at about ten miles an hour, rolling over the speed bumps as smoothly as possible. "Pilar, I'm not a child, you know. I'm a big girl now."

"I suppose," Pilar muttered.

"So will you let me drive on the street?" Fern pleaded.

"All right. Just for a little bit," Pilar said. "Make a left out of the parking lot, but don't go onto Bristol Street. Just drive through the neighborhood."

Delighted, Fern made a wide turn out of the parking lot onto Flower Street, almost bumping a parked car, and made a right at a stop sign. A ball shot out between two parked cars, followed by a small boy. Fern slammed on the brakes. *Maybe the parking lot wasn't so bad after all,* she thought, watching the boy grab his ball and wave at her. She waved back weakly before proceeding.

After a few more minutes of slow, cautious driving, Fern looked sideways at her sister. She was burning to tell her about last night's ritual. Maybe she could ask her about Rogelia. "So Marina and I did some magic last night."

"You mean like with a Ouija board? You shouldn't be messing with that sort of thing," Pilar lectured in her most annoying big-sister tone.

"It wasn't like that." Fern bit the inside of her cheek to keep herself from saying anything more. She tried to back-pedal. "We lit candles, like in church. You know, for a prayer."

"You shouldn't be playing with matches, either," Pilar warned.

Fern rolled her eyes. When would Pilar get over this protector routine?

"If you forgot to put out a candle and something caught fire, I'd be in trouble." Pilar quickly spat out the words.

Fern was completely caught off guard. "*You'd* be in trouble?"

"Remember the time you dropped my curling iron on your arm?" Pilar said defensively. "Your blister was the size of a tangerine."

"I was three!" Fern exclaimed. "What did you expect?" Fern glanced over at Pilar before turning down another street.

"And I was only fifteen. How could anyone have expected me to be responsible for you then?" Pilar folded her arms over her chest in a very characteristic manner.

"I didn't ask to be the youngest in the family," Fern snapped. "No one's ever around. Mom and Dad are always out dancing or on some second honeymoon."

"Being the oldest was no picnic," Pilar retorted. "Ramon and Raymond got all the privileges since they were boys. I had to wear dresses, tights, and party shoes every day when we lived in Colombia. And you get to run around barefoot with twigs in your hair." Pilar pulled something out of Fern's tangled locks and threw it out the open window.

"Why take it out on me?" Fern turned to glare at Pilar, forgetting momentarily that she was driving a two-thousand-ton car. Without warning the road took a sharp bend to the left. Fern felt a powerful bump as the car went straight over the curb. A painful jolt shot under her rib cage, and her head whipped straight back. The car ran over the sidewalk into a low wall three bricks high, smashed hard into a chain-link fence, and settled on top of it. In immense shock, Fern watched a few grapefruits fall from the tree in front of her.

A slightly built man with a barrel chest, a large mustache, and a Caesar haircut bolted out of the house, down the asphalt driveway with grass in the cracks, and up to the broken chain-link fence. Pilar jumped out of the car and approached the man, who had begun yelling in rapid Spanish as soon as he saw all the damage. In her patent-leather knee-high boots, Pilar stood a couple of inches taller than the man.

Fern slumped over and rested her head on the steering wheel. Her arms dangled by her sides. She stared down at the fringes of her batik miniskirt as her eyes teared up. She'd never get her driver's license with an accident report before she even got her learner's permit.

"Are you okay?" a voice asked.

Fern jerked her head up. A really hot guy, probably sixteen or seventeen, with shoulder-length hair and gorgeous liquid brown eyes, was crouched outside her car, looking in her window. His long eyelashes and perfect complexion mesmerized Fern. Her heart thumped wildly against her chest as she checked out his muscular build through his white tank. Her eyes fell on the tribal-looking tattoo wrapped around his fine bicep.

"Are you hurt?" Even his voice was hot.

"No, I'm fine," Fern purred. He had long, graceful fingers. Piano fingers, her mother would have said. She wanted to reach out and touch his silky-smooth reddish brown skin, but when she stared into his eyes again, the oddest thing happened. Flickers of light flashed like several small stars around his head. The lights sparked on and off at random. It was like watching a miniature fireworks show. She whipped off her sunglasses for a better look.

The surge of loud voices caught her attention, and Fern turned to look through the windshield. Pilar and the man were shouting at each other, but to Fern's utter surprise, Xochitl stood behind the man. In the middle of all the commotion, she heard Xochitl say, *"Papá, fue un accidente.* It was an accident."

"Dad"? This was *Xochitl's* house? Fern unbuckled her seat

belt and started to get out of the car, but the hot guy was blocking her way. Not that she cared.

"I saw that you were barely moving, and—I thought . . . ," he stammered, then smiled. "My name is Tristán."

Fern watched curiously as the flickers above his head dulled, then turned into a gray light that billowed and grew. She had no idea what to make of it. Had she hit her head on the steering wheel or something?

"What's your name?" Tristán asked.

Wake up, she told herself. *Give him your name before he decides you aren't worth his time.* "Fern," she finally blurted out.

"Well, I'm really glad you're okay, Fern," Tristán said.

Fern was about to give him her best smile when to her horror, the gray cloud spread down Tristán's head and over his shoulders. Fern rubbed her eyes hard to make sure some dirt or accident debris hadn't flown into them and distorted her vision, but when she opened them, the grayness hadn't gone away.

Whatever that is, it can't be good, she thought.

"Are you sure you're okay?" Tristán asked, his chocolate brown eyes filled with concern.

Fern stared at Tristán and that ugly gray light. She usually didn't mind a little danger or the unexplained, but that gray color was so lifeless and bleak, it terrified her. When she turned and looked at the other people on the scene, everyone seemed normal. Fern was so freaked out by it that she thought it might be best to ditch him as soon as possible. She opened the car door and stepped out.

"Yes, I am," Fern said reassuringly.

Tristán momentarily touched Fern's shoulder. Prickles of white-hot electricity raced through Fern's entire body.

"Maybe I'll see you around sometime." He shuffled his feet from side to side, as if he was a little nervous.

How cute, Fern thought. At that moment the gray light began to pulse all around him. She shrank away from him. "You'll have to excuse me. I've got to talk to my sister," she said.

"Yeah, of course," Tristán said.

Fern gave him a closed-lip, semismile but then hesitated a moment to look into his beautiful eyes. *Should I give him my number?* she wondered. But then he smiled and turned to leave. Fern fell back into the car seat. As she watched Tristán walk across the street, she could see the gray cloud following him like a pending thunderstorm. Which meant Fern wouldn't be running after him, at least not today.

Before Fern could get back out of the car, Pilar was already climbing into the passenger seat. Fern leaned back as if she was expecting her big sister to rip into her.

"Everything's okay. I told Mr. Garcia that we'll pay for the damage," Pilar said soothingly. She put a hesitant but reassuring hand on Fern's shoulder. "And we'll take care of this without Mom and Dad."

With a great sigh, Fern relaxed her shoulders, which had been hunched up somewhere around her ears. "Thank you *so much,* Pilar," she said.

"You should thank that daughter of his. She's the one who calmed him down and got him to listen to me," Pilar said while searching through her pocketbook. "I'm going to write him a check, and then you're going to pay me back with cheap babysitting labor. Got that, Fern?"

"Okay," Fern said distractedly. Although she was grateful that Pilar was helping her and not chewing her out, she was really moved to hear about what Rogelia's granddaughter had done. Fern wanted to thank her, but when she looked out the window, Mr. Garcia also seemed to be searching for Xochitl, who was suddenly nowhere to be found.

That was weird. Hadn't she just been out there a second ago?

"I'll be right back," Pilar said as she ripped a check from her checkbook. "And you should get comfortable in the passenger seat."

Fern had a feeling that this test drive with Pilar might be her last, but as she looked around the neighborhood for a sign of either Xochitl or Tristán, she hoped she hadn't seen the last of them.

Seven

Moments later, Xochitl ducked down an alley around the corner from her house. The deafening sound of Fern's car crashing into their fence had reminded her of the horrible accident that had killed Graciela. Now that Xochitl was away from the mangled fence and the car sitting haphazardly on her lawn, she could begin to relax. Slowly she imagined that with each breath she was pumping her body back into the realm of visibility. The colors of her skin, clothes, and hair filled in like a magical watercolor painting until her body became solid once again.

The sun's rays beat down on Xochitl's brown skin, giving her a toasty feeling, the total opposite of the clamminess and fear she'd felt at the accident scene. She closed her eyes, wishing she could be hanging out with Graciela back home right now. She needed some comfort. Without her sister, Xochitl felt terribly vulnerable.

"Graciela," Xochitl begged quietly, "please come visit me. I need to talk to you." She sighed, exasperated. She never thought it would be so difficult to speak to her sister's spirit.

Aside from an orange tabby cat that scampered across the cement-covered alley that ran between the rows of houses, there wasn't a person in sight. She stepped onto Occidental Street and peered into the crowds of people walking up and down the sidewalk but saw no familiar face.

Xochitl stared into the large sycamore trees growing up from the parkway, hoping to catch a glimpse of her sister in their branches. Graciela had been her anchor, her rock. The idea of her twin being dead was too final. She looked up to the sky, longing to see her sister's face in a cloud formation.

"Graciela, please. I can't stand this loneliness anymore," Xochitl begged.

When nothing happened, a wave of desperate isolation washed over Xochitl. She needed to talk with someone or to be with someone she knew. Then Xochitl thought of Nana, who was at the Peralta house and had said Xochitl could come see her anytime she needed. So Xochitl set off toward the bus stop at the next corner. She shaded her eyes to look down the street. A bus slowly rumbled toward her.

In front of the bus, Fern and her sister drove along in their station wagon. Pilar honked the horn as Fern leaned out the passenger-side window, yelling and waving. They pulled the car over to the sidewalk a few feet before the bus stop while the bus came to a halt right in front of Xochitl.

Xochitl hesitated. She looked from the bus to Fern, who

had jumped out of the car and was heading straight toward her. The door of the bus opened, and the driver, an old man with a toupee like a rat's nest, glowered down at her. "Are you coming or not?" he growled.

As Fern approached, she gave Xochitl a broad, easygoing smile. She remembered what Nana had said about needing friends. Xochitl gathered all her inner strength and shook her head at the driver. "No, I'm staying," she said.

Xochitl watched the bus rumble off, leaving a cloud of toxic fumes in its wake.

"Hey, I've been looking for you," Fern said. "I wanted to say thanks, but then you disappeared on me." Fern hesitated as she turned to look at the back of the retreating bus. "Were you going somewhere?"

"I was going to see my nana," Xochitl said.

"If she's at Marina's house, we can take you," Fern suggested. "I'm spending the night. Come on, my sister Pilar will drive us." Fern held up her index and middle fingers and crossed them. "I promise I won't get behind the wheel."

Xochitl laughed. "Okay."

Fern led the way to the car. As she opened the back door, she gave Xochitl a once-over, "Isn't it hot in those pants?" she asked, then hopped into the backseat.

"Not really." Xochitl followed Fern into the station wagon. The truth was, Xochitl was a little hot, but since she didn't have a lot of clothes, there hadn't been a wide selection to choose from this morning.

"Pilar, this is Xochitl. She's going to Marina's house with us."

Pilar twisted around from the driver's seat. "It's nice to meet you, Xochitl. Sorry about your fence. We'll get it fixed."

Xochitl nodded. "Thanks."

Fern turned sideways to face Xochitl. "So what are you and your nana going to do?" she asked.

"I don't know. She isn't really expecting me," Xochitl said, looking out the window. There were lots of antiques shops, a bank or two, an Irish pub, and an old-fashioned soda shop. There wasn't an empty lot or a patch of dirt to be seen. She couldn't get over how many cars there were, or how impatiently people drove in California.

"Why don't you hang out with me and Marina?" Fern suggested.

Xochitl bit her lip and didn't answer at first. "I would not want to impose," she said rather formally. This was all moving a little fast for her.

"Oh, no. It would be great to have you with us," Fern said enthusiastically. "Marina and I were just saying the other day how much we wanted to get to know you."

"Really?" Xochitl turned around. She scanned Fern's topaz-colored eyes, hoping she was sincere.

"Yeah, really," Fern replied earnestly.

They pulled up in the long circular driveway in front of Marina's large beige Tudor-style house. Jasmine grew along the frame of the house, up the turret, and around several huge windows. Palm trees stood in clumps on the bright green front lawn. Xochitl couldn't get over how much the Peralta house looked like a miniature palace.

"Thanks for the ride, Pilar," Fern said as she jumped out of the car. "And for, well, for everything."

"What are big sisters for?"

Marina came out the front door wearing a midnight blue sarong covered with sequins and a magenta bathing-suit top. She strolled up to Pilar's car. A blast of heat enveloped Xochitl as she exited the station wagon.

"Have fun!" Pilar called as she drove away.

"Marina, Xochitl is going to hang with us!" Fern said excitedly. "And I've got some juicy news to share."

"Awesome," Marina said, smiling at Xochitl. "Let's get inside. The air-conditioning is on. Man, it's baking out here."

Marina led Xochitl and Fern up the flagstone walkway to the house. On either side of the path, white roses bloomed alongside lavender bushes and irises. "Can you swim, Xochitl?" Marina asked as she opened the oaken, Spanish-style front door to reveal a large, terra-cotta-tiled entryway. "I'm dying in this heat, and I was just waiting for Fern to get here so I could take a dip in the pool."

"I used to swim in the river at home," Xochitl said, staring at the vaulted ceilings.

"Great," Marina said. "I've got a suit for you. Fern, did you bring yours?"

"I'm wearing it," Fern replied, showing off the red strings tied at the back of her neck. "So let me tell you—"

"In a minute, Ferny; let's get settled. Xochitl, can you stay the night?" Marina asked. "My family's at the movies. They'll be back in a couple of hours."

"Well, I should call my dad," Xochitl said, slowly returning her gaze to Marina.

Marina grabbed a cordless phone from the shelf of an antique hall tree and handed it to her. Xochitl smiled shyly and took the phone. She looked into Marina's eyes and saw a lot of kindness in them. Xochitl hadn't intended to stay overnight, but now that she was here, it seemed like a good idea.

"We'll wait for you in my room." Marina turned and headed down the hall.

Xochitl wandered into the living room. She stepped onto the plush carpet lined with vacuum paths.

Fern's voice drifted to Xochitl from the hallway. "So I crashed Pilar's car and met this really cute guy."

"Well, it's early, something exciting could still happen," Marina teased.

"But there's more," Fern replied. Their voices were cut off when Marina's bedroom door closed.

Xochitl sat on the upholstered beige couch and dialed her home number. Her father picked up right away. *"¿Bueno?"*

"Papá, it's Xochitl."

"Where have you been?" asked Mr. Garcia. "You disappeared *again*, didn't you?"

Xochitl didn't respond. Her father just didn't understand how much that scene was like the accident in Mexico.

"Where are you?" Mr. Garcia asked.

"I'm at the Peraltas'," she replied.

"Good. Nana is with you," her father said, comforted.

"Marina asked me if I can spend the night," Xochitl said. "Can I?"

"Yes. It will be good for you to be around people your own age," Mr. Garcia said. "But I want you to check in with your nana."

Xochitl walked to her nana's room in the garage. She could hear Marina and Fern giggling across the hall. She knocked on Nana's door three times and then opened it slowly.

"What are you doing here?" Nana said, setting the iron upright. She had been using it to press a taupe linen dress that looked like it must belong to Mrs. Peralta. Nana turned down her radio, silencing the man singing a bolero.

"Fern's sister Pilar brought me," Xochitl explained, glancing at the pile of clothes yet to be ironed. Suddenly it felt a little strange to be hanging out with one of the people who employed her nana. "I'm spending the night."

"Que bueno." Nana smiled. "That's very good. I knew they would be a nice match for you."

Xochitl bit back the words she was longing to say. Everyone thought they knew what was best for her. "Yeah, well, I'm going to go now," Xochitl said. And yet, she thought as she walked across the hall to Marina's room, being in a house like this and meeting new friends was all she had dreamed about only three months ago.

When Xochitl opened Marina's bedroom door, she saw Marina digging into her chest of drawers, which matched the desk, which matched the bed, which matched the nightstand. Xochitl also noticed the garish pink and green decorations. Yikes.

Marina threw Xochitl a yellow bikini. "Here ya go."

Xochitl held up the tiny bathing suit. "Um, don't you have anything bigger?"

"Marina only has bikinis," Fern said. "She likes to show off her curves."

"Nah-uh," Marina protested.

Xochitl continued to examine the little yellow patches of material, wishing she could make the thing grow.

"Oh yeah? Then how come you wear triangle tops, which only happen to make the most of your bodacious cleavage?" Fern retorted, throwing out her chest for emphasis. She then turned to Xochitl. "Last year, Marina would be all insulted if any guy even noticed she had a big chest. This summer she's all about flaunting it."

"I'm *not* flaunting it," Marina shot back, turning red in the face. "Triangle tops are the only ones that cover my, my ... girls."

Fern burst out laughing.

"You know I don't like being so big," Marina said.

Xochitl mused how strange it was that Marina and Fern were talking so intimately about body parts. She had never discussed anything like this with anyone but Graciela.

"Wear a tankini, then," Fern suggested.

Marina shook her head. "No way. How would I show off my tan tummy?"

"You're one messed-up chicky," Fern said with a shake of her copper curls.

"Hmph," Marina snorted. "At least I can be compassionate about feeling shy. I totally understand if you don't want to wear this, Xochitl." Marina took back the yellow bikini, pulled open another drawer, and took out a black one-piece suit. "I wear this to pool parties. When I'm not in the mood to show off anything," she said pointedly to Fern.

Fern shrugged. "Whatever you say."

"Can I have a T-shirt, too?" Xochitl asked.

"Sure." Marina took out a superlarge dark blue T-shirt with a soccer ball streaking across the front, and handed it to Xochitl.

"Thanks," Xochitl sighed.

The pool at the Peralta house was kidney-bean shaped and surrounded by large rocks. Between the rocks grew birds-of-paradise, king palms, and several plumeria trees in full bloom, sending their sweet, soft perfume into the air. Xochitl stared in amazement at the waterfall at the far end of the pool, which made a gentle gurgling sound, and the dragonfly twinkle lights strung copiously over the latticework around the patio. The opulent beauty of the backyard felt like forbidden fruit. How could she really let herself enjoy all this with Graciela gone?

Marina stepped down the tiled pool stairs, carefully testing the water. "It's a saltwater pool. No chemicals."

"Hooray for no chemicals!" Fern did a cannonball, sending water all over Marina and the blue slate deck.

Marina retaliated by squeezing water between the palms of her hands, creating a stream directly aimed at Fern when she resurfaced.

"Ahh!" Fern yelled.

Xochitl stepped back to avoid getting wet and to distance herself from Marina and Fern. Their playfulness reminded her of the closeness she had shared with her sister, and it was making her ache all over.

Marina dove into the water and then popped back up a few seconds later, her hair glistening. "Come on, Xochitl. The water feels great!"

"Don't make me come get you," Fern warned, wagging a finger in Xochitl's direction.

Xochitl paused for a moment longer. Even though she might feel a little uncomfortable and out of place, she longed for companionship. When she had left Guadalajara, she had hoped for exciting adventures, new friends, and big opportunities. She seemed to have it all at her fingertips now. She just needed to convince herself to go for it. Xochitl took a deep breath and made up her mind and dove cleanly into the pool. The cool freshness of the water changed her entire attitude almost instantly. She swam the length of the pool before taking a breath.

"You're a good swimmer," Fern observed.

"Race you!" Marina challenged.

"I'm out," Fern said as she dog-paddled to the opposite end of the pool. "I'll ref you two, though."

"All right," Xochitl said, pushing her wet black hair out of her eyes. She smiled shyly, then took off the T-shirt and placed it on the pool deck.

"Ready, set, go!" Fern called.

Xochitl cut through the water like an Olympic gold medalist. Every weekend, she and Graciela would float down the river and then race back against the current. Xochitl easily passed Marina and touched the end of the pool first.

Fern whistled. "She smoked you!"

"Wanna race again?" Xochitl asked with a surprising amount of enthusiasm.

"You're on!" Marina said.

Fifteen minutes and three races later, Xochitl was crowned the victor. After the final race, Xochitl swam another lap just to feel the silent water rush past her. She rejoined Marina and Fern at the other end of the pool.

"No one has ever beaten me on my own turf," Marina panted.

"Looks like you've met your match," Fern said.

After floating in the pool for a half hour, they dried off with the whitest, fluffiest towels Xochitl had ever used. A warm, sultry breeze whispered through the trees, sending pink and yellow plumeria flowers fluttering and spinning to the ground at their feet as they headed back to the house. It was like paradise for Xochitl.

When they ambled through the kitchen, Rogelia was busy at the stove. "My specialty," she said, offering the girls three steaming mugs of hot cocoa with tiny marshmallows floating on top.

"Thanks," Fern and Xochitl said simultaneously.

Nana gave Xochitl a special smile as she handed her the mug. Xochitl felt a strange mix of comfort and grief. Nana had made her delicious cocoa every Saturday night in Mexico. Xochitl thought of how she used to fight Graciela for more marshmallows. When would getting a simple treat like this not bring with it a rush of sadness, too?

Marina received her cup of cocoa like it was the Holy Grail itself. "Thank you so much, Rogelia," she said appreciatively. "I don't remember the last time anyone made me cocoa." She took a sip. "Mmm. This is really good." She reverently carried the cocoa in front of her as she trod carefully toward her bedroom.

Fern lifted both palms and scrunched up her shoulders. "Whatcha gonna do? She's just a little kooky," she whispered to Xochitl before following Marina to her room.

Xochitl hesitated. She looked down at the melting marshmallows.

"Go on," Nana urged Xochitl, patting her on the back.

Xochitl nodded and walked down the hall. She felt twinges of nervousness again. Swimming was something she could do well, and it made her feel confident. But what would they do in Marina's room? What would they talk about? Xochitl sighed as she walked into Marina's bedroom with trepidation.

Marina sat at her desk looking at her computer. Music came from the speakers. "Do you like Nickelback? They're my favorite band. They have really good lyrics."

"I've never heard of them," Xochitl admitted.

"I'll burn you a CD," Marina said.

"I don't have a CD player," Xochitl said. "I left it at home in Mexico."

"I've got one you can have." Marina stood up and crossed the room to her closet. She dug something from under a pile of clothes. "Here you go." Marina handed Xochitl an ancient boom box.

Xochitl hesitated. "You don't have to."

"It's okay, she's got *tons* of stuff," Fern said.

Xochitl accepted the CD player. "Thanks," she mumbled. She wasn't used to getting handouts. It felt really weird. She sat down on a hugely overstuffed pink beanbag chair.

Fern sprawled out on Marina's bed. "Hey, speaking of music, I heard Los Lobos is coming to town. Even if you can't speak Spanish, Marina, you can still sing 'La Bamba.' Plus, it'll be good for you to hear some Mexican *corridos*. Pilar said she'd order the tickets online. We'll have to pay her back, of course."

"That sounds like fun," Marina agreed. "Wanna come, Xochitl?"

"I don't think I can go to a concert," Xochitl said. "My dad is really traditional about me going out without an adult."

"Pilar is an adult," Fern said. "Most days."

"I don't think he'd approve," Xochitl said softly.

"Well, maybe he'll change his mind," Fern said. "The concert isn't for another month or so."

"Maybe," Xochitl agreed. Inside, she knew it wasn't going to happen no matter how many times she asked.

Suddenly a girl with perfectly kept blond hair burst into the room. "Marina, where are my Lucky jeans? I know you wore them last." She began rifling through the piles of clothes on the floor.

Marina leaned over, pulled a pair of jeans from under the chair, and threw them at her. "You said I could wear them, Monica."

Marina's sister caught the jeans in the air and inspected the rear of the pants. "Probably stretched them out with your fat ass."

"Get out of here," Marina demanded.

Monica closed the door in a huff.

Marina sat back down, exasperated. "Sisters can be so annoying."

"*Marina,*" Fern admonished.

"Oh my gosh," Marina said immediately, covering her mouth with her hand. "I'm so sorry."

Xochitl looked suspiciously from Marina to Fern. *I guess they know about Graciela.* Xochitl braced herself for the questions, willing herself not to vanish into the air. That would only bring about more questions, of course.

"We heard about what happened to your sister," Marina said.

"The accident must have been so scary," Fern said.

Xochitl tried to respond, but she could only nod.

"I heard you didn't end up with any injuries," Marina said, awestruck.

"Your nana is a *curandera*, isn't she?" Fern asked.

Marina whipped her head around, staring in shock at Fern. Fern shrugged and lifted her hands, palms up, as if to say, *What? You want to know as bad as I do.* Marina bit her lip and glanced at Xochitl.

"She stopped the voices in my head the other day," Marina said. "But I heard them again the other morning. It's so creepy."

"How did your nana do it?" Fern asked.

Silence blanketed the room. For one dreadful moment Xochitl thought she should leave and seek refuge in Nana's room. As much as she wanted the company of friends, she did not want to talk about her nana's magic. She had completely lost faith in it and had no intention of delving back into the world of *curanderismo* anytime soon. Even though Nana had calmed down Marina, she had not been able to save Graciela.

Fern got up and scrambled over on all fours to plead at Xochitl's knees. "Today I met this really cute boy, Tristán. I thought he was gorgeous, but then this horrible gray light appeared all around him. I don't understand it, but maybe your nana could help explain it."

Marina placed her hand over Xochitl's slightly trembling hand. "We want to be your friend, regardless of whether you tell us or not."

Fern put her hand over Marina's. "But we are dying to know." She looked intently into Xochitl's dark brown eyes.

A dark suspicion rose in Xochitl's mind. *Why are they so interested in magic and Nana's secrets?* Xochitl wondered. She wasn't sure if they truly wanted to be her friends or if they were using her to get to her nana. A bad feeling sat like a heavy rock in the bottom of Xochitl's tummy.

"Fern, don't be so insensitive." Marina pushed Fern's shoulder so that she fell over.

Fern got back up on her knees, glared momentarily at Marina, then turned softer eyes to Xochitl. "I need to get to the bottom of this. The magic doesn't have to stop after one night. Why can't it go on forever? The spell we did seemed to work."

"We asked for magical powers," Marina explained to Xochitl.

"Marina hears voices," Fern said. "Though I'm not exactly sure how that qualifies as a power. It seems more like a problem to me."

Marina threw a pillow at Fern, then turned her attention to Xochitl. "I gotta tell you, hearing voices isn't something that brings on a happy feeling. Makes me feel like I'm going to be locked up in a white padded cell."

Fern caught the pillow and put it under her knees. "Well, Xochitl?" Fern asked.

The silence dragged on. Xochitl felt increasingly uncomfortable the more Fern and Marina pushed, but then she remembered how Graciela used to tease her for her skepticism and distrust. Graciela had always been the openhearted one, while Xochitl was afraid to let people get close to her. However, now that Graciela was gone, maybe it was time for Xochitl to live more like her sister had.

"Nana is a *curandera*," Xochitl began tentatively. "She heals people, working mostly with herbs. She does spiritual work, too, kind of like spells, but maybe not exactly what you might call magic. She's like a shaman, but that term is mostly used for men. Back home, everyone called her Mamá. She taught me some things." Xochitl pushed some stray strands of her long black hair behind her ear. "But I haven't had any lessons since my sister, Graciela, died."

Xochitl knew she was leaving some information out. Nana had wanted to continue teaching her the ways of the *curandera*, but she had refused. It was just too painful without Graciela.

"Do you miss it?" Fern asked. Marina shot her another warning look. "What?" Fern said to Marina.

Of course, I do, but . . .

"I miss Graciela more," Xochitl answered plainly. "And magic can't bring her back." Xochitl's eyes welled with tears. "Actually, Nana's magic wasn't even strong enough to prevent the accident."

"Do you think she would teach us?" Fern asked.

Xochitl hesitated. "I don't know. . . ." The pressure was too much.

"Just ask her," Fern suggested.

"She doesn't take on strangers as students," Xochitl said, hoping to stop this conversation.

"Marina isn't *that* strange," Fern said.

69

"Hey!" Marina protested.

"I'm kidding," Fern said reassuringly. "We won't bug you about it forever, Xochitl. Just ask her this once."

"Okay," Xochitl relented, figuring Nana would say no anyhow. She got up and walked out of Marina's room and across the hall to her nana's room. She knocked once, then entered. Nana was kneeling reverently and meditating at her altar. Xochitl didn't want to disturb her, so she started to back up.

"What it is, *mija*?"

Xochitl was always impressed with Nana's sharp hearing.

"Nana, Marina and Fern want to learn *curanderismo*, and they would like you to teach them. You don't have to, though." Xochitl chewed on her bottom lip. Looking around at the hanging herbs and crosses and at the altar, Xochitl had a bad feeling she had made a mistake in asking Nana.

"Will you return to your lessons as well?" Nana kept her eyes closed and her head bowed.

Xochitl felt panic rise in her throat. This was not going well at all. To get herself out of this, she would have to make it seem like Marina and Fern were looking for something flashier than *curanderismo*, which they probably were. "I don't think they are serious, Nana. I mean, they might think your magic is like Harry Potter or something," Xochitl said.

"I'll be the judge of that," Nana said, opening her eyes and turning to face her granddaughter. "I insist that you work alongside them, too."

"Why?" Xochitl whimpered. "What's the point of learning magic if you can't save the people you love from dying?"

"It's not wise to use magic tricks to avoid life's difficulties, Xochitl," Nana replied calmly. "Death is part of life."

"Well, what if they think we're weird?" Xochitl sniffled a little. "First you wanted me to have friends, and now you're willing to scare them off."

"We are weird," Nana said matter-of-factly. "Who would want to be normal?"

Sometimes Xochitl thought her nana had forgotten what it was like to be a teenager.

"Come back with your friends in fifteen minutes," Nana said.

Xochitl took a deep breath and returned to Marina's room, where her nana's new apprentices were awaiting the news. "She said to be ready in fifteen minutes."

"Oh my gosh, this is so cool!" Fern squealed. "I'm so excited. Let's eat something." She got up and led the way to the kitchen.

"Why do you always eat when you're nervous? If I did that I'd never fit into my jeans," Marina asked as she and Xochitl followed Fern.

"Dunno." Fern shrugged. "But it works for me. I'll make quesadillas."

Fern whipped together the first quesadilla and handed it to Xochitl on a plate. Xochitl tore off a corner and took as long as possible to chew, gnawing on it until the cheese dissolved. Fifteen minutes could take forever, as far as Xochitl was concerned. *They have no idea what they've gotten themselves into,* she thought. Stalling for more time, she started to pick individual pieces of melted cheese off the plate.

"Come on, Xochitl, it's time," Fern pleaded.

"Okay," Xochitl grumbled as she pushed herself away from the table. As she led the way, she had the distinct feeling she was walking to her execution. Tentatively, Xochitl pushed open the door to her nana's room. On the altar sat four glass advent candles: blue, green, white, and red. The heady scent of copal incense filled the air.

From the doorway, Xochitl, Fern, and Marina watched as Rogelia held a bundle of dried sage to the flame of the white candle, which burned brightly in the center of the altar. The sage caught fire. Rogelia blew on the sage to extinguish it and waved the bundle around the altar, letting the smoke waft over all her sacred items.

"Come closer. I don't bite," she laughed.

Fern ventured in first, Marina followed, and lastly Xochitl stepped into the room. Xochitl watched Fern and Marina carefully. She fidgeted, shifting her weight from side to side. Nana wielded the ash-tipped torch over Marina, then Fern, like a conductor with his baton. She beckoned to Xochitl. Reluctantly, Xochitl took a few steps forward and allowed Nana to waft the sage smoke around her. Nana gestured for them to sit on the bed after she had blessed each of them with the smoke and kissed their foreheads. Xochitl sat on the bed between Fern and Marina.

Rogelia crushed the sage's burning leaves in an abalone shell. Slowly, she turned to face the girls, making eye contact with each of them. "Why are you interested in *curanderismo*?" she asked.

"I've always been curious about magic," Fern spoke first. "After we did a ceremony the other night, I began to see a strange light around this guy."

"Auras," Rogelia said simply. "You are seeing auras. Auras are a magnetic energy force around people, plants, and every living thing. If you use your ability to see the energy around plants, you can match medicine with sickness." Rogelia turned her gaze to Marina.

"I've heard voices in my head a few times since the ceremony Fern and I did, and it would be nice to not be so freaked out by it and maybe even figure out what they're saying," Marina said.

"Marina, it sounds to me as if you may be an *espiritualista,* sometimes called a medium or *clairaudio,*" Rogelia said, sounding impressed. "There aren't many true *espiritualistas.*" Nana turned to face Xochitl, but it was obvious to Rogelia that her granddaughter was not going to reveal anything. "Xochitl has learned the ability to focus on the space around her, changing her energy so there is more attention on the space rather than matter. To others it seems as if she has disappeared."

"I knew it!" Fern exclaimed. "You did that after I crashed into your fence."

Xochitl avoided her nana's look of disappointment.

"Manipulating energy can bring healing and harmony," Rogelia said tersely. "But it can also be abused to avoid difficult situations."

Xochitl sat on her hands to keep them from trembling and tried to regulate her shallow breathing. She was sure Marina and Fern were going to think this was all too strange and make a run for it.

"Marina, since you hear things others cannot, you will pick up sounds in the distance, as well as the voices of spirits visiting the earth plane. Take all the electronic equipment out of your room so you can slow down the communication. People who have died often connect to those on earth through phones, computers, televisions, iPods, and fax machines. They will flicker lights, and zap phone lines, too, but there isn't much you can do about that."

Rogelia turned to face Fern. "Fern, your ability to see auras is part of clear seeing, or being clairvoyant. With practice, you may be able to deepen your skill and have visions into the past, or future, or perhaps see the spirits living among us. I want you to get rid of as many mirrors in your room as possible."

"But my closet doors are mirrored," Fern said.

"Cover them with a sheet," Rogelia advised.

Xochitl shuddered to think how deeply her nana was asking her friends to delve into this magic. In the movies, people blinked or snapped their fingers and objects flew around the room or someone zipped off on a broom. But that wasn't what it was like in reality. When someone entered Nana Rogelia's house of magic, they had to alter their life and ways of thinking to make certain magic happen. Xochitl knew all too well what it took to conjure the natural forces, call upon the elements, and direct the energy where she wanted it to go. Now Nana was about to test Fern's and Marina's dedication, like she'd tested Xochitl and Graciela long ago. As she watched Fern and Marina giggle with excitement, Xochitl wondered if these girls would make it through the training—and if they didn't, would they still want to be her friend?

Eight

"Marina!" Her mother called from somewhere in the house. "We're home! Where are you?"

"It's my mom," Marina said apologetically.

"We'll wait," Rogelia said. "Go see what she wants."

Marina pulled open Rogelia's door and floated toward the kitchen, deep in a fog of concentration. She didn't know what an *espiritualista* was, but it sounded good. No, better than good—simply sweet. Marina smiled, thinking how Rogelia had called her powers a gift. Pulling back her shoulders, she stood a little taller than usual as she walked down the hall.

Her mother was sifting through the bills on the kitchen counter. She stood as formidable as ever in her silk blouse, pencil skirt, and heels, but for once Marina didn't notice how intimidating she was.

"What do you want, Mom?" Marina said impatiently. She was kind of annoyed that her incredible introduction to *curanderismo* had been interrupted.

Marina's mother raised an eyebrow in suspicion. "What are you so irritated about?"

Marina stared off into the distance, not really paying attention to her mother. Everything became blurry as she concentrated on the slight sounds of her house, like the humming of the refrigerator, the faucet running in a bathroom, and her sisters, Samantha and Monica, arguing behind the closed door of Monica's bedroom.

¡Marina, despierta! a voice commanded in her head. The voice sounded young, like a girl her own age.

Marina snapped her attention back to her mother, who suddenly came into sharp focus. She was watching Marina quite intently.

"What are you up to?" Marina's mother asked. "Where were you just now?"

"I was just hanging out with Fern in Rogelia's room," Marina answered quickly. "Rogelia's granddaughter, Xochitl, is here, too." She widened her eyes to appear guilt free.

Marina's mother continued to scrutinize Marina for any detection of a lie, but finding nothing but benign innocence in her daughter's expression, she returned to sorting the mail. "What are you doing in the maid's room?"

"What's the matter with hanging out with Rogelia?" Marina asked defensively.

Ever since Marina could remember, someone had cleaned their house, with the exception of the girls' bedrooms. When

Samantha was born five years ago, they got their first live-in maid, meaning that between Monday and Friday, Marina could leave anything anywhere in the house, and almost like magic it would be neatly put in its proper place within minutes of her walking away from it. It dawned on her that she had never paid one bit of attention to their former maids. What kind of person did that make her?

"Hanging out with the maid," Marina's mother said contemptuously. "Next thing I know, you'll be hanging out in the barrio." Sarcasm dripped heavily from the last word.

"Rogelia is more than a maid," Marina objected. "She made us the best cocoa ever tonight." She recalled how comforting that simple gesture had been.

Marina's mother glanced briefly at her, then flipped open her *OC Metro* magazine. "That's why I hire Mexican maids. They're always so devoted, domestic, and . . . you know, loving."

Indignation and confusion bubbled up in Marina's head and heart. She watched her mother pour herself a glass of red wine. Why was she talking about Rogelia like she had been bought from a dime-a-dozen-maid service? As if you could hire someone to love your children. As if that was all Mexican maids were good for. "Why would you say something like that?" Marina snapped.

Watchale, came a warning voice in Marina's head.

Marina's mother's left eyebrow rose so far that it disappeared under her perfectly styled bangs. Her right eye lowered into a menacing slant. Her lips thinned and quivered with barely concealed anger. It was the look that could silence Marina and her siblings in an instant. "What did you say?" she asked in a threatening voice.

"Nothing, Mom," Marina said, smiling apologetically. Rather than face off with her mother, she decided to swallow her anger. Rogelia was waiting for her, and there was magic at hand. "Do you mind if I go back?" Marina asked politely.

"No, that's fine. I just wanted to know where you were," Marina's mother said, picking up her wineglass and magazine and heading toward the den. "One more thing. Don't pick up any bad habits from Rogelia's granddaughter. After all, she lives in the barrio."

Marina quickly turned around and nearly sprinted down the hall. Had her mom always been so snobby about their maids? And what was her deal with the barrio?

When Marina stepped back into Rogelia's room, she sat between Fern and Xochitl on the bed and shrugged off her thoughts about her mother. She grinned eagerly at her friends, then turned her full attention to Rogelia.

Rogelia smiled warmly at the three of them as though she was surveying a mound of clay sitting in the center of her potter's wheel, just waiting to be molded.

"*Curanderas* work very closely with nature," Rogelia said. "When you are disconnected from nature, you are disconnected from yourself. You will be learning how to recognize and learn from nature's patterns. This requires courage and dedication."

Rogelia took a rabbit's foot from her shelf and handed the furry totem to Xochitl, who hastily passed it to Fern. Fern gave Xochitl a quizzical look before accepting the rabbit's foot.

Rogelia let her gaze rest on Xochitl. "This talisman from the rabbit is very sacred. Rabbits represent fear." She looked at Marina and Fern. "Many years ago, Sorceress and Rabbit took a long walk through the woods. Rabbit became hungry. Sorceress picked up some stones and turned them into bread crumbs. Rabbit hesitantly ate the bread but did not say thank you. Later on, Rabbit stumbled and Sorceress healed her friend with herbs."

Marina nudged Fern, who stared, mesmerized, at Rogelia. In fact, she had to pry the talisman out of Fern's hand so that she could rub it intently.

Rogelia continued her story. "Rabbit trembled. 'You scare me,' he said. 'I've never seen anyone do the things you do. Stay away from me,' he said. Deeply hurt, Sorceress said, 'From now on, Rabbit, you will be afraid of everything.' The following morning Rabbit sensed Wolf's presence. 'Don't eat me, Wolf!' " Rogelia made a terrified face and held her hands up above her head.

Fern laughed.

Rogelia smiled appreciatively before continuing. "From that day, Rabbit became afraid of all things, and forever calls these fears to him." Rogelia stared at each girl in turn. "When you begin your journey into *curanderismo,* you may encounter many hidden fears. Do not be like Rabbit and talk endlessly about your fears, as if you do not have the power to conquer them. Whatever you focus on grows. Think about what you want, not what you don't want."

Marina decided she really liked learning from parables. Perhaps these were the kind of stories she had missed by not knowing much about her Mexican heritage or her grandmother.

From the altar, Rogelia picked up a seven-day advent candle that featured an image of San Miguel, or Saint Michael, his foot pinning down a demon, on the front. "With the power of truth on his side, San Miguel gives us courage and strength to overcome fears." She set the candle down.

Rogelia pointed to the red, blue, and green advent candles and in turn lit each one. "The red candle represents Fernanda. The blue candle is for Marina. And Xochitl is symbolized by the green candle. Take a stick here." She pointed to a cup filled with wooden skewers. Fern, Marina, and Xochitl each selected a stick.

"I would like you to commit to learning with me for one season. Tomorrow will be the first day of summer."

"Summer solstice," Fern chimed in with a huge smile.

"Yes." Rogelia smiled at Fern's enthusiasm. "Over the next week, I will have a *plácita* with each of you individually," Rogelia continued.

"Sorry, I don't speak much Spanish," Marina said timidly. Maybe one of these days she should learn the language. "What are *plácitas*?"

"*Plácitas* are heart-to-heart talks," Rogelia clarified. "Please bring an item you intend to barter or trade for our time together whenever possible. The barter can be food, gifts bought or handmade, flowers, anything that shows your appreciation. Your gift exchange will keep the energy flowing. After I have spoken with each of you, we will have a *limpia*, or cleansing. During the *limpia* we will work on strengthening your spiritual gifts. You will each need to bring something that corresponds with each of the four directions."

"Like what?" Marina asked. She had no clue what to bring. But Rogelia's confidence in her made her feel the distinct possibility that she could enter the realm of magic and perhaps someday wield its power.

Rogelia pointed to a bunch of chamomile flowers in a vase on her altar. "Each of the four directions is represented on this altar and is essential in life. These flowers represent earth and the north, which is symbolized by our body. The bowl of water honors the west and the fact that our bodies are seventy-five-percent water. The incense smoke celebrates the eastern direction and air, our life-giving breath. With our breath we give thanks—the most important prayer there is." At this point Rogelia picked up a cluster of yellow copal resin and dropped it onto a white-hot piece of charcoal in a small black cauldron. Incense smoke billowed from the cauldron. "The candle and its fire symbolize the heat or energy in our body and correspond to the south. The fifth direction is spirit, which is not shown but is always here, and will be symbolized by your presence."

Marina leaned forward to look into the cauldron. The copal chunks had begun to melt and gave off a strong overly sweet smell. Marina picked at the nail of her ring finger and tapped her left foot nervously. Something about the power symbolized by the incense gave her the heebie-jeebies. She felt like she was entering a new world where nothing would ever be the same again. She was scared but at the same time entranced.

Rogelia pulled out a journal covered with black feathers. "These are crow feathers. Crow is a guide to the Spirit World, to mystery, and to the left direction, which represents feminine wisdom. You will share this book, taking turns recording your dreams and desires, or how you are progressing with me. Whatever you want to write or draw is fine with me as long as you are honest." Rogelia looked over her new apprentices. "Do you agree to my terms?"

Marina and Fern nodded solemnly. Xochitl hesitated, then agreed.

Rogelia handed the journal to Xochitl. "You are the first

because you have been with me the longest." She smiled. "I want each of you to insert the stick I've given you into the flame of your candle at the same time. From the flame that represents your individual spirit, I want you to light the candle of San Miguel, who will protect and guide you on your journey with me."

Together Fern, Marina, and Xochitl gathered the flames from their individual candles, then lit the San Miguel candle. Almost immediately the individual candles flickered, then went out.

"That is so cool," Fern whispered.

Rogelia smiled slyly as she set the San Miguel candle prominently in the center of her altar. She turned and clasped her hands in front of her. "I will watch over this candle as I watch over the three of you. We will not need to make appointments for the *plácitas*. The candle will stay lit for seven days. In that time, you will know when you are ready to talk."

Xochitl stood up as though she understood some unspoken signal that their lesson was over. "*Gracias*, Nana," she said almost in a monotone.

Marina and Fern leapt off the bed. Rogelia placed her hands on Marina's shoulders. "You are ready for this. Just be willing to be open and honest." Rogelia turned to face Fern. "Be prepared to alchemize." Lastly, she faced her granddaughter. "Just show up, *mi amor*, and the rest will take care of itself."

Xochitl smiled wanly, then led the way out of the room. Fern and Marina stumbled over each other in a race to get back to Marina's bedroom.

Once they closed the door behind them, Fern crooned, "This is better than I imagined." She dug out her torn Sierra

Club T-shirt and a pair of striped flannel boxers from her dirt-stained, pumpkin-colored JanSport backpack.

"Really, Xochitl," Marina said. "It's like learning from the nana I never had." She took out a lavender paisley Victoria's Secret sleep shirt and cotton sleep pants from her dresser and handed them to Xochitl. "This should do."

"You've never had a nana?" Xochitl asked, taking the clothes.

"She died a month before I was born," Marina said as she chose a cami-and-shorts set with a scripted *VS* on the cami. She walked to her closet and pulled out a sleeping bag, a fleece blanket with Tinker Bell flying across the sky, and a goose-down pillow. "And my dad's parents dropped off the face of the earth when he did."

"Oh," Xochitl said.

"My mom talks about my nana like she was some kind of saint. I don't know," Marina said. "It's kind of hard to feel connected to someone so flawless and perfect."

Fern took the sleeping gear. "I'll sleep on the floor. Xochitl, you can sleep on the trundle."

Marina pulled back the cover for Xochitl and hopped onto her bed. None of the new friends she made in her posh neighborhood were as easy to be around as Fern or even Xochitl. She was a little surprised that she felt this close to Xochitl after such a short time. Part of this quick bond had to do with the fact that Xochitl had borne witness to Marina's first bout with the voices. Not only did Xochitl refrain from treating Marina like a psycho, but she had also helped in the healing, which was intriguing in itself. Xochitl had a real down-to-earth vibe that Marina had never felt in anyone but Fern.

"What does *'watchale'* mean?" Marina asked as she punched her pillow into a comfortable form.

"It means 'watch yourself' or be 'careful.' Why?" asked Fern.

"I thought it was something like that," Marina answered. "I heard one of the voices say it tonight, right before I almost talked back to my mother."

"*You,* talk back to your mother? Why?" Fern asked.

Marina shrugged but didn't answer. "Hey, you guys ready to go to sleep?"

"Sure," said Fern, though she sent Marina a puzzled look.

Marina turned over in bed. She turned off the lamp on her bedside table. "Night."

When her family had moved to Orange Olive, Marina had found it so easy to walk away from the old neighborhood. The barrio, as her mother would call it. And now she wondered what she had left behind. She had never learned Spanish, and she didn't know much more about being Mexican than how to make tacos without using premade shells. A desire to learn more about this part of her culture ignited like the flame of the San Miguel candle.

In the silence that followed, she heard the voice of an older woman say, *Welcome home, mi'jita.*

Nine

Early the next morning, Fern rolled over in her sleeping bag and looked out Marina's bedroom window. She watched brilliant rainbow-colored sparks dance upon the morning light that shone through the tiny slits between the horizontal blinds. As the colors played, she wondered if she would ever see lights like this in an aura, especially the more she worked with Rogelia.

And then her mind wandered into boy territory. Why did Tristán have that gray aura? What was he doing now? Probably sleeping. It was still early.

A door in the hall creaked open. Immediately, Fern closed her eyes and pretended to be asleep. She figured it was

Marina's youngest sister, Samantha, who loved to wake up at the crack of dawn and beg Fern to play Candy Land. Footsteps shuffled down the hallway in the opposite direction from Marina's room.

"Buenos días, señor," Rogelia said in a hoarse whisper.

"Buenos días, Rogelia," Marina's stepfather responded. "I'm off to work. Have a good day." The front door opened and closed.

Fern's eyes shot open. The coast was clear; she wasn't about to be attacked by a bouncing, hyper five-year-old. Rogelia was awake and alone in the house. Maybe Fern could talk with Rogelia now and ask her some questions. It was really early, though, and she didn't have anything to barter. Fern sat up and looked at the alarm clock on Marina's nightstand. It was 6:45 a.m. What was she thinking? Who in their right mind would get out of bed at this hour?

Apparently, she would, especially when her interest in a cute boy was on the line. Fern quietly unzipped the sleeping bag and whipped back the cover. Carefully, she curled up her legs and slid them out. She tiptoed out of the bedroom and sneaked down the hall. Rogelia's door was ajar, but she wasn't inside. Fern padded softly to the kitchen.

Rogelia stood with her back to Fern. The healer pulled a stainless-steel teapot off the stove and poured the steaming water into two blue ceramic mugs. She rolled closed a small, unmarked brown bag that sat on the counter in front of the cups and tucked the bag into her apron pocket. The *curandera* turned and smiled at Fern. She handed Fern a mug. "Let's go to my room."

"How did you know I was here?" Fern asked, taking the mug. She looked into the cup and saw a mound of chopped green leaves at the bottom.

"Intuition," Rogelia said as she walked down the hall. "You'd be amazed what happens when you pay attention to it."

Rogelia pushed open the door to her bedroom and allowed Fern to walk in first. Fern settled herself onto Rogelia's bed. She watched the candlelight of the white San Miguel candle. Rogelia had lit a votive under a crudely drawn picture of the flaming Sacred Heart, another under a Huichol weaving of a jaguar, and a third under a statue of the Virgen de Guadalupe.

"Intuition is like a nudge, a gut feeling," Rogelia said, taking the cup of tea from Fern and scooping out the green herb with a rattan strainer. She handed the tea back to Fern. "I felt that you needed me, so here I am. This is *yerba buena* tea."

Fern took a sip of tea. "It tastes like peppermint."

"That's because *yerba buena is* peppermint," Rogelia laughed. "What did you want to talk about?" She adjusted her blue shawl over her shoulders.

"I, um—I just wanted to ask you about auras," Fern stammered.

"Yes," Rogelia said empathetically. "It is strange when you first begin to see the light."

"You could say that," Fern said. "It's like someone is running a special-effects show inside my head."

Rogelia chuckled quietly. "I am guessing you would like to learn more about the auras and why you see them and others don't? When they show up? Are they real? No?"

Fern nodded.

Rogelia swirled her tea and took a long sip before answering. "Every living thing has a spirit at its center. The energy forms circles around the center like rings around a pebble when you throw it into water. The first few circles take form as the bush, or animal, or person. After that, the next circles of energy are the aura. *¿Entiendes?*"

Fern nodded again, showing that she understood.

"When you first begin to see auras, you notice only random flickers. But you must be patient. Every sighting of an aura means something. Your job will be to assess what the aura intends to show you. The message will be unique for everyone. This is why you must learn to trust *your* intuition."

"How do I do that?"

"Listen to your body. You might experience prickles, heat or coldness, strong instincts, nudges, hunches, and gut feelings," Rogelia said. "Intuition will grow stronger each time you use it. It's like a muscle that way. I use intuition in my healing work, both as a *curandera* and a *mamá*."

"Can you use intuition in relationships?" Fern asked, thinking of Tristán and his captivating eyes.

"That's an excellent place to use intuition," Rogelia replied. "For example, I have been asked to make a remedy for Marcela Cabrera, a woman in our neighborhood. Her six-month-old son, Gabriel, has colic, and she hasn't slept in weeks. Do you have any idea what kind of herb I would use for little Gabriel?"

"No," Fern said automatically. How would she know that?

"You answered that quickly," Rogelia said. "Is there nothing you have ever had to eat or drink that has settled an upset stomach or calmed you when you were nervous?"

"Oh," said Fern, suddenly remembering something. "Once my mother gave me chamomile tea after I ate too much cake at Marina's eighth birthday party."

"*Manzanilla,* or chamomile, is an excellent remedy for stomach pains, and it will help the baby sleep," Rogelia explained. "I have the chamomile herb, it's this one"—Rogelia pointed to the hanging herb—"but I need some oil to rub on

Gabriel's tummy. I would appreciate it if you would go to a store in downtown Santa Ana, by Fourth Street, and get me some almond oil. That can be our exchange for this little *plácita*."

"Okay," Fern agreed.

After lunch that day, Fern, Xochitl, and Marina headed off to downtown Santa Ana. Once they rounded the corner onto Fourth Street, the area became crowded with mothers pushing strollers, businessmen strutting like peacocks, and dowdy but friendly women passing out business cards and flyers from store entrances advertising legal services, cleaning services, and clothing sales. The girls walked past the Plaza Fiesta, where fluttering triangular flags displayed Mexico's national colors of red, green, and white. Above the banners, three much larger flags—one for California, one for the United States, and one for Mexico—waved atop fifty-foot poles. A carousel of horses with flaking paint spun giggling children in circles.

A short, wiry old man with a bad hip, wearing a cowboy hat, plaid shirt, jeans, and a belt with a humongous buckle, limped past the Panaderia and shouted "*¡Hola!*" to someone driving by in a lowrider. The familiar scent of tamarinda juice wafted from a cart parked on the corner of the sidewalk between pale pink two-story art deco buildings with teal awnings that protected the signs of various clothing, jewelry, and shoe stores on either side of the plaza.

"So how are we going to find this place?" Marina asked, looking around uncomfortably.

"We're looking for the smell of copal," Xochitl said. She narrowed her eyes and scanned the storefronts for the location of the *botanica* that burned the signature scent many great healers used. "Finding the best botanica, or healing center, can be as tricky as locating a magical portal to a parallel universe. Graciela was good at this. It's harder for me."

Fern giggled at the way Xochitl looked like a bloodhound tracking a raccoon. Still, she was almost envious of how far ahead of her Xochitl was when it came to Rogelia's magic.

"Look," Xochitl said, pointing. "See that crazily colorful window display for the Mexicana Botanica across the street? The one with the touristy Aztec wall hangings and *mocahetes*? It's like they're trying to appeal to Americans who think they're something because they've traveled, like they're amateur anthropologists."

"Like major coffee chains that think because they use a picture of a poor barista in their advertising, they're suddenly all about cultural diversity and free trade?" Fern piped in more strongly than she had intended.

"Yeah, something like that," Xochitl said, laughing. "That place is obviously too commercial—not enough soul. We're looking for the dense feel of magic." Xochitl paused, and her mouth kind of twisted as if she had tasted something sour. "But even the best magic can't do everything."

"You never know," Fern said hopefully.

"Yeah, you never know." Xochitl stopped short and whipped around. "There it is." She pointed to the sign over one storefront and read aloud, "Four Crows."

Fern swung open the gate of a white picket fence and Marina and Xochitl followed. Fern's feet crunched over thousands of tiny gray and black pebbles covering the courtyard. Rhythmic Native American music echoed from inside the shop. To the left, water trickled in a concrete fountain with a center column in a large circular basin lined with coins.

Around the fountain, chairs, benches, and sofas were set as if for a gathering of friends. To the right, in a smaller area, a forest of hanging flowers and plants flourished in pots of every shape and color. A four-foot dream catcher hung from a post where a Hopi ladder leaned. A shaggy willow tree dropped leafy branches onto the patio like long feathers.

Above the door, a bumper sticker read IGNORANCE IS THE MOST DANGEROUS THING IN SOCIETY. Fern pranced into the store, already head over heels in love with the place.

Ceramic bowls and statues of eagles, mountain lions, coyotes, wolves, and horses rested on every shelf. Shield drums and painted buffalo skulls lined the walls. Bone, turquoise, and seed bead jewelry rested next to essential oils in a wood and glass case. Wild turkey, hawk, and imitation eagle feathers hung from threads or were stuffed into jars. Large, clear quartz crystal points, tumbled semiprecious stones, and bundles of white sage, red cedar, flat cedar, and piñon were piled in baskets next to sticks of fifty or so kinds of incense.

"I love how it smells like Rogelia's room in here," Fern said as she inhaled deeply. The store had an earthy scent that also reminded Fern of the woods, a place that made her feel really connected to nature.

"Glad to see you're okay," a familiar voice said.

Fern turned around to find herself face to face with Tristán. She grinned but said nothing. He smiled, revealing perfectly white straight teeth. They just looked into each other's eyes. Fern felt like she was in one of those Mexican *novelas* her grandmother watched whenever she came to visit from Colombia.

"Can I help you find something?" Tristán asked Fern, still gazing deep into her eyes.

"I don't know," Fern replied distractedly. She stared at the carving of a bear claw hanging from a leather cord that rested just below Tristán's Adam's apple. Suddenly, she was very conscious of the fact that she was wearing a ratty Sierra Club T-shirt and sweatpants. Why hadn't she thought to put on something cute and sexy? Well, she obviously hadn't thought she'd run into anyone she cared to impress.

Marina giggled. "We'll just go over here," she said, and pulled Xochitl away to look at the irregularly shaped dream catchers fashioned from driftwood.

"Do you work here?" Fern asked.

"A few hours here and there," Tristán said.

Fern's knees felt wobbly, and it was a little hard to catch her breath.

"Were you looking for something in particular?" Tristán asked.

"Uh, yeah. We need some almond oil," Fern muttered. Never before had she been so taken with a guy. She felt like her skin was on fire and a volcano was erupting in her chest.

"It's over here," Tristán said.

Fern followed Tristán to a row of plastic bottles filled with various base oils. Tristán deftly maneuvered through the store. His black hair was pulled back into a low ponytail, tied with a string of rawhide. *He's even better-looking than I remember, and taller, too.* Suddenly, a sunshine yellow light began to float around Tristán. The soft color moved around his head and slowly drifted over his shoulders and down his arms. It was a happy, bouncy aura. *Ooh, a new color. Very interesting.*

Tristán grabbed a bottle off the shelf and turned to face Fern. "Almond oil is good for just about anything. What do you need it for?" Tristán asked.

"Now, why would I tell you that?" Fern asked teasingly.

She was stalling for time. Why would he have a gray aura one day and a yellow one another? Could auras change? Why had she seen the aura around only Tristán and no one else? Fern looked over at Xochitl and Marina, who were now testing the different sounds the drums made. She couldn't see a flicker of light or the faintest shadow around either of them.

"Usually almond oil isn't used alone. Maybe I can help you find something else, like an essential oil, to match your specific intention," Tristán said.

"Do you practice *curanderismo*?" Fern was completely awestruck.

"No, but my aunt Alma owns this shop," Tristán answered. "And I've learned some things along the way. She teaches the traditions of our people."

"Your people?" Fern asked. "That's kind of a funny way to put it."

"I'm Tongva—California Indian from Los Angeles," Tristán replied, raising his refined chin a little higher. "I just moved down to Orange County from Whittier a couple of weeks ago."

Fern was flabbergasted. "Is there an active Indian community in Orange County?"

"Yeah, pretty much," Tristán said. "We have powwows here at the store a couple of times a year. Auntie Alma teaches basket weaving with pine needles, and Uncle Jimi is a wingman for the Bear Dance."

"What's a Bear Dance?" Fern breathed.

"It's a ceremony that honors the healing energy of the bear. Tongva are bear people," Tristán said proudly. His yellow aura took on a golden hue, particularly around his necklace.

Fern stared at the bear claw. "That is so cool. I think it's so important to keep a strong connection with the animals and earth."

"Like the Sierra Club?" Tristán asked, nodding at her shirt.

Fern looked down at her T-shirt and laughed. "Yeah, I'm a fanatical tree hugger. Right now I'm part of a team fighting the developers who want to build homes on the Bolsa Chica wetlands."

"Hey, Uncle Jimi is involved with that. The Tongva had a village there years ago," Tristán said.

"That's where they found those thousands-of-years-old cogs," Fern added fervently. "They still haven't figured out what they were used for. . . ." Fern trailed off because Tristán was smiling at her. "What?" she asked.

"It's just really cool to hear someone else be so dedicated to helping our causes." Tristán took a small bundle of dried sage leaves out of a woven basket. "Here." He handed it to Fern. She stared at his outstretched hand, which glowed yellow from his aura.

"Thanks," Fern whispered. She stared down at the gift and ran her finger over the soft leaves. She looked up at Tristán, and a thrill rushed through her when she thought of how much they had in common.

"Fern, did you find the oil yet?" Marina asked as she and Xochitl joined them. In her arms, Marina held a roll of charcoal, an abalone shell, several white taper candles, a packet of copal resin, and a few tumbled semiprecious stones.

"I hear there's a meeting next Friday at Bolsa Chica." Tristán handed Fern the almond oil. "Maybe I'll see you there." He sauntered over to the cash register.

Marina raised her eyebrows at Fern and walked over to place her items on the counter, then dug through her purse for her wallet. Fern reached into her back pocket and handed Marina a crumpled five-dollar bill.

Tristán looked up from ringing up the sales to glance at Fern. He smiled shyly at her. Without smiling back, Fern studied Tristán, looking around his head for his aura. He seemed to grow nervous under her scrutiny. Suddenly, the yellow light around Tristán faded, then darkened and became more like the gray cloud Fern had seen before.

I knew it, Fern thought. *It was just too good to be true.*

Ten

A week later, Xochitl sat at the kitchen table on a Thursday morning, looking around the empty room. The quiet seemed unbearable. She missed family breakfasts in Mexico. She missed the smell of frying *nopales*, the sound of her brothers fighting, and the task of braiding her sister Amelia's hair. But most of all, she missed Graciela. When her father had earned enough money for their passage, the rest of the family would move to California, but Graciela would never return. All she had in this foreign place was Nana and Papá.

The phone rang on the kitchen wall, directly above Xochitl's head, shocking her back to reality. Xochitl picked it up. "Hello?"

"I can't wait for Rogelia's next lesson!"

"Fern?" Xochitl asked, trying to get her bearings.

"Yeah. Listen, Xochitl," Fern began. "We want to do another spell. We've got enough stuff. I already talked with Marina. She's all set to do the ceremony at my house tonight. My parents will be out dancing for a while. Do you think you can sleep over?"

Xochitl looked out the kitchen window to the backyard. The fear that Marina and Fern were more interested in *curanderismo* and spells than they were in being friends raised its ugly head once more. Why were the girls so excited about spells? "I don't know," Xochitl said reluctantly.

"Come on, Xochitl," Fern begged. "It wouldn't be the same without you there. We need your expertise."

Xochitl rolled her eyes. It was obvious Fern and Marina didn't understand how bizarre and superstitious *curandera* magic from Jalisco, Mexico, could be. At least the kind her nana practiced had its share of different ideas.

Fern and Marina probably think magic is all hocus-pocus, swishing wands, and getting someone to fall in love with you, Xochitl mused. No, magic from Mexico was much more serious than that. It wasn't about tricks or bending someone's will. It required faith—something she currently lacked—and dedication to observing nature.

"Please say you'll come, Xochitl," Fern implored.

"I've got to . . . ," Xochitl began, but there was nothing she could even think of to lie about. All she had to do today was sit around by herself and be sad.

"Xochitl, I know you're all alone there. Your nana is at the Peraltas' until tomorrow night, and your dad's got to be working. Don't mope by yourself. We want you with us."

Xochitl looked around the deserted kitchen. Going to Fern's would be a distraction. . . .

"Please say you'll come," Fern begged.

"Okay," Xochitl agreed. Moments later she hung up the phone, wondering if she had done the right thing.

As the day wore on, Xochitl began to feel very nervous about another sleepover and casting a spell. She didn't want to be doing magic of any kind. It had failed her. Around five o'clock, she decided to call Fern and tell her she had a stomachache, but before she could pick up the phone, there was a knock at the door. When Xochitl opened it, she found Fern and Marina standing on her porch.

"I had an intuition that you might back out, so we came to get you," Fern said, smiling broadly.

Xochitl couldn't help returning Fern's smile. "All right," she relented. "Let me get my things."

❀ ❀ ❀

Once they were all settled in Fern's bedroom that evening, they decided they would do the spell at midnight. Xochitl stared at the mural on Fern's wall.

Fern followed Xochitl's gaze. "Do you like it? When I got home from my last visit to Colombia, I stuck that burlap coffee sack up there." Fern pointed to the decoupaged, blown-up pictures of her and a man pouring beans into the sack. "That's Uncle Carlos. He's a barista and grows the best coffee in Sierra Nevada de Santa Marta, Colombia. He has seven kids, and I ran absolutely wild with them when we visited my dad's family. My aunt Ibis reminds me of your nana."

Oh great, thought Xochitl. *Now all they'll talk about is magic.*

"I'm really enjoying hanging around your nana," Marina said. "She's taught me a lot."

"I'm beginning to think I can see more colors in auras now because of her," Fern said. "I saw another aura around Tristán when we were in Four Crows. I think it's weird that it would change color and that I would only see it around Tristán. I looked and couldn't see anything around either of you. Do you think some people don't have auras?"

"No, Nana said auras are around all living things," Xochitl answered before she could stop herself. If she was so adamant about not discussing magic, she scolded herself, why was she contributing to the conversation?

Marina scratched her bare leg. "Hey, maybe your ability to see auras comes and goes."

"Yeah, Rogelia said something like that," Fern conceded. "Maybe with time and more lessons, I'll see them around other people."

"So you've got your magical powers," Xochitl said. "Why do we need to do another spell?"

"It's kinda cool," Marina said.

"It's not as if you've never done this before," Fern chided.

"Mexican magic is different," Xochitl muttered. She sat on a cushion in front of the bay window in Fern's room, clutching an orange polka-dotted pillow under her chin.

Xochitl wondered what would happen if she tried to disappear. Could she slip out of Fern's house unnoticed? Maybe she should have disappeared when she heard them knock on her door. Too late for that, but she could still go invisible now. Xochitl closed her eyes, slowed her breath, and focused her attention on the spot just above her belly button, the place her nana called the solar plexus. She imagined pure invisible light taking over her physical form, almost like it would erase her fingers, her hands, then her arms. She began to feel the floaty sensation that always preceded her disappearances.

Just then, Xochitl felt a hand clutch her arm just above her elbow. Awareness flooded her body, and she felt the heaviness of the earth plane. Her eyes flew open.

"Promise not to vanish"—Fern held tight to Xochitl—"and I'll let go."

"What makes you think I was going to?" Xochitl asked.

"Just a hunch," Fern replied as she let go of Xochitl and walked over to her bed. She flopped on her tummy facing her friends.

"Can you really disappear?" Marina asked.

"Yes, when I want," Xochitl said sulkily.

Marina whistled, impressed. "Do you want to right now?"

What could she say? *You are taking this magic thing all wrong. It doesn't fix problems, not the ones that matter, anyway. Not only that, but I'm totally out of my element here and my head is spinning and yes, I would love to disappear right now.* But Marina and Fern had been so nice, she couldn't bring herself to say these things, which she was sure would hurt their feelings.

"I can't imagine what it must be like to be in your shoes," Marina said, breaking the awkward pause. She pushed herself on a swing chair that was bolted to the ceiling.

"So let's do a little magic to improve our situation," Fern suggested.

"Magic isn't a cure-all," Xochitl said.

"No, but it can help you create a life of your choosing," Fern said firmly.

"Where did you hear that?" Marina asked while toying with the fringes of a throw pillow.

"Read it in our spell book," Fern said as she thumbed through *Magik for Teens*. "Xochitl, are we closer to a full or dark moon?"

"The moon will be full on Monday."

Xochitl's village in Mexico didn't have many night lights, so the stars and moon shone bright. It was second nature for her to know the moon's cycle and whether the moon was getting larger or smaller. She could also have told Marina which constellations were out at this time of year and the Aztec myths regarding their origins. But she wasn't about to open that can of pinto beans. She didn't want to hurt her new friends, but the idea of their proximity to her heart made her feel a little crowded and overstimulated, like waking up to a ten-person mariachi band playing in your bedroom.

Fern flipped through the spell book for a moment, then reported, "Okay, a waxing moon, getting bigger, is the perfect time to ask for things you want."

"I want a good hair day," Marina announced.

"You always have a good hair day, with your Pantene-perfect straight and shiny hair," Fern joked.

Marina made a wounded face at Fern. "No more jealousy. I like your curls."

"Thanks. But let's make another wish or two or three," Fern said.

"I want my mom to get off my back," Marina said. "She's got a new rant now."

"What is it?" Fern asked.

"I don't want to talk about it," Marina said coolly.

"Fine," Fern sighed. "I want to fall in love, just a little bit."

"You already are in love. With Tristán." Marina whomped Fern with the throw pillow.

"Am not!" Fern shrieked.

"I think you would make a good couple," Xochitl said quietly.

Fern blushed, then changed the subject. "Oh, and I want to save the Bolsa Chica wetlands from being developed."

"You're such a good person," Marina jibed. "When I grow up I want to be just like you."

Fern threw the pillow to Xochitl. "Hit her for me."

Xochitl threw the pillow at Marina. Marina caught the pillow in midair and tossed it back to Xochitl. "What do you want?"

Xochitl looked back and forth between Fern and Marina. She hugged the pillow and then lowered her eyes. "I want my sister back."

"Oh, Xochitl." Fern jumped up from her bed and put her arm around Xochitl's shoulder.

"Nana always says you can't go back in time." Xochitl blinked a tear away. "Let me see the book."

Marina handed the book to Xochitl. She opened it at random to the page about summoning the spirit of a loved one. Of course. Speaking to Graciela was what Xochitl wanted more than anything. She glanced at the spell's ingredients and quickly committed them to memory. She might as well try it. After all, spells from this book had worked for Marina and Fern. But this spell would have to be done in private and wasn't something she was ready to share with Fern or Marina. Xochitl's neighbor Mrs. Benitez had asked her to walk her pampered poodles a few days ago. With the money she earned, she could buy the ingredients she needed to cast the spell to speak with Graciela.

Scanning the book's pages, Xochitl wracked her brain to think of something normal, something fun and lighthearted to wish for. She looked up from the book. She saw Marina's walk-in closet with clothes spilling out of it. "I want new clothes," she announced confidently. It was a vague and re-mote desire, something she and Graciela had both dreamed about. When Xochitl had journeyed to America, she had brought only as many clothes as she could carry in a very small suitcase. Nana had picked up a few things for her from garage sales. All her clothes were practical and completely lacked style.

When the magical midnight hour struck, Fern drew the circle. Quietly, almost as if she didn't want to, Xochitl called in the four directions. Marina led the meditation. Fern rubbed oil on four white candles so roughly, she nearly broke one candle.

Xochitl watched the ceremony unfold like something out of a dream. Marina and Fern seemed almost greedy as they asked for their multiple desires. Xochitl didn't often do rituals like this. The spiritual work or magic she and Nana created was designed for a specific need, usually for a healing of some sort, not for a slew of wants.

Later that night, Xochitl slept fretfully, imagining all sorts of unformed nightmares. She hadn't exactly been taught that their ceremony tonight was wrong. But instinctively, it hadn't felt right.

⌘ ⌘ ⌘

The next morning, low, dark clouds crept along the hori-zon, threatening a rare summer storm. Xochitl, Fern, and Ma-rina sat around the pine kitchen table while Fern's mom served them pancakes with real maple syrup. Fern's mother had the kind of flawless, sculpted face that looked good even without makeup. She was dressed in an elegant crepe blouse and jeans with bejeweled appliqués that made her legs look long and trim.

"You were up late last night," Fern said critically to her mother.

Fern's mother ruffled the top of her daughter's curly hair. "This is why I'm so lucky to have such an independent daughter. I never worry about my girl."

Fern gave her mother a feeble smile.

"Let's go to the Block today," Marina suggested. "I don't have to be home until dinner."

"What's the Block?" Xochitl asked.

"This really cool outdoor mall," Marina said. "They have tons of hip clothes stores and usually tons of eye candy." She took a bite of pancake.

"Eye candy?" Xochitl repeated, bewildered. She felt a wave of guilt wash over her. She and Graciela had planned to shop at American malls together.

"Cute guys!" Fern said.

"But then, Fern already has a favorite eye candy," Marina teased.

"What's this?" Fern's mother asked, setting a glass jug of orange juice on the table.

"Nothing, Mom," Fern said, casting a warning look at Marina and Xochitl.

Marina kicked Xochitl under the table, and they both burst out into squeals and snorts of suppressed laughter.

"Stop it," Fern hissed at them. "Mom," Fern said loudly to cover her friends' laughter. "Can you drive us to the Block?"

"Sure. I heard Ann Taylor is having a shoe sale," Fern's mother said.

Fern rolled her eyes. "Mom, you already have a hundred pairs of shoes. The more you buy, the more waste is jammed into the landfills."

"Yes, but I just got this beautiful turquoise dress to wear dancing with your father, and I need shoes to match it," Fern's mother said. She kissed the top of Fern's head. "I'll try to find something biodegradable, okay?"

"They sell those?" Marina inquired.

"Hush," Fern's mother said with a sly smile.

⌘ ⌘ ⌘

Fern's mother drove the girls to the Block an hour later. "Just pull up to the front, Mom, and let us out before you find a parking spot. We'll take the bus home," Fern said.

"Well, I didn't think you'd go shopping with me," Fern's mother said lightly. "I do have a reputation to uphold."

"Puhleeze," Fern said as she got out of the car.

"Thank you, Mrs. Fuego," Marina and Xochitl said together.

They waved goodbye and fell in with the crowds. Xochitl felt a little claustrophobic around so many people. It seemed like everybody and their brother was out today. The busy shoppers crowding the mall kept bumping into her. It was as if she was only half-visible. Xochitl felt only partly in her body, like she was waking up from a really believable dream but hadn't opened her eyes yet. This had never happened to her before. She considered becoming completely invisible, but then she would surely lose Marina and Fern.

Xochitl looked around incredulously at all the clothing shops, where mannequins wore bright summer clothes and jewelry sparkled in display cases. Music blared from an overhead speaker. Cart vendors stationed in the wide walkways sold everything from cell phone covers to bath salts to dog clothing. She was finally shopping at an American mall with

American friends. This mall even had flashing billboards. *This is what you wanted*, Xochitl told herself. *Don't blow it.* Xochitl steeled herself against her fear of being overwhelmed and lost in confusion.

"Where to first?" Fern asked.

"Let's go to Planet Beauty. It might not be the MAC counter at Macy's, but I need to get some new lipstick and some blush," Marina said, shaking her abundant hair out of her face. "Then we can hit the Hollister store. They've just come out with the cutest miniskirts, and I'm dying to pick up a couple."

"A couple?" Fern asked.

"Yeah, I've got some money left over in my debit account this month," Marina said. "You want me to buy you something?"

"No," Fern said. "You know I prefer to choose my clothes at vintage shops because I like them, not to follow fashion trends."

"You don't have to get testy," Marina said. "I'll buy Xochitl something. Okay, Xochitl?"

Xochitl nodded mutely. She stared in awe as they passed the Edwards Theater and the outsized silver strips of movie reels fashioned into benches. A circle of palm trees stood in front of ten-foot-tall images of famous movie stars. Brilliant fuchsia and vibrant orange bougainvillea covered the walls. Jugglers, a bouncy house, a bucking bronco, and a climbing wall provided entertainment for small children in the large plaza in front of the theater. *This is a bit much.*

"Whoa. Did the lights always flash like that?" Fern asked, looking up at the blown-up pictures of well-known actors above the theater.

"What lights?" Xochitl asked.

"There, see those lights?" Fern pointed to the billboards and shop signs.

"I don't see anything." Marina said. "Is it an aura?"

"How can it be? It's over a billboard," Fern replied. "Wow, it's giving me a headache. Let's get inside."

Xochitl sighed with relief as they headed toward the doors of Planet Beauty. At least she wasn't the only one craving a little peace and quiet.

Fern pulled open the store's glass doors and was immediately sprayed with perfume by a woman wearing a white smock. "It's called Diva," she said with a plastic smile. "Like it?"

"No," Fern said rudely as she stormed past her.

A man in a business suit rammed into Marina. "Why don't you like your boss?" she asked Xochitl. "I didn't know you had a job."

"What?" Xochitl asked confusedly. The store was just as crowded and noisy as outside. She was feeling really uncomfortable and had to close her eyes to concentrate on breathing properly.

Just then, a frumpy woman with frizzy brown hair bumped past the girls without seeming to see them; she appeared lost in her own thoughts.

"I don't think you have bad acne, Fern," Marina said sympathetically.

"Oh my God, what are you talking about now?" Fern asked, laughing. "For once, my face is clear."

"I don't know," Marina said as she arrived at the makeup counter. "I just thought I heard someone say . . . Oh, forget it." Marina reached out to take a lipstick.

Dance music piping from the loudspeaker grew louder and louder in Xochitl's ears. Xochitl tried to calm her breathing.

She was beginning to feel consumed by all the noises, sights, and smells, like she had when they were in Guadalajara. She felt like she was falling into a dark pit. Graciela would have recognized the signs. She would have realized that Xochitl was too freaked out to concentrate on turning invisible. Her sister would have seen the growing look of panic in Xochitl's eyes.

"Let me put some makeup on you, Xochitl," Fern said. "You're looking kind of pale."

"I think I need to rest." Xochitl sat down on the black metal stool in front of the counter and took a shuddering breath. She needed to calm down. She tried to focus on the advice Graciela would have given her and imagine a peaceful setting.

Fern grabbed a Q-tip and dipped it into chestnut-colored eye shadow. Her hand trembled as she applied the shadow to Xochitl's eyelids. Fern blinked several times. She bent over Xochitl for so long, Xochitl thought she might scream if she didn't get some space. Fern finally succeeded in smearing the makeup on Xochitl's temple.

"Fern, what are you trying to do? Make her look like Count Dracula?" Marina asked.

"My left eye," Fern complained. "I can't see out of it very well."

"Not a good time to be putting on makeup, then," Marina said.

Xochitl picked up a mirror and looked at her face. There was more color than white in her almond-shaped brown eyes. Streaks of dark eye shadow were smudged all over her lids. She took a cotton ball and with a shaking hand wiped her eye clean.

Marina dabbed rouge onto Xochitl's cheeks. She leaned

back to inspect Xochitl's face and cringed. "Xochitl, I hate to tell you this, but your face is getting all blotchy."

"Ooh, I can see a shadow around you, Xochitl," Fern said. "No color, just waving lines, pulsing like crazy. Speaking of crazy, Xochitl, stop breathing like that."

Xochitl twisted her cotton bracelet so tightly it almost broke. "I . . . can't . . . help . . . it!" she gasped. "It's so stuffy in here. I really don't like crowds." She yanked on the bracelet as if she could wrench Graciela back from the cosmos to be with her on earth.

"Maybe we should go," Marina said. "I'm not feeling so hot myself."

Once they got outside, Xochitl, Marina, and Fern linked arms, forming a moving wall as they stumbled down the walkway between the stores. Fern staggered toward a guy standing next to a vending cart of massage oils. Xochitl pulled on Fern's arm just before she crashed into him.

"Watch out," Xochitl said, and looked back at the cart. She wanted to take some of the oil and pour it over her chest. She felt like her skin was on fire. Her breathing came in rasps. Her legs were like lead weights, but she forced herself to get as far away as possible from the hordes of people, clashing sounds, and blaring lights.

"I'm trying, but I can't see," Fern said. "My eyes are burning."

"Oh my God, the voices are starting again," Marina whined. "Only . . ." She paused and stared in disbelief at all the strangers whizzing past her. "I hear them. All their thoughts. It's so loud."

Fern gripped Xochitl's arm and closed her eyes. "These lights are too bright. I can't make out shapes properly."

"I . . . told . . . you we asked . . . for . . . too much last night. Supposed . . . to ask for . . . one thing . . . at a time," Xochitl panted. She clutched her throat. This had never happened before. They were in big trouble.

"You never said that. Oh man. Your face and neck are really getting red and bumpy," Marina said. "You look like you have malaria or something."

"Let's get out of here." Fern dug into her purse for her sunglasses, found them, and put them on. "I can't stand this glare. You don't think I'm going blind, do you?"

"Xochitl, we need to go see your nana," Marina said.

"No way!" Xochitl objected. "Do you have any idea how much trouble I will be in? We'll have to . . ." She tried to breathe deeply and slowly, but the overwhelming number of people and their jarring energy made it difficult. "We'll have to hope it goes away once we get out of here."

Eleven

As they weaved through the crowd at the mall, Marina heard snippets of thoughts from every person passing by.

God, these shoes hurt, complained a woman in a tweed business suit with high heels.

No one remembered my birthday, sulked a teenage boy dressed in tight black jeans, with straight shaggy hair and eyes darkened with black eyeliner.

The bombarding noises gave Marina an earache. She closed her eyes and reached cautiously to massage the groove behind her earlobe. She moved her jaw from side to side to redirect the pain, but the earache refused to lessen. The intense pain seemed not only to shoot through her ear but also to send a constricting tightness to her heart.

"What are you doing?" Xochitl asked.

"My ear hurts," Marina said. "And I'm about to lose it."

You'll be all right, came a calming voice in Marina's head. It was one of the soothing voices she had heard before. This one sounded like an older woman. *You will be fine once you get to Rogelia's.*

"You look like a cow chewing grass," Fern said.

"What'd you say?" Marina asked loudly.

"Come on," Xochitl said, picking up the pace. "Let's . . . get . . . to . . . the bus stop."

Marina looked over at Xochitl, who was still panting. Fern stumbled and clung to her for dear life. How would they get out of this?

Just then the skies opened, sending heavy raindrops down on them. By the time they reached the bus stop some five blocks from the mall, they were drenched.

Despite her condition, Marina fidgeted uncomfortably, trying to decide the best place to stand or sit. She turned her head from side to side, sending her wet hair flying. She had no desire to be seen at the bus stop. They were a little too close to driving age to be seen waiting to ride a bus, especially in the rain. Marina felt shivers of embarrassment race up her arms. She thought about calling her mom to ask for a ride and laughed to herself. How would she explain the state she and her friends were in?

Fern looked at Marina and Xochitl. "You look like a pair of drowned rats."

"That makes you a fuzzy drowned rat," Marina shot back. She laughed nervously. They really did look a mess.

Xochitl had her eyes closed with her hand gingerly pressed to her chest, working hard to calm her breath. A dumpy-looking man with a potato-shaped body stuffed into a too-small suit leered at them.

Marina didn't wait to hear what he had in mind. "Pervert," she spat at him as she pulled her friends by the hands to the other side of the bus stop.

Fern fumbled frantically through her purse.

"What is it?" Marina asked. She cupped her hand to her ear, hoping to decrease the sharp pain.

"I can't find my wallet," Fern whimpered. "And my eye hurts like hell." She lifted her glasses and raised her face to catch some of the raindrops in her eyes.

The northbound 43 bus hissed and moaned as it stopped in front of the girls. Xochitl pulled Marina and Fern aside. "You need to look at this." She pulled down her shirt collar. The scarlet rash racing across Xochitl's chest shone like Rudolph's nose against her mocha-colored skin.

"Oh no," Marina groaned. She turned to Fern. "Ferny, look at me."

Apprehensively, Fern lowered her face from looking skyward to her friends. Both Marina and Xochitl gasped with horror.

"What is it?" Fern asked.

"The skin around your left eye is practically swollen shut," Marina said.

Fern peered at her wobbly reflection in the bus mirror. Only a slit of a cotton-candy pink revealed itself underneath her puffy eyelid. "It's as if I've been fighting with Oscar de la Hoya. What if I go blind?"

They were in deep trouble. Marina thought she might go deaf from the high-pitched tone ringing in her ear. "Can we see your nana now?" She turned around wildly, searching for

Xochitl, but Xochitl was nowhere in sight. "Xochitl, this is no time to disappear! We need you. Come on, we have to stick together."

Xochitl slowly materialized. Only the dumpy man noticed, which caused him to keep his distance. Xochitl looked sheepishly at her friends. "Sorry. Okay, let's get to Nana."

Immediately, Marina bit her lip. A terrible thought occurred to her. It was almost dinnertime on Friday. Rogelia wouldn't be working at her house until Monday morning, almost three days away. What if their conditions got worse? Although she knew her mother didn't like her hanging out in the barrio, Marina didn't see much of a choice here.

Necessitas la ayuda de Rogelia, a soft girl's voice said urgently yet calmly in Marina's head. It was strange how comforting and familiar this voice sounded, despite the fact that it spoke in a language she didn't understand.

"We'll have to take the south bus"—Xochitl took a raspy breath—"to Santa Ana." She grabbed Fern's and Marina's hands and dragged them across the street.

"Slow down, I can't see straight," Fern complained, stumbling as she tried to keep pace with Xochitl.

"That's why I've got your hand," Xochitl explained patiently.

"Guys, I don't know about this," Marina said worriedly, reluctantly trotting behind Xochitl.

You need Rogelia, Marina heard the harmonious voice of the older woman say adamantly. *She will heal you.*

Xochitl reached the other side of the street and guided Fern up the curb. She turned to face Marina. *"¿Qué pasó?"* Xochitl panted. "What's the problem?"

"Nothing," Marina lied. What was she supposed to say? *I'm sorry, but you see, my mom is going to freak when she finds out*

I've been to your house because, well, you live in the barrio and she doesn't think it's a safe or good enough place for me. But for you, it's perfectly okay.

Xochitl hastily boarded the southbound bus and flashed the driver her bus pass. Marina guided Fern onto the steps.

"I—I still can't . . . ," Fern stammered as she fumbled with her purse.

Marina glanced nervously at the driver. She clearly heard him thinking that he should throw them off the bus for disorderly conduct. "I got it," Marina said, paying both their fares, since Fern had still not unearthed her wallet.

Fern staggered down the aisle to where Xochitl sat trying to catch her breath. She plopped herself down on the lap of a homeless-looking fellow with straggly hair, a dirty sunburned face, and a stained army field jacket. "Ohmigod," Fern squealed as she jumped up.

Marina took Fern by the arm and led her to the seat next to Xochitl. "What are you doing?" Marina looked at the bum, who groggily looked around him. His only thoughts were about where he could lay his head to sleep.

"I didn't do it on purpose," Fern wailed. "I'm telling you *I can't see!*"

"What is happening to us?" Marina asked as she helplessly watched the bus pull away from the curb and head toward Santa Ana and the barrio her mother so detested. On the other hand, they were heading for Rogelia, and this provided Marina with a small amount of relief.

Even though hardly anyone spoke on the bus, Marina could hear a jumbled orchestra of their thoughts. She pressed her fingertips to her ears, hoping to drown out the internal dialogue of thirty people. It was as if the voices were inside her head and she couldn't stop them no matter what she did.

She watched the raindrops race after each other, hoping to distract herself from the excruciating pain in her ear and what she would say to her mother. Thunder boomed in the distance. Before long, many of the signs no longer announced their wares in English but in Spanish. Yellowed newspapers lay scattered against graffiti-marked walls. One garden featured lush banana trees, trumpet vines creeping over cinder-block walls, and jewel-toned flowers.

"This is it," Xochitl announced. "This is our stop."

Holding on to Fern, Marina followed Xochitl off the bus. They raced down a few streets until they arrived at the little white and green bungalow-style house where Xochitl lived. Rogelia stood inside the front door, clad in her knitted shawl, as if she was expecting them.

"Come in. Come in." Rogelia held open the screen door, beckoning them with her hand.

Fern, Xochitl, and Marina scurried up the wine-colored steps and into the house. There was no hallway, so they stepped directly into the living room. Mr. Garcia sat in a patched armchair reading *La Opinión*, the Spanish-language newspaper. Next to him a stack of four or five books lay beside a 1970s reading lamp with a large, tubular goldenrod lampshade. Tattered books were neatly lined on a wooden shelf behind him. He looked up blankly and laid his cigarette in a clay ashtray. "Ai." Mr. Garcia shook his head in exasperation. "Xochitl, get your friends dry clothes. Mamá?"

"We'll take care of it," Rogelia said. "Come on, *niñas*."

Xochitl dashed off to her bedroom while Marina and Fern followed Rogelia down the stark white hallway into Rogelia's room. This room looked very similar to the one Rogelia kept at the Peralta house, with the hanging bunches of herbs, wooden crosses, and pictures of the Virgin Mary and La Virgen de Guadalupe. Marina felt she had never truly stepped into a Mexican home until this moment. Despite the pain in her ear, she began to feel that they were going to be okay. Rogelia had lit about a hundred votive candles: on the altar, on sconces, and on the shelf where she kept her crystal skull, her eagle's wing, and an extra supply of saint candles.

There were also many pictures of the Garcia family adorning the walls. Marina heard a humming coming from the photographs, as if the people pictured were talking to her. She stepped closer to a picture of Xochitl and Graciela with their arms wrapped around each other's shoulders, standing knee-deep in a wide river banked by dark green plants. Marina heard the distant echo of laughter and running water. They had been identical twins. Both had long black hair, brown eyes, and heart-shaped faces.

"No one could tell them apart except for their mother and me," Rogelia said quietly.

Marina contemplated how sad it would be if either of her sisters, Monica or Samantha, died. Especially Monica, since they were only one year apart. She didn't think she could bear the pain.

Xochitl returned with dry clothes. Marina flinched as she pulled her wet top over her ears. She would faint if this pain didn't subside soon. Settled into the dry clothes, Marina, Fern, and Xochitl sat huddled together on the edge of Rogelia's bed.

"What happened?" Rogelia asked firmly as she plucked flower heads from the hanging herbs and placed them in a bowl of water.

"We did a spell," Fern admitted.

"Why are you girls so impatient?" Rogelia asked. "I still need to have a *plácita* with Xochitl and Marina before we are ready to move forward. I was intending to have the *limpia* next Friday, but obviously we'll need to wait an additional week so you all can learn the value of patience. Look at you, *mi'jita*." She pointed to the angry red rash on Xochitl's chest. It had recently crept up to her neck.

Xochitl's lip quivered. Marina knew without reading Xochitl's thoughts that she wanted more than ever to disappear. Marina grabbed Xochitl's hand and squeezed it. No one spoke. Rogelia set a small black cauldron on a small table covered with a bloodred scarf. She lit a charcoal and placed it in the cauldron. Rogelia leaned close to the charcoal and blew on it until the edges turned chalk white. She sprinkled copal resin inside. The incense smoke immediately wafted into the air.

"It wasn't Xochitl's fault," Marina said protectively.

"What wasn't Xochitl's fault?" Rogelia asked. "Spit on your finger and rub your neck behind your ear," she told Marina.

Baffled, Marina looked at Xochitl for reassurance. Xochitl nodded, and Marina could hear her silently say, *It's okay, you can trust her.* Dubiously, Marina spat on her fingertips and began to rub her neck. This was bizarre. But if it could help, Marina was all for it. She glanced up at Rogelia.

The healer's voice resounded in Marina's head. *What have you done?*

Marina didn't want to answer. But she knew that at the onset, Rogelia had said this journey would require honesty, so she trusted that she wouldn't get in too much trouble for telling the truth. "We asked for a lot of things during a ritual and we cast several spells."

Rogelia took a cloth from a shelf on the wall and dunked it into the herb-infused water. "When you open the door to the spiritual realm, it's like finding another world that has been existing right alongside your world. Every creature, animal, plant, even the planets have their own communication going on all the time. You just haven't been aware of it until now. You must enter this other world slowly, so that you can grow accustomed to the constant barrage of new information."

"Lie down," Rogelia said kindly to Fern, who obeyed without delay. Rogelia picked up the tea-soaked cloth and placed it over Fern's eyes.

"Ahh," Fern moaned.

"Where did you learn about this spell?" Rogelia asked as she moved Marina's fingers directly behind her ears and gently guided them in small circles until Marina could do it on her own.

"From a book I bought," Marina said. The more she rubbed her neck, the more her earache subsided. As the pain slowly lessened, she felt a quiet come over her. When she glanced around at her friends, she was relieved that she could no longer hear their innermost thoughts. Marina looked into Rogelia's warm brown eyes and felt immense gratitude.

Rogelia sighed. "Books are wonderful resources," she said. "But you must allow the information to sink into your mind, body, and soul with the passage of time. If you rush through your learning, stacking spells and magical information on top of each other, everything will collide in one big mess. It's as silly as getting behind the wheel of a car without knowing the rules of the road."

"Just like the woman in Moonlight Midwifery said." Fern whispered as she lifted the washcloth momentarily.

"Continue to read the book if you like, but please do not do any more spells for now," Rogelia requested. "I will speak with Marina and Xochitl, and we'll have our *limpia* in two weeks. Please remember to bring something that honors the four directions of east, north, west, and south."

Fern, Marina, and Xochitl nodded. Marina tried to convey her dedication to conform with her eyes. She felt there was nothing she would ever do again to interfere with the trust and responsibility Rogelia was placing in her, especially because Rogelia made Marina feel protected and safe.

Rogelia broke open an aloe leaf and squeezed the plant's juice, which dripped into a jar. She passed the jar through the incense smoke. She expertly drizzled aloe juice on Xochitl's rash, and taking another cloth, she placed it over Xochitl's chest. Then Rogelia shook her rattle over the girls and sang. She picked up her cauldron and carried it through the room, filling every corner with incense smoke.

⌘ ⌘ ⌘

The sky was ink black by the time the healing was complete and all the girls' ailments had disappeared. Marina anxiously dialed her home number from a phone hanging on the kitchen wall. She hardly had time to cross her fingers before her mother answered.

"Mom—"

"Where have you been?" Marina's mother yelled.

"Mom, I'm okay," Marina said consolingly.

"I've been worried sick about you! I want you home right now."

Marina's eyes darted to where Xochitl stood talking to Fern in the living room. Could they hear her mother shouting? "Mom, I can't get home," Marina whispered, covering the mouthpiece so no one could hear what she was saying. "I'm at Xochitl's."

Dead silence filled the line.

"Hello? Mom?" Marina said softly. Her breathing came in ragged rasps. "I need you to come pick me up."

"I've told you not to hang out in the barrio," Marina's mother said coldly. "Have Pilar drive you home."

"She can't. Danny and Miguel are already asleep," Marina protested. She had already asked Fern about this.

"Well, I'm not coming to get you," Marina's mother said with finality. "Have Mr. Garcia drive you, and you'd better be home by ten!"

Marina glanced at the kitchen clock. "Mom, it's already nine-thirty."

"Then I suggest you hurry."

Marina stared at the receiver. Her mother had hung up.

Marina poked her head into the living room and saw that Mr. Garcia had fallen asleep on the couch, his snoring ruffling his mustache. There was no way she was going to disturb him. Marina thought about asking Rogelia for a ride, but then she remembered that Rogelia didn't have a driver's license—in fact, her mother drove Rogelia home every Friday afternoon.

How am I going to get back home in a half hour?

There was only one solution—run.

"I've gotta bounce," Marina said to Xochitl and Fern, then bolted out the door before either of them could say goodbye.

Marina dashed to the bus stop, praying that she'd catch a bus before they stopped running for the night. The rain continued to fall, but it had become more of a drizzle. When she was half a block away from the bus stop, Marina saw the bus pull away in front of her.

"No!" Marina cried. She sprinted after the bus and caught it at the stop light. Marina pounded on the bus door, startling the driver. The driver shook his head. "Please!" Marina screamed as tears filled her eyes. If she missed this bus, she would miss her curfew. If she missed her curfew, her mother would ground her for a month.

The light turned green and the bus driver took off, leaving Marina coughing in a cloud of toxic fumes. A gang of tattooed skinheads turned around in their seats at the back of the bus and laughed at her.

Cold sweat beaded Marina's forehead as she started to run again. It was all she could do. Although Marina played soccer, she was no track star. After sprinting for several blocks, she felt so sick to her stomach she thought she would vomit.

The distance between Xochitl's house and her house was five impossible miles, but a stitch pierced Marina's side once she reached mile one. Yet she had to keep running. Marina reached a section of road when the street lanterns became spaced further apart, making for long dark stretches. There was no sidewalk, but merely a thin bike lane to separate Marina from the cars that raced at fifty miles an hour beside her. On the other side was a cavernous black ditch.

Another ten minutes passed, and Marina had slowed to a walk, clutching her side and feeling like she was holding in bodily organs. She was sweating profusely but shivering from the cold and fear. This was it. She'd never make curfew now.

No, no, mi'jita, *help is on the way,* a voice echoed in Marina's head. It was the older woman's voice returning to encourage her.

"What are you talking about?" Marina asked out loud, irritated that the voice could be so calm when she was evidently in danger. "It's cold, it's dark, and I'm all alone."

Nothing is going to happen to you while I'm here, said the voice.

"What am I doing?" Marina asked herself. "I must be crazy to be talking to myself."

You're talking to me, the voice said calmly.

"Who are you?" Marina asked.

At that moment, an olive-green Pontiac Grand Prix drove up behind Marina, then pulled to the side of the road in front of her. She stared fearfully at the brake lights. Could this be the help she was told about, or was it danger? The voice didn't answer.

Marina had no one to rely on but herself. She decided to walk between the car and the ditch. When she reached the passenger window, Fern's crush, Tristán, leaned over the seat to ask, "What are you doing out here so late?"

"I'm running home. I need to make my curfew, or . . ." Marina bit her lip to keep from finishing the sentence, in addition to preventing herself from crying. The desperate situation her mother had placed her in made Marina feel ashamed and exposed.

"Get in," Tristán said. "I'll drive you home."

Marina slipped into his car. A rush of relief swept over her. But at the same time, she hoped Tristán wouldn't ask any embarrassing questions. No matter how many times Fern tried to convince Marina that her mother was the one who needed therapy, Marina felt self-conscious each time her mother treated her so unkindly, especially in public.

"Which way?" Tristán asked.

"Down Peralta Hills Road till it ends, then turn right on Lincoln and left on Bixby," Marina said.

"Got it," Tristán said.

Marina looked out the window. She rubbed her hands together, grateful to be in a warm car. What should she say? She wanted to make sure they stayed far away from why she was out here in the dark running for her life.

"My family used to own this land," Marina said, fishing for conversation.

"My family lived here before people owned land," Tristán said simply, staring straight at the road ahead of him.

"Oh," Marina said. "You're Indian."

"And you're Spanish," Tristán replied with a quick glance in her direction.

"Well, Mexican," Marina corrected. "Mexican American, I guess."

"It takes both Spanish and Indian people to make Mexicans," Tristán said jokingly.

Marina felt like she had just been schooled, but with kindness, not spite. She had never considered the people who had lived here before her family arrived or what had become of them. And even though she was sick of hearing her mother's ranting about their illustrious family history, she often found herself telling others that her Spanish ancestors were the Peraltas of Peralta Hills or the Yorbas of Yorba Linda and had been in Orange County for two hundred years. Until Rogelia and Xochitl had come along, she had never thought about those less fortunate than herself. Now it seemed like reminders of her privileged life were coming at her from all directions.

"How long have you and Fern been friends?" Tristán asked.

"Since preschool," Marina said.

Tristán nodded thoughtfully, as if he was impressed by the long relationship. They drove in silence for a bit. Marina glanced sideways at Tristán. He seemed very comfortable in the quiet. And he wasn't nosy. *The strong, silent type,*

Marina laughed to herself. That ought to give Fern a run for her money.

"Has Fern always been a tree hugger?" Tristán asked.

"Always," Marina answered. "She rarely wears shoes."

"Nature separators," Tristán declared.

Oh God, they even talk alike, Marina thought. "Turn right at the next block, we're almost there," Marina said.

"So, um, does she have a boyfriend?" Tristán asked quickly.

"Not this week," Marina said flippantly.

Qué malo, the girl's voice reprimanded in her head.

Marina wasn't sure what the voice meant, but she could tell by the tone that it wasn't exactly a compliment. And in truth, she was making Fern sound like she ran through guys like they meant nothing to her.

"Oh," Tristán said, disappointed.

"It's not like that," Marina said quickly. "Fern rarely acts on her crushes." Marina looked Tristán directly in the eyes. "At least so far."

De la qué té salvaste, the girl's voice said assuredly.

Marina sighed, still unsure of what the girl was saying. But somehow she felt confident that she had recovered Fern's reputation. She absolutely needed to learn Spanish.

Tristán turned onto Bixby and cruised along slowly, waiting for Marina's direction.

"My house is the third one on the left. The one with the lights shining on the palm trees," Marina pointed.

Tristán whistled low as he pulled up to Marina's house. "Nice crib."

"Yeah. Hey, thanks for the ride," Marina called as she jumped out of the car. "I gotta get inside."

Marina ran to her house and burst through the door. The time on the microwave read 9:59 p.m. Monica flew out of her bedroom, her blond hair whipped up into a neat ponytail, her hazel eyes blazing with apprehension. She breathed a sigh of relief when she saw Marina and gave her a big hug.

"I'm all right," Marina said, pulling away from her sister's tight embrace.

Marina walked into the kitchen. Her mother stood at the sink with her back to Marina. "Mom, I'm home."

Marina's mother's shoulders fell, then quickly tightened up. She turned and Marina was surprised to see her nose was red and her eyes were watery.

"Mom?" Marina asked.

Her mother barely looked at her before disappearing up the stairs to her bedroom, where she remained for the rest of the night.

Twelve

While the skies continued to sprinkle, Xochitl held an um-
brella over herself, Fern, and Rogelia. Huddled together,
they staggered down Occidental Street, which was lit by old-
fashioned, two-pronged street lanterns. Normally Fern would
have skipped playfully through the rain, maybe even sung at
the top of her lungs. But their disastrous attempt at spell
crafting and her concern about Marina kept her subdued.

"Will Marina be okay?" Xochitl asked.

Fern was momentarily startled. How did Xochitl know
what she had been thinking?

"She usually pulls through," Fern answered, choosing
her words carefully. She wasn't sure how much she should

divulge. Typically, Fern was not the best at keeping secrets, except the ones closest to her heart. And she knew Marina felt mortified when her mother lashed out at her. Fern silently wished Marina's mom could feel that kind of humiliation.

"*A cada puerco le llega su sábado,*" Rogelia said wisely. "Everyone gets what's coming to them in the end."

Fern looked suspiciously at Rogelia. Was her mind a newspaper for everyone to read?

"I do work in the Peralta house," Rogelia said crisply. "I see a lot."

"Oh. Yeah," Fern replied.

Obviously, Rogelia was going to be a powerful ally to have in their corner.

Fern rubbed her eye, grateful that she could see clearly and that it no longer hurt. They passed a small crowd standing under the flat yellow glow of the lamppost. Fern's friends from the neighborhood, Analisa Esparza and Cara Limon, were talking to a couple of boys. Fern's heart leapt to her throat. With a pang of jealousy, she thought one of them was Tristán, particularly since he had an ominous-looking gray cloud around him. However, when she got a closer look, she recognized the two guys as Ruben Gomez and Salvadore Ramirez. It was the first time she had seen color in an aura around someone other than Tristán. Her lessons with Rogelia were showing results.

Fern sighed in deep relief, but then she quickly felt uneasy. Ruben had a bad reputation as a player. He broke more hearts every week than she cared to count. He was a smooth sweet-talker with one thing on his mind. Could the gray aura mean that the person it covered like a cloak was not to be trusted and someone who didn't really care about you?

"What is it?" Rogelia asked when she saw Fern's dazed expression.

"Uh, nothing," Fern said. "Here's my house." She pointed to a bright yellow house whose sunshine orange and cobalt blue trim shone cheerfully even at night.

Rogelia scanned the windows for a sign of life. "Are your parents asleep?" she asked with an edge to her voice.

Fern tried to remain indifferent about her parents' frequent late nights with everyone but Pilar. But sometimes it was tough to hide that she didn't like being in the house alone. If only her parents knew that she kept a bat under her bed because she was afraid of intruders.

"No," Fern said, guarded. "They're probably still out dancing."

"I don't like it," Rogelia grunted.

"Now she's never going to stop," Xochitl chuckled.

"I'll be fine. I'm often home alone," Fern said. *Oh. I shouldn't have said that*, Fern thought.

Rogelia clucked her displeasure. She pulled her blue knitted shawl tightly around her shoulders.

"It's okay, really." Fern smiled brightly at Rogelia. The healer shook her head disapprovingly. Nervously, Fern gave Xochitl a quick hug. She clasped her cold fingers around Rogelia's warm hands and shook them. "Thank you, Doña Rogelia. I'm really looking forward to the *limpia*."

Rogelia looked straight at Fern, as if with her unwavering stare she could see through Fern's forced cheerfulness. Fern smiled uneasily and spun away. She thought compliments would get Rogelia off the scent of her discomfort with being alone. No such luck.

Fern ran up the empty driveway and the few short stairs

onto the patio landing. As quickly as she could, she dug out the key from the clay planter holding a large calla lily plant. She waved goodbye to Xochitl and Rogelia as the key turned the lock.

"Hasta luego," Xochitl called. "See you later."

Fern stepped inside and flipped on the porch light for her parents.

❀ ❀ ❀

All week Fern thought of Tristán, but she hadn't the nerve to visit him at Four Crows. She could be outright ballsy in most situations, but when it came to these crushes of hers, she preferred the safe route. On Saturday morning, Fern awoke from a dream of Tristán and her on a date together. They were walking along the beach, barefoot, holding hands, and talking about their shared passions, like hugging trees. Then they got a huge vegetarian pizza from Native Foods and gobbled it down with glasses of iced hibiscus tea. Just before they were about to kiss, Fern had woken up.

Fern looked up at the chandelier she had bought from the Second, her favorite thrift store. The morning light flashed through the crystal points. She was disappointed to be in her bed and not in Native Foods with Tristán. She yawned and stretched, trying to recapture the happy haze of her dream. Maybe she would see Tristán today. Would he come to Bolsa Chica? She thought of his warm brown eyes and the way he cared about the same things she did.

Then she thought of his storm cloud of an aura and how it made her question whether Tristán was a player like Ruben. Ugh. Why couldn't she just shake the image of his occasional gray aura and let herself like him wholeheartedly, without interruption?

Fern threw back the covers and got out of bed. She pulled on her Bolsa Chica Stewards tank top and a pair of Levi's. She pushed aside the floral, crinkled voile curtain she'd gotten from Cost Plus to cover her mirrored closet doors. She twisted around and checked to make sure her backside looked good in these jeans. Marina wore designer brands, like True Religion or Seven. Fern preferred the look of classic jeans on which she could sew patches over the tears or in well-chosen locations. Her patches were of the varied places she had been to, such as the Grand Canyon or Oaxaca, Mexico, and were scattered all over her jeans like stickers on an old-time steamer trunk. Fern slid into her favorite Teva hiking sandals and shuffled down to the kitchen. She poured herself a bowl of Honey Nut Cheerios and sat down at the table to enjoy her breakfast.

Fern's mother stumbled into the kitchen rubbing her eyes. She wrapped her baby blue chenille robe tighter around her waist as she beelined for the coffee machine.

"Mom, remember I need you to take me to Bolsa Chica this morning," Fern said.

"I can't," Mrs. Fuego mumbled, sipping her coffee. "I was up until three in the morning. Why don't you call your sister?"

⌘ ⌘ ⌘

Thirty minutes later, Pilar, Fern, and her two rowdy nephews, Danny and Miguel, drove down the 55 freeway to Huntington Beach. The boys' black spiked hair glistened from the sun streaming in through the sunroof. They began bouncing in their seats when their mom turned onto Pacific Coast Highway. A few miles later, Pilar took a right into the Bolsa Chica wetlands parking lot. A flock of white terns flew low over the lagoon as Pilar parked the car.

"I'll be a couple of hours, Pilar," Fern said, getting out of the car. "We've got a lot of work to do today."

"We're going to the beach across the street," Pilar said. "Just call me on my cell when you're ready."

"I'm going to ride my new bodyboard," Danny announced.

"Bet I'll catch more waves than you," Miguel challenged.

"Will not."

"Will too."

"Bye, guys," Fern said, and turned away from the car.

The scent of sweetgrass floated in from the fields. She felt jitterbugs doing their fancy dance in her stomach as she walked along the pickleweed growing beside the path leading to the front entrance. *Is Tristán here?* she wondered. Fern looked at the people milling about. Mostly, she saw the familiar faces she had seen over the last seven months, while she had been working with the Bolsa Chica Stewards and the plant restoration project. She glanced behind her and saw Tristán talking with a cute girl with a long black ponytail. Fern turned away quickly before he saw her spying on him. *Who is that girl?* In her search for Tristán, she didn't see the rock protruding out of the sand in front of her and stubbed her toe, nearly losing her balance.

"Are you okay?" Tristán asked, hastening toward her.

Fern chuckled nervously. "I can be a bit of a klutz." She put her foot gingerly back on the ground.

"I noticed," Tristán said, stuffing his hands in his pockets and backing away with a bit of a grimace.

"Hey!" Fern said.

Tristán smiled. "Only kidding. I'm glad you're not hurt." He wrapped a strand of hair around his ear.

Fern felt her anger melt like an ice sculpture in hundred-degree weather, especially when she noticed a cobalt blue aura forming around his head. Sparkles of white light flashed like stars in the nighttime sky. *That is so much better than gray, it's not even funny.* "So, you made it."

"Yeah, Uncle Jimi came with me," Tristán said, pointing to a man with a long silver braid that fell to the small of his back. He was facing the opposite direction, watching a brown pelican flying in the air.

"Uncle Jimi really wants to help stop the development here, too. Come on, I'll introduce you."

Before Fern knew what was happening, Tristán took her hand and led her through the pickleweed to where his Uncle Jimi stood at the edge of the lagoon. He interlocked his fingers with Fern, and she felt her heart swoop. Tristán had the warmest touch, and their hands felt perfect together.

"Uncle Jimi," Tristán said, dropping Fern's hand.

Instantly, she felt the coldness in her palm where his skin had made contact with hers.

Uncle Jimi slowly broke his affectionate gaze at the pelican's flight and turned his brown, moon-shaped face toward them.

"I wanted to introduce you to Fern," Tristán said.

"Oh, the girl you told me about," Uncle Jimi spoke in a gruff but kind voice.

He talked *about me?* Fern wondered.

She glanced over at Tristán, who was staring at his Vans tennis shoes, a red flush spreading up his neck. The blue aura softened in color, melting into a lavender hue before turning rosy pink and spilling over his shoulders and down the length of his body. For a moment, Fern found it difficult to concentrate on anything but Tristán and his aura.

"It's very nice to meet you," Uncle Jimi said, shaking

Fern's hand. "I'm really glad to see young kids like you and Tristán get involved in saving the land."

"I think as much land as possible should stay wild," Fern said.

"It's more than wilderness we're protecting here," Uncle Jimi replied. "Every October we have a pilgrimage to Native American sacred sites in Orange County, and Bolsa Chica is one of those stops."

"I didn't know that," Fern said.

Tristán pointed to a plateau of eucalyptus trees deep in the wetlands. "They sing and pray up there, where there used to be a Tongva cemetery."

At that moment, a woman with a ruddy complexion, light blue eyes, and long strawberry blond hair stepped up to a raised berm, or mound of sand. Everyone turned their attention to her. "Thanks for coming, everyone. For those of you who don't know me, my name is Kim Bradfield. We're going to work on maintaining the trails and watering today. Shovels are to my right, and the water is over by the trucks in the parking lot, as usual. We'll be meeting in a couple of hours right back here to discuss how we can help protect the wetlands. In just six weeks the courts decide whether or not to pass the Bolsa Chica Restoration Project, which would help protect the land from developers."

Tristán gestured for Fern to choose between the shovels or the watering truck. "What do you want to do?" he asked.

Fern shrugged. "I usually work on the trails." *How will I concentrate if he chooses to work with me? What if I drive the shovel into my toe?*

"Sounds good," Tristán said.

Fern walked over to the tools and selected a yellow shovel with a blunt edge. "We can start over the bridge." She pointed to a wooden walk-bridge that stretched across a small lagoon and connected the entrance of the park to the beginning of the trails. As she walked nervously over the bridge, she thought, *I should say something funny and clever, but what?*

Once on the trails, Fern immediately found a few potholes to fill in with dirt. She tried to relax and get into the groove of her work, but Tristán smelled so clean and fresh. Fern looked down at her shovel. She tried to peer at him through her hair, but only a couple of copper ringlets escaped her tangled mass, not nearly enough to conceal her eyes. Tristán caught her trying to steal a look and smiled. If only she had hair like Marina, who could pull that sheet of thick hair over her face as if she had six layers of extensions. Fern seethed with hair envy as she stared down at the packed-sand trails littered with seashells.

"So how did you find out about Bolsa Chica?" Tristán asked.

"You don't want to know," Fern said. This was not how she would have preferred to start a conversation.

"Try me," Tristán insisted.

Fern began slowly as she dumped a shovelful of dirt into a hole and packed the earth down. "I'm an artist, you see. I'll paint or draw with anything." Fern looked up. Tristán's aura was still pink. She took a deep breath and plowed ahead. "At the end of last year I got hold of a spray can and created these really funkadelic peace signs to protest the war."

"Funkadelic?" Tristán smiled.

"Yeah," Fern said shyly.

"Where did you paint them?" Tristán asked while digging into the earth on the side of the trail.

"At my school." Fern smiled nervously and scrunched her nose.

Tristán chuckled and gazed at Fern in astonished appreciation. "You've got guts."

"You could call it that." Fern smiled as Tristán's aura changed colors again. This time a lime green light shone around his head. It was the kind of bright green in a rainbow, like the one she had seen when playing with the crystals at Moonlight Midwifery. Green was by far her favorite color.

"So, as ironic as it is, while trying to create awareness for peace, I got busted for tagging and had to volunteer community service hours." Fern rested on her shovel and looked around at the rolling hills of tall grass that rose above the inlets and lagoons of blue-green water. "My hours were up months ago. I just fell in love with this place. And I really like Kim. She asks my advice about how to get more kids involved to protect Bolsa Chica."

"You're an amazing girl." Tristán reached out and squeezed her hand.

Fern shivered from his touch. She loved how Tristán adored her passion. She was sometimes teased for her enthusiasm, and here Tristán was complimenting her for it. "How can anyone not see the beauty of these wetlands? You know, they want to build nine hundred houses here. It's already home for two hundred species of birds, and over fifty types of mammals."

"And it's been the ancestral home to my people for thousands of years," Tristán said.

"Exactly. It just burns me up when I think what some people are willing to throw away for the sake of money." Fern rammed the shovel into the dirt.

"I'm sure a passionate girl like you has a plan." Tristán smiled coyly at her.

Instead of making her feel weak at the knees, this time Tristán's smoothness made her think of Ruben and the possibility that Tristán could share his player ways. How could she tell if he was being honest? Then again, if he could help her cause . . . She'd have to just wait and see. Plus, he was really hot. Fern just loved the way his long eyelashes rimmed his eyes. And she couldn't get enough of watching that tattoo on his bicep move when he shoveled.

"I was thinking, if we could get hundreds of people to just hold hands across the wetlands and get enough press here, we'd put some real pressure on those bigwigs that are making all the decisions," Fern said. "It would show that people care."

"I think it's a great idea," Tristán said.

"But how do we get people here? What about security? Permits? And all that red tape?" Fern complained.

"If you believe in something, you've got to go for it," Tristán said, looking intently into Fern's eyes. "Come on, I'll help you talk with Kim."

Thirteen

The church bells chimed out from the Saint Jude's Catholic church in downtown Santa Ana, muffling the sounds of the creaking gate as Xochitl entered the courtyard of Four Crows. She stepped inside as cautiously as if she were about to commit a robbery. She wasn't, of course. She had just come here to get sandalwood oil, which had been Graciela's favorite scent, and the other special ingredients for the spell to summon her spirit. Still, Xochitl felt a little like she was scheming, purposefully trying to hook her sister from the cosmos. Nana had warned her it wasn't okay to continually pester someone's spirit to visit the earth plane. But she needed to speak with Graciela.

Xochitl headed for the glass case of essential oils. She had finally earned enough money walking her neighbor's dogs to buy the things she needed—though now her lats were sore from the dogs pulling on the leashes. Xochitl reached into the case and took out a bottle of sandalwood oil and a bottle of oil that combined the essences of frankincense and myrrh. She selected a couple of sandalwood incense sticks from a display in a woven-pine-needle basket next to the cabinet.

Xochitl picked up a packet of loose sage leaves. If she'd still been in Mexico, she would have had an abundance of sage to burn for a ceremony. Graciela and Xochitl had often accompanied Nana on her trips into the fields to gather the herb. She turned around to head toward the cash register and nearly jumped out of her skin when she saw Tristán watching her from behind the counter. She should have become invisible when she entered the store and just left some money on the counter.

"I didn't mean to scare you," Tristán said. "You came in so determined. I thought I had better not disturb you."

"I didn't see you," Xochitl muttered.

"I noticed," Tristán said warmly.

Xochitl put the oil, incense, and sage on the counter without saying anything. She wasn't used to being the one who didn't notice other people. Usually it was others who didn't notice her.

"Where are your friends today?" Tristán asked as he rang up her items.

"They aren't part of this," Xochitl said quickly. "It's kind of personal."

"I get it." Tristán put her goods into a small brown bag. He folded over the top of the bag twice, as if he was just as concerned to keep her mission secret as she was, and handed it to Xochitl. "Good luck."

She took the bag, put it in her backpack, and slung the pack over her shoulder. "Thanks."

As she stepped out the door, Xochitl thought of how much Tristán reminded her of her brother Tano. He never told a soul any of her secrets. Both guys had that quiet, confident air about them. Xochitl sighed. She missed her family. She patted her pocket, where she kept her mother's last letter.

Xochitl hopped on her bike and rode through Santa Ana's artists village. The colorful buildings and brown-faced people seemed to mock her pain. Everywhere she went reminded Xochitl of home. But then she rode past red, white, and blue banners, remnants of the recent Fourth of July celebrations, and she remembered how very far away from home she really was.

Xochitl rode her bike along the asphalt trail that ran above the Santa Ana River. Once she could smell the sea in the air, she got off her bike. Walking her bike, she carefully descended the dirt incline into the alluvial woodland that flourished to the left of the river trail.

Midmorning rain drizzled on Xochitl as she tiptoed along the animal path bordered by tall marshland grasses. Until rains had flooded the area, the murky creek to her left had been a sandy dirt trail wide enough for a truck to drive through. The three-inch-deep water actually had a small current and was home to what sounded like hundreds of croaking frogs. A rustling caught Xochitl's attention. She watched the white fluff of a cottontail rabbit disappear under a pile of sycamore leaves.

Seeing the rabbit made Xochitl think of Nana's lesson about how rabbits represent fear. She wondered if the animal sighting was an omen of some sort. *Fear has nothing to do with my mission today,* she told herself. She was excited to do the spell that would help her speak with her sister. She needed to talk with her, to somehow begin to understand how her life had changed so drastically and so quickly. Xochitl dismissed the rabbit as a coincidence.

Xochitl held on to a low sycamore branch and leapt over a particularly muddy track. She continued through the dense undergrowth beneath a sprawling oak tree and crept deep into the forest canopy. She was completely hidden from the trail when she stopped. She debated turning invisible to avoid being seen by anyone passing by, but since she wanted to see Graciela in the physical form, it made sense for her to remain flesh and bones, for now.

Xochitl faced north, the direction that connects to family. She dug in her backpack and took out the picture of Graciela and herself at the river, propping it up against a small tree stump. Looking at the photograph of her sister, Xochitl distractedly twisted her wishing bracelet. Then she took out the bag from Four Crows, lit a dried sage leaf with her lighter, and allowed the smoke to waft over her entire body. When the leaf was nearly burned down to her fingertips, she dropped it to the ground and carefully stomped on the leaf until the smoke disappeared.

Xochitl willed herself to relax as she lit the sandalwood incense and stuck the bottom of the stick into the soft dirt. She took out orange slices, a tamale from her neighbor Mr. Soto, and peppermint candies and placed them on a small paper plate. Xochitl dripped three drops of each essential oil onto her palms and held her hands up toward the San Bernardino Mountains.

"I welcome the four directions to this ceremony," she said. "Please bless me with your presence. And Great Spirit, if you make Graciela appear, I'll promise to believe in magic and miracles again. Do we have a deal?"

The wind blew the trees above, sending oak leaves flying past her. Xochitl felt a chill of anticipation. She stared at the picture and spoke to Graciela as if her sister were there under the oak tree.

"Graciela, I miss you more than you can imagine. You would have loved America, if only . . ." Xochitl broke off, not wanting to give any room for memories of the accident to come rushing back to her. She changed the subject. "You'd like Fern and Marina. They are exactly the two friends that we would have wanted to meet. It's so hard to go on without you, living the dream we were supposed to be sharing side by side."

Xochitl paused and looked around at the moss growing on the thin branches of the trees and bits of fluff floating on the air from the cattails.

"I came to this spot because it's near the river, just like this picture of us. And I thought you'd like the fact that you can smell the ocean from here, too."

The wind blew the branches above her, sending a small shower of leaves to flutter around Xochitl.

"Where are you, Gracie?"

For twenty minutes, Xochitl looked for a sign from her sister. Eventually, she had to admit to herself that Graciela wasn't going to show herself today. Would she ever reappear, or was she lost forever? Xochitl noticed a sleeping lizard with zigzagged stripes basking in the sun. She remembered one of Nana's lessons that lizards were known as dreamers in the Spirit World. Maybe this ceremony was like opening the door, and Graciela would appear in a dream? It wasn't enough. She wanted to talk to her now.

Devastated that Graciela hadn't appeared, Xochitl grabbed her backpack and shoved in her things, including a fistful of dirt and a few oak leaves that got caught up in her angry frenzied movements. She got back on her bike and rode home thinking about the day she and Graciela had first learned to ride two-wheelers. Graciela had fallen more but had learned to ride first. Xochitl had feared how hard she might hit the ground, so it took her longer to find her balance. She could ride hands free for blocks on end now, but Graciela would never ride again.

The wind lifted the scent of honeysuckle and jasmine into the air as she turned into her neighborhood. A group of older women laughed on rocking chairs, gossiping in Spanish. Mr. Soto, the tamale man, pushed his small metal cart, sealed tight to keep warm the dozens of tamales his wife had made that morning. Xochitl remembered countless Christmases making tamales at home with the family. Mamá used to scold Xochitl and Graciela for spreading the masa too thick. Mariachi music floated out of Mrs. Ramirez's house.

"Xochitl!" Fern called from somewhere behind Xochitl as she whizzed past.

Xochitl put on the brakes and turned to see Fern practically sashaying down the sidewalk.

"Where have you been?" Fern asked.

"Just riding around," Xochitl said.

Fern gave her a quizzical look. Xochitl didn't think she had quite pulled off a sense of lightheartedness. How could she?

Fern smiled knowingly but didn't press Xochitl for additional information. "I'll walk you home," Fern said happily with a bounce in her step.

Xochitl got off her bike and began to push it alongside Fern as they walked down the street. *How is it that Fern and her sunshiny enthusiasm pops up when I'm missing my sister the most?* Xochitl wondered. A flock of screeching green parrots flew overhead.

"I was at Pilar's," Fern said cheerfully. "She made the yummiest vegetarian empanadas."

"I thought empanadas were made of meat," Xochitl said.

"Pilar makes them special for me," Fern said. "So I just have to tell you, I am so excited about the *limpia*."

Xochitl grimaced and feigned excitement. "Yeah." But there was no way she could muster the same enthusiasm as Fern. Since she couldn't summon Graciela, Xochitl had very little desire to talk about magic, especially because she couldn't ignore the nagging feeling she got now and then about Fern's sincerity. When Fern or Marina talked like this, Xochitl still got a little worried that they were using her to get closer to Nana.

"Have you already got the items to honor the directions?" Fern asked.

"I'm working on it," Xochitl said.

"We're still on for Friday, right? What time is Rogelia going to meet us at your house?" Fern asked, forging right ahead, not seeing that Xochitl would rather disappear than have this conversation.

"Nana and Marina will take the bus over Friday afternoon," Xochitl replied.

Fern giggled.

"What?" Xochitl wondered.

"Nothing." Fern tried to cover up her laughter by biting her lip.

"What?" Xochitl prompted.

Fern caved in immediately. "Haven't you noticed how uncomfortable Marina is riding the bus?"

"She was acting weird the day at the mall. I thought it was the spell," Xochitl said.

"Well, I hope you don't take this the wrong way," Fern began. "Marina is a product of her new environment. Ever since she moved to that fancy house, she's been caught up in appearances. She only buys popular clothes and stuff. And the bus, in her mind, just isn't . . ." Fern trailed off.

"She doesn't think it's cool to ride the bus?" Xochitl offered.

"It's beyond uncool," Fern said. "It's more like she's afraid to be seen as low class. But that's mostly her mother's baggage. It's not really what Marina is all about."

"Oh," Xochitl said. She couldn't even begin to understand this concept.

"I've tried to help her feel better by telling her taking the bus is an environmentally conscious thing to do." Fern shook her head hopelessly and sighed dramatically. "Whatever. She'll get over it eventually, if I have anything to do with it."

Xochitl stopped walking at the end of her driveway. "See you later," she said. She just wanted to be alone.

"Bye." Fern waved and walked on to her house.

Xochitl opened her front door to find Nana sitting on the couch in the living room knitting a green shawl. Her father sat at the kitchen table, poring over bills and drinking a Modelo.

"Xochitl, where have you been?" Mr. Garcia asked. "You haven't read to me today."

Xochitl groaned inwardly but didn't answer. Ever since she had learned to read English, Xochitl and her father had looked up a new English word in the dictionary every day. Spanish had been Xochitl's first language, but Mr. Garcia had kept an eye on the future and made sure his children learned two languages. Eventually, they read the classics, devouring a chapter or two a night. Reading with her papá used to be one of her favorite things to do.

"I'm not in the mood, Papá," Xochitl said.

"You used to love reading with me," her father said sullenly.

"Yeah, well, I guess it's not the same when you don't have to fight for it," Xochitl replied, staring at a picture on the wall of their entire family.

With two sisters and three brothers, getting alone time with Papá had always been a precious commodity to Xochitl. Now that she had him all to herself but didn't have Graciela, time with her dad made her feel terribly lonely and homesick.

"Have you written back to your mother yet?" Mr. Garcia asked.

"No," Xochitl said. In fact, she hadn't even read Mamá's entire letter. She had only read the first line, which called her "a blooming flower," in reference to the name Xochitl, and hadn't been able to continue. Graciela used to tease Xochitl that the name "closed flower" was a better fit for her. There were just so many memories wrapped up in the smallest things.

"Ai. See that you do. She's worried sick about you," Mr. Garcia said.

"Let the poor thing be, Sebastian," Nana said. "Xochitl, come sit with me." She patted the couch beside her and smiled warmly at her granddaughter.

"I'm going out back." Mr. Garcia rose from his chair and exited through the back door.

"Ven aqui," Nana coaxed.

Xochitl hesitated, then turned around and sulked into the living room. She plopped down on the couch next to her nana. Nana put down her knitting needles and began to stroke

Xochitl's hair. "Healing from your grief is going to take time, *mi'jita*. You need to reach out to the people who want to help you."

Xochitl spun her bracelet around her wrist but kept quiet.

"I'm really glad you have made friends with Marina and Fern," Nana said.

"Well, your magic works," Xochitl griped. "Most of the time."

Nana looked at Xochitl thoughtfully. She placed her arm around her granddaughter's shoulders and gave her a squeeze. "This has been hardest on you. I know how much you miss Graciela."

Xochitl felt a hard lump in her throat. "I still can't believe it's happened. I can't believe that Graciela is really dead. It's like a bad dream, the worst dream ever." Tears began to fill her eyes. She looked down, so that her long hair covered her face and she could allow the tears to fall. "I wish I could wake up and find that it's all been a horrible mistake."

Nana took Xochitl's hand in her own and caressed it gently, compelling Xochitl to talk even more. "Everything is so different here. The way people dress, how they speak to their parents, how fast everybody lives their lives. My head is just spinning, and it seems like there is no time to catch up."

Nana nodded in understanding. "It's a different world," she agreed.

"It would just be so much easier to handle all these changes if Graciela were here," Xochitl ventured.

"I'm not denying the truth in that, *mi'jita*," Rogelia said softly.

"I just can't let her go," Xochitl cried.

"El tiempo lo cura todo," Rogelia said soothingly.

"Time might heal wounds, but it's not going to make me forget Graciela, ever," Xochitl said adamantly.

"No, but I have the feeling that not only time but your new friends will help heal your broken heart," Rogelia said. "If you let them."

A horn honked outside. Rogelia moved back the white cotton drapes. Xochitl looked out the window. She could see Marina's mother in her car, parked in the driveway with the motor running. She was inspecting her nails.

Nana gathered up her knitting and packed it into a canvas book bag. "I'll be home Friday afternoon. Be ready for the *limpia*."

"Why is Mrs. Peralta here? You don't usually go to the Peraltas' until tomorrow morning," Xochitl said. She was just beginning to get to the bottom of her feelings, and she wasn't ready to let Nana go.

"Mrs. Peralta needs me to watch Samantha. They're going to some charity benefit tonight." Nana kissed Xochitl on the forehead. "Would you like to come with me?"

Xochitl shook her head. "Can't Marina watch her own sister?"

Nana stood and shuffled toward the door. "Marina doesn't have many obligations." She blew Xochitl a kiss. "I love you, Xochitl. You will make it through this."

Xochitl watched Nana get into Mrs. Peralta's car through the living room window. A hollowness filled Xochitl's stomach. She hadn't thought it was possible to feel more alone than before she had begun her little *plácita* with Nana. But she did.

fourteen

On Monday morning, Marina rubbed the sleep out of her eyes as she sprawled on her queen-sized bed. Even after she rolled over, her hair remained spread like an open fan on her silken pillowcase. She touched the top of her head and felt the static electricity as individual strands followed the movement of her hand. She looked out to the backyard and watched the palm trees wave their fronds back and forth in the blustery wind. Marina sighed happily. She loved windy days.

Good morning, mi amor. The woman's voice sounded in Marina's head.

Buenos días, said the girl's voice cheerfully. These two voices were becoming familiar, so that Marina no longer feared them.

Marina got up and shuffled down the carpeted hall, trying to gather up as much electricity as possible. Monica was just coming groggily out of her bedroom, her usually tidy hair in a single disheveled dark blond braid. Perfect target.

Marina scooted up to her sister and poked her shoulder with her index finger. The electric jolt pulsated against Marina's finger with such force she thought her fingernail might pop off.

"Ow!" Monica rubbed her shoulder. "Jerk!"

Marina giggled and trotted to the kitchen to avoid her sister's retaliation. When she got there, Marina saw Rogelia cleaning a weekend's worth of dirty dishes.

"Good morning, Rogelia," Marina said as she took a box of waffles from the freezer, pulled out two waffles, and shoved the box haphazardly back in the freezer. She popped the waffles into the toaster.

"Buenos días," Rogelia said.

"Buenos días," Marina repeated nervously.

Monica came into the kitchen and grabbed a breakfast bar out of the pantry. "Have you got anything for Grandpy's birthday?" she asked Marina.

"No, I haven't found anything yet," Marina replied, taking the waffles out of the toaster and buttering them. She had been agonizing for weeks over what to get Grandpy for a present. She loved him the most of all her older relatives, and it worried her to think she hadn't yet found the right gift.

"Better come up with something soon," Monica said as she headed back to her bedroom. "The party is in less than two weeks."

"I know." Marina set her plate of waffles on the granite counter, pulled out a high-backed wooden chair, and sat down. Next to her on the counter, Rogelia had made a pile for each family member of personal items such as clothes, mail, and homework. Marina felt awkward as she looked at a stack of her earrings, her favorite pair of fuzzy socks, and a couple of her *Lucky* magazines. A twinge of guilt shot through her stomach. As she pulled her stack closer to her plate, she felt squeamish thinking about how Xochitl's grandmother was now responsible for picking up after her laziness.

"Sorry about leaving this around, Rogelia," Marina said. "I promise to keep my sloppy ways to my bedroom."

"It doesn't bother me, Marina." Rogelia set the last dirty glass on the rack of the dishwasher and closed the door. "It's my job."

"I just meant, well, I've never known anyone who has worked for us. Not very well, at least. The woman who cleaned the house before you came, Anna? I couldn't even tell you her last name."

Marina waited for a response from Rogelia as she dried her hands on a dish towel. She half expected Rogelia to say something nice that would help her feel better about not delving into the personal lives of her former maids. She wanted Rogelia to think well of her. But Rogelia said nothing to assuage Marina's guilt or let her off the hook.

"El conocimiento es plata entre los pobres, oro entre los nobles, y una joya entre los principes," Rogelia said as she walked across the kitchen to the pantry and got out the broom.

"What does that mean?" Marina asked.

Rogelia thought for a moment before answering. "Literally, it means 'knowledge is silver among the poor, gold among the noble, and a jewel among princes.' But the reason I tell it to you is to say that no matter who you are in life, knowledge is valuable. And knowledge about others, particularly the people who affect your life—or in this case, pick up your dirty laundry—is one of the most important things you can gain. It means you respect them."

" 'Respect' is a big word in this house," Marina's mother said, sauntering into the kitchen, her high heels clicking hard against the tiled floor. "Something I don't seem to get enough of." She grabbed an apple out of a large maroon ceramic dish. "Marina, make sure you get outside for some exercise and don't laze around all day."

"It's summer vacation," Marina said. "By definition it means I'm supposed to lie around and do nothing." *Yeah, I'll get outside,* Marina thought. *Long enough to erase the tan lines on my back.*

"See what I mean, Rogelia? No respect." Marina's mom opened the pantry and took out a water bottle. "At least clean your room, Marina. You should have more pride in yourself."

"What does cleaning my room have to do with my pride?" Marina asked.

"Just do it, Marina, or I'll take away your cell phone for a week. I'm off to work." With a backward wave of her hand, Marina's mother left through the front door.

"She's in a bit of a twist," Marina said haughtily with a flip of her hair.

An uncomfortable silence hung in the air. Rogelia made no comment of agreement or dissent and merely continued sweeping the kitchen in her quiet, contented way. A kind of peace exuded from Rogelia. Marina never felt content, despite her comfortable life, all the clothes and electronic toys she wanted, and the fact that she didn't really have chores or responsibilities aside from cleaning her room. What would it be like to feel as satisfied as Rogelia seemed? How did she do it? Marina longed to be closer to Rogelia, to learn her secrets, but didn't know how.

"Mas val dar que recibir," Rogelia said confidently.

"What?" Marina asked, bewildered.

" 'It is more blessed to give than receive.' I find peace in my service to others."

Was this supposed to be an answer to her unspoken question? "I don't really like hard work," Marina said.

"Not many of us do, but there is a great sense of satisfaction when you conquer something uncomfortable or unfamiliar and make it your own. That's something to be proud of."

⌘ ⌘ ⌘

Following Rogelia's wisdom, Marina thoroughly cleaned her room. Exhausted by the effort it took to tackle weeks of discarded clothes, makeup, and jewelry, and to dust the furniture, Marina retired to the pool. The wind had died down, and she caught some rays while lying on a chaise lounge. She had just picked up her magazine when, somewhere in the house, she heard Samantha howling in pain. Marina put her magazine down on the glass table to go help Samantha and saw the blur of Rogelia hustling toward the crying little girl. Rogelia had become Samantha's nanny in addition to the Peraltas' housekeeper and was quicker to respond to Samantha's needs than their mother had ever been.

Marina walked into the house and followed the sounds of Samantha's whimpering and Rogelia's soft singing. She peeked around the corner into the living room. Rogelia sat on the dark green wing chair with Samantha on her lap. She took a bandage out of her apron pocket and carefully put it over a scrape on Samantha's knee.

"*Sana, sana, colita de rana. Si los sanas hoy, sanarás mañana,*" Rogelia sang.

"What's that mean?" Samantha asked, tugging on one of her pigtails.

"It means," Rogelia crooned, " 'Heal, heal, frog tail is in sorrow. If I rub today, you'll be healed tomorrow.' "

Samantha laughed. "That's silly."

"That's why it works." Rogelia chuckled, tapping Samantha's nose with her finger. "See? You have stopped crying. It is a song I have sung to every one of sixteen grandbabies and five children." Rogelia kissed Samantha's nose. "Let me make you a peanut butter, honey, and banana sandwich. That's your favorite, no?"

Samantha nodded. Rogelia guided Samantha's legs to the ground. Marina ducked into the kitchen and poured herself a glass of water. Out of the corner of her eye, she watched as Rogelia and Samantha entered the kitchen hand in hand. Rogelia took the whole-grain bread from the breadbox and laid several slices on the cutting board. While Rogelia cut the bananas, Samantha tried to sing the Spanish song. Rogelia made three sandwiches, put each on a plate, and handed one to Samantha.

Samantha gave Rogelia a tight bear hug around her middle. "You're so squishy," Samantha said, then bounded to the table.

"That's not nice, Samantha," Marina said.

"I like being squishy," Rogelia answered with a smile. She handed Marina a sandwich. "I noticed you haven't had any lunch."

A weird sad feeling came over Marina as she gratefully took the sandwich. She watched Rogelia sit down next to Samantha and felt a void in the place her own nana ought to have filled. She had never had a grandmother to kiss her scraped knees, sing to her, or make her lunch. Was this little scene something she could have experienced if her nana had lived? Marina joined Rogelia and Samantha at the table. She took a bite of sandwich.

"This is the best sandwich I've ever eaten," Marina said.

"Mmmmuhmo," Samantha tried to talk, but since the peanut butter had stuck to the roof of her mouth, she just nodded fervently in agreement.

Marina and Rogelia laughed. Marina ruffled Samantha's hair.

"What was your town in Mexico like?" Marina asked Rogelia.

"It was beautiful," Rogelia said. "It was surrounded by a ring of mountains, and so green. Oh, you should have seen my garden."

"I thought most of Mexico was a desert," Marina said. "Except for beach towns like Puerto Vallerta."

"I suspect there is a lot about Mexico you don't know," Rogelia said.

⌘ ⌘ ⌘

That afternoon Marina sat in her bedroom painting her toes a cool cranberry color and thought about what Rogelia had said earlier. She wasn't sure she was ready to start cleaning houses, but maybe she could take on a bit more responsibility. She applied a sparkling quick-dry overcoat, and as she was weaving tissue around her toes, her bedroom light flickered twice. Marina looked up at the lights.

Go see Rogelia, the woman's voice said.

The lights flickered twice more. At this point, Marina

needed no more persuasion. She jumped out of bed. Without knowing how she knew, she was sure it was time for her *plácita*. She hobbled to the front yard and plucked a handful of gardenias. Quietly, so as to not draw any attention from her family, she took a bowl out of the cupboard and filled it with water. She put the flowers inside and carried it down the hall.

Marina tapped lightly on Rogelia's door. While she waited for Rogelia to answer the knock, Marina glanced behind her. What would her mother say if she saw Marina going to Rogelia's room? Rogelia opened the door.

"Come in," Rogelia said.

"These are for you." Marina offered Rogelia the flowers and quickly walked in the room.

Rogelia took the gardenias and placed them on the altar. The familiar copal scent filled the room.

Rogelia sat on her bed and picked up a pair of knitting needles. "I was hoping you would come see me," she said, patting the bed beside her. "Come sit down."

Marina stepped inside and carefully avoided the dangling herbs on her way across the room.

"Do you know how to knit?" Rogelia asked.

"No," Marina said, settling onto Rogelia's bed.

"Would you like to learn?" Rogelia asked.

"Sure," Marina answered.

Rogelia held up a basket of yarn balls. "Pick one."

Marina was surprised to see a ball of soft yarn almost the exact same color as her cranberry nail polish. "I love this color," she said, picking up the yarn.

"Take a knitting needle in each hand." Rogelia handed Marina two wooden knitting needles. "Now let the yarn hang over the needles like this," Rogelia instructed. "And I'll show you how to get started." She guided Marina's hands in knitting. "Knitting is easy once you have done it a short time, and it's very good for meditative work."

"What's meditative work?" Marina asked as she clumsily maneuvered the needles around the yarn.

"Do you ever get really upset over something someone says or something that happens, and no matter how hard you think about it, you just can't get any peace?" Rogelia asked.

Marina looked up from her knitting. "Sometimes I get stomachaches trying to figure out why my mother is so strict with me."

"Well, meditative work only requires the use of your hands, not your brain. While you work, you get the answers to tough questions. The more able you are to quiet your mind, the better you will be at calling on the voices in your head to help you."

"Oh," Marina said.

"Housework is like that, too," Rogelia said. "Do you know why I do not charge money for *curanderismo* services?"

"No," Marina answered quietly.

"While I clean house my mind is free to wander. I imagine my clients being healthy, happy, and free from whatever ails them. While I dust, or sweep, or vacuum, the *remedios* I need to cure others come to me." Rogelia took Marina's knitting and placed it on the bed beside her. The healer held Marina's hands in her own and studied the lines of her palms for a moment. Then she added a chunk of copal resin to the charcoal. "How long has your family lived in Orange County?"

"Two hundred years," Marina answered.

"That's a long time and a lot of family history packed into one place," Rogelia observed.

"There are little monuments all over this area—one at the

Santa Ana River down the road that marks the spot where a big battle was fought during the Mexican-American War." Marina looked at Rogelia. The healer encouraged her with a smile. Marina continued. "Across the river at Camelot, the miniature golf place, there used to be an Indian village. You know the yellow house on the top of Oceanview Street? That was a flour mill in the 1800s. Before that it was the hacienda of the Yorbas." Marina gained momentum. "And down Buena Vista Road is Orange Olive School, an elementary school with a hidden room that has one-hundred-year-old desks and inkwells draped in cobwebs. Across Glassell Street, there was a Sunkist orange-packing house, and before that it was the horse corral for the Yorbas. Fern read about the archeological dig when they found horseshoes and stuff." Marina smiled. She couldn't help feeling a little pride at the extent of her family history. She ignored the irony of how she sounded like her mother.

"It sounds like you live on a place of power. A vortex," Rogelia said. "Very similar to how the Spanish Mexico City was built upon the ancient Aztec capital of Tenochtitlán. People are drawn toward places of power even if they don't know why."

"The only vortex I know about is the black hole called a dryer that steals my socks every week," Marina said.

Rogelia chuckled. "The kind of vortex I am talking about is a swirling center of intense and immense energy, like an invisible, stationary tornado. Fantastic things happen in vortexes."

Marina wondered if the vortex had anything to do with spells. Maybe spells had more punch to them if you performed them in a vortex.

"Did you ever hear voices before you and Fern cast the spell?" Rogelia asked.

Marina shook her head. "No, but sometimes before I'd

go to bed, I'd hear noises like the sounds of a busy city. It was all jumbled."

"The night after your first spell casting, there were clear voices?"

"Yes."

"How many do you normally hear?"

"Two." Marina paused. This would be the time to ask the question burning inside her. She couldn't afford not to ask Rogelia now that they were alone together. "I've been hearing voices pretty much daily ever since the first spell. I'm kind of getting used to them, but I can't help but wonder if I'm going crazy."

"No, no, *mi'jita*," Rogelia laughed. "You have deepened your ability to hear. You have become a doorway, the channel, for these spirits to speak through you."

A channel? Will I start sprouting commercials next?

Rogelia chuckled. "No, you won't be advertising anything strange. These voices are your friends."

Marina stared at Rogelia, still amazed at her mind-reading abilities. "I wish I knew who they were," Marina said.

"You can't summon people from the other side, just for the asking," Rogelia said. "They will reveal themselves when the time is right."

Marina sighed. Well, at least she felt better now that she understood a bit more about the voices. Of course, there was one more thing she wanted to ask Rogelia. "Will you teach me Spanish?" Marina asked.

"I would love to," Rogelia answered. "What do you want to know?"

"Anything and everything," Marina said excitedly. "It feels weird that I don't know the language. And I've always wanted someone to teach me at home."

"Two hundred years is a long time to be a Mexican minority in the United States," Rogelia said.

Marina shook her head dismissively. "Someone in my family should have had the courage to stay true to their Mexican roots. My mom just goes on about being Spanish."

"Some people think Spain is a more impressive homeland than Mexico. There was and still is a lot of pressure to assimilate," Rogelia said. "For years nearly every authority figure in America told Latinos that their children would have a better life if they gave up their customs and language. Your relatives weren't the only Mexican Americans to abandon their culture."

"I didn't realize they were doing it for me," Marina said, looking down at her cranberry painted toenails.

"It's not easy to give up your language, your ways of life." Rogelia gripped Marina's hands. "Repeat this word: 'valentia.'"

"*Valentia,*" Marina repeated. "What does it mean?"

"Courage," Rogelia said. "Now say *corazón.*"

"*Corazón,*" Marina said.

"That means 'heart,'" Rogelia said. "You see how the words 'courage' and '*corazón*' are similar? That is no accident. The words come from the same root. Follow your heart and you will have courage."

Fifteen

Friday afternoon, Fern admired her finished artwork on the poster announcing the Hands Across the Wetlands demonstration. She couldn't wait to show Tristán, who would be coming over any minute. A pile of crumpled sketches spilled out of her wastebasket onto the floor in the corner of her bedroom. Throughout the week, she had tried pastels, oils, and charcoal and finally settled on watercolors as the best medium to depict the wild beauty of the Bolsa Chica wetlands. Fern shook her hand. It was cramped from days of endless work.

The doorbell rang. Fern checked her reflection in the mirror and decided that this green tank dress she was wearing really set off the summer highlights in her hair. She pinched her cheeks for a little color and inspected both her left and right profiles. Rolling up the poster, she held it behind her back as she raced barefoot to the front door. She took a deep breath to settle her nerves before she opened the door.

Tristán stood on the threshold smiling. His hair was swept back and fell in dark waves to his shoulder. His soft blue plaid shirt hung loosely over his cargo shorts. "Hi," he said.

"Hey," Fern replied, holding on to the front door for support. She smiled back at him, locked in a moment of near rapture.

Tristán looked around Fern inside the house. "Um, can I come in?"

"Oh yeah, of course." Fern blushed, recovering her senses. Why was she always acting like a lovesick puppy around him? She stepped aside so Tristán could enter.

There was a long silence while they stood there staring at each other in the entryway. Fern grinned at Tristán until she realized what a dork she must seem like, just gawking at him. Abruptly, she slammed the door. "Let's go over our plans in the backyard." Fern turned quickly and led the way through the house. Tristán admired the black-and-white photographs of nature in silver frames adorning the indigo painted hallway.

Her mother was in the den listening to music playing on a classic turntable when they entered the room. She moved her fingers in time to the soulful sound of the Gipsy Kings's music.

"Mom, this is Tristán," Fern said. "He's come over to help me plan that demonstration I was telling you about for Bolsa Chica."

"It's very nice to meet you, Mrs. Fuego," Tristán said politely.

Fern's mother stood up from the floral-upholstered armchair to shake Tristán's hand. "It's very nice to meet you," she said. Reaching for a bowl of caramels on the teak coffee table, she offered some treats to Tristán. "Would you like some candy?"

"Thanks." Tristán took a piece.

While he selected a candy, Fern's mother mouthed in her daughter's direction, *Nice* eye *candy.*

Fern glowered at her mother, took Tristán by the forearm, and dragged him toward the back door. "We'll be going now."

The Fuegos' backyard was a jungle of plants and luscious flowers, statues of all shapes, and colorful ceramic wall hangings of celestial orbs, animals, and flowers. Fern led Tristán down a mosaic walkway to a stone bench and two rattan chairs. Behind the sitting area, attached to the backyard fence, was a mosaic design of a large parrot sitting on a banana tree.

"I don't remember telling you my last name," Fern said, sitting down on the bench.

"I know a lot about you, Fernanda Isabel Fuego," Tristán said, sitting beside Fern.

"Oh," Fern said shortly. *He found out my middle name. He's sitting so close. I'm going to faint.*

As Tristán settled into his seat, Fern caught the merest glow of a soft pink light over Tristán's head.

"So what are you hiding?" Tristán asked.

"Huh? Oh yeah." Fern pulled out the poster and handed it to him. He unrolled it and examined it for a full minute without saying anything.

"Well?" she asked anxiously. Fern noticed that the subtle pink light slowly began to rise and emanate from the top of Tristán's head.

"You're good," he said, obviously impressed.

"You're just saying that." Fern looked away and stared at the mosaic parrot.

"No, I'm not. This is really beautiful work," Tristán insisted.

"Thanks," Fern whispered, pulling the spaghetti strap of her dress back onto her shoulder.

Tristán followed Fern's gaze to the mosaic on the wall behind them. "Did you do that, too?" he asked.

"Yeah," Fern said. She had worked for hours getting all the right colors and shapes. It had been difficult and time-consuming, one of her longest projects. She was stoked that she'd had enough stamina to finish it.

Tristán whistled. "You're an amazing artist."

"I've had good teachers," Fern said, glancing at Tristán. Waves of pink light floated around his head, dancing in a gentle, hypnotic way.

"Maybe you're a good student," Tristán observed. "Is there anything you can't do?"

Fern laughed. "Not that I can think of. As a matter of fact, I talked to my old art teacher, and she said her printing company will donate the cost of producing five hundred posters. She'll send them to press as soon as the art is ready."

Tristán took another look at the poster. "I'd say it's ready. I've got good news, too. My uncle Jimi knows a few of the people from Red Nation Security Guard. They keep the peace at the powwows. They've agreed to come to our fundraiser."

"And Kim called yesterday to tell me she got the permit from the city," Fern said.

"It's really coming together," Tristán said.

"Yeah, I can't believe it," Fern admitted. She stared as Tristán's pink aura gradually glided down his head to his shoulders.

"Why not?" Tristán asked.

"I don't know," Fern said. "I guess sometimes I find it easier to dream about things than actually going out and doing them."

"Yeah, I heard that about you," Tristán confessed.

"What else did you hear about me?" Fern asked, taking back the poster. She rolled it up and set it beside her on the bench. She looked up to see that the rosy aura had grown to about three inches wide and was floating around his head, shoulders, and arms.

"I'll never tell," Tristán said, holding up his hands in defense.

"Come on," Fern pleaded. The aura still undulated around Tristán, but more pressing at the moment was finding out what he had learned about her.

Tristán pointed to Fern's bare feet. "You don't like wearing shoes."

"Shoes are nature separators," Fern declared.

"Uh-huh," Tristán agreed.

"That's not fair," Fern protested with a laugh. "I'm at a disadvantage here."

"What do you want to know?" Tristán asked.

Fern thought for a minute. What should she ask? She had an open field and nothing was coming to mind. "When is your birthday?"

"March twentieth," Tristán replied.

"Spring equinox," Fern said. "The day of balance."

"That's me," Tristán said lightly.

"Okay, you know my middle name. What's yours?"

"Ernesto," he replied with a slight grimace.

"Family name?" Fern asked sympathetically.

"Grandfather's on my mother's side," Tristán confirmed.

"Any brothers or sisters?"

"Two brothers," Tristán answered. "Okay, what else?"

Fern squeezed her eyes tight, trying to come up with a clever question. "What's your favorite ice cream flavor?" she blurted out.

"Chocolate chip," Tristán said resolutely.

"Me too," Fern said.

"Glad to hear it," Tristán said, smiling.

Fern noticed a dimple in his right cheek. *How adorable is that!* She giggled. She looked around Tristán. The rosy light around him gave her a warm and cozy feeling. Rose was a very romantic color. Fern found it very interesting how the auras appeared different sometimes and wondered what made them do that. She just knew that the *limpia* with Rogelia today would help her understand Tristán's auras better. After all, it was Friday the thirteenth. What better day for magic?

"Anything else?" Tristán asked.

"That's all for now," Fern said. "But I may come up with other questions later."

"Then I'm fairly warned," Tristán said. "But you'd better be sure you're ready for the answers, because I'm a tell-all kind of guy." At that moment, his phone rang. Tristán fished his cell out of his pocket. He looked down at the window and laughed. Quickly, he sent a text message.

Fern frowned. *What does that mean? Like kiss and tell? Oh man, why does he have me going one way one minute, then off in the opposite direction the next?*

166

Tristán shoved the phone back into his pocket. He tapped Fern's hand, sending a shiver up her arm. "So what's next on our to-do list for Bolsa Chica?" he asked. "We've only got another three weeks until the hearing, right?"

"Uh, right," Fern said, distracted by her mixed-up feelings about Tristán. "As soon as the posters are ready, we need to put them up on business windows and stuff like that."

"She's not only an artistic genius, she's also resourceful," Tristán complimented.

Fern blushed. "Are you always this nice?"

"Only when it's deserved," Tristán said, moving his chair closer to Fern.

Her teeth chattered nervously. "I gotta go to Xochitl's now."

Tristán noticed a small red flower on the ground and handed it to Fern. "Can I walk you?"

"Sure. It's just right around the corner," Fern said, holding on to the flower with a trembling hand. "I've got to get something first." Fern stood up and led the way back along the mosaic path and around to the front of the house. "Be right back." She left Tristán standing at the front door.

Fern ran to her room and grabbed a wool book bag with a bird stitched on the front in bold colors of orange, gold, teal, and apple green. Fern put the red flower in her bag, thinking she might be able to use it for the *limpia* later today. The flower could represent heat or fire to correspond to the southern direction, as she certainly was burning up at the moment. Prickles of excitement and confusion surged through her as she slipped into her rubber flip-flops. She really liked Tristán, but simultaneously she felt such a strong reluctance to move forward with him.

What if the gray aura she had seen around him meant he would break her heart? And what was with the other colors? Yellow could mean cowardice or happiness. Blue could make her sad, and green reminded her of nature and a feeling of connection and belonging. Fern sighed heavily. Then again, she could be totally wrong about what the colors meant. She just had no idea what Tristán's changing auras meant. She trotted back to the entryway, where Tristán waited for her. "I'm off to Xochitl's," Fern called to her mother.

"Cool bag," Tristán said as Fern closed her front door.

"It's from Colombia," Fern said proudly. "Like me."

"Were you born there?" Tristán asked.

Fern turned right at the end of the driveway and headed down Occidental Street toward Xochitl's house. "No, but my brothers and sister were born in Bogotá. I'm the first generation to be born in the United States," she said.

"So you're the baby of the family," Tristán concluded.

Fern pushed Tristán's shoulder. "Watch who you're calling baby," she countered.

"Artistic, resourceful, *and* feisty," Tristán said with a wink. "Quite a combination."

Fern looked intently at Tristán. All she saw around him now was that same pinkish color she had seen since they'd been in the backyard. Where had the gray aura gone?

"What?" Tristán asked.

"Nothing," Fern lied. "This is it." She pointed to Xochitl's house.

"This is the house you crashed into," Tristán said.

"I didn't crash into the *house*," Fern retorted. "I merely hit the fence."

"Mangled the fence," Tristán corrected. "But it looks fixed now."

"Yeah, my sister Pilar had it replaced right away," Fern said. "I'll be babysitting my nephews until I'm eighteen to pay it off."

"Let me know when the posters are ready, okay?" Tristán said. "I want to help you put them up."

"Okay," Fern said. Before she could say or do anything stupid, she ran up the few steps to Xochitl's front door. Once at the doorstep, she turned to look back at Tristán.

He waved and broke into a big grin that once again revealed the tiny dimple in his right cheek. "See you!"

Fern felt both hot and cold all over. Tristán just stood there for a second. He kicked a rock in the road, then turned and walked away. As he did so, the pink aura immediately changed to gray again and made its familiar yet totally unwanted creep down his body.

Sixteen

At that same moment Fern was saying goodbye to Tristán, Xochitl was staring at the letter from her mother she'd received several days ago. She hadn't written back yet. Mamá was sure to call if she didn't scribble down something soon. Xochitl set the letter on her dresser. She had the gnawing feeling that she was purposely avoiding everything that could make her feel better, but she couldn't help it. She had cried endless tears over not reaching Graciela the other day. The mound of used tissue spread over her dresser was proof of that.

Xochitl pulled the feather-covered journal from under her bed and frowned at it. She leaned against her bed, opened the journal, and leafed through its blank pages. Taped to the back of the book was a sealed envelope. She glared at it uneasily for a moment. She guessed that it was another one of Nana's tricks to force her into opening up before she was ready. What good had it done Xochitl to share her feelings with Nana before she left for the Peraltas' last week? Absolutely none. And now she was supposed to write something that would make her feel exposed and vulnerable to Marina and Fern.

Even though they were nice girls and Xochitl was truly beginning to like them, the idea of having them read something she wrote made her feel nauseated.

She flipped the journal pages back to the front of the book. She didn't know what to write about. All she felt was this vast emptiness. To even explain what she was feeling, she would have to delve into her own emotions, and that felt very scary. Back home in Mexico, Xochitl had always liked writing poetry, but she had only ever let Graciela read it. Without pausing to think too much, Xochitl put pen to paper.

The silent womb, the darkness before creation.
Pregnant space, waiting breath, the air of inspiration.
In the black hole where nothingness abides
The absolute stillness of a deep cave
Shut out the senses you rely upon
Hear no compliments nor criticism
See no glory nor despair
Feel not the cold floor nor stifling heat
Smell not the acrid dampness of the earth
Taste not the flavor of saliva
Be nothing and a window opens

Follow the mystery of emptiness
With the rise and fall of your breath
This cave holds possibility of knowing
Be nothing and you will
Discover yourself in the
Refuge of the Black Cauldron

A refuge was what she needed—a place to go and just heal, maybe sleep, until all the pain went away. Xochitl closed her eyes and imagined the bliss of warm water at the hot springs she and Graciela used to visit in Mexico. She visualized the steam rising and her own body turning into mist. As she relaxed, she allowed her physical form to collapse into the empty space of her solar plexus. She began to feel lightheaded. Gradually, her hands, then her arms, began to fade, until she disappeared completely.

Nana knocked on Xochitl's door, then opened it a little and poked her head through. "Are you ready?" Nana looked around the empty room and snorted in frustration. "Xochitl, I know you are here. I can feel your energy."

Nana stepped into Xochitl's bedroom and with unnerving accuracy walked directly to where Xochitl sat on the ground next to her bed, invisible. "Marina and Fern are here."

Slowly, Xochitl materialized from thin air. There was no hiding from Nana.

"*¿Que tal?* Why would you disappear right now?" Nana asked.

"I don't want to go today," Xochitl protested.

"You can't use your vanishing ability to run away." Nana took Xochitl's hand and pulled her to her feet. "Marina and Fern are good girls. *Son niñas buenas.* Give them a chance."

"All right," Xochitl muttered.

"Meet me in my room," Rogelia said before leaving.

Xochitl closed the journal. She still had to gather the things to bring to the *limpia* ceremony. From her backpack Xochitl pulled the picture of Graciela, to represent the north. A few oak leaves from the river trail where she had tried but failed to speak with Graciela's spirit fell out. She picked up a leaf and examined it. There weren't many oak trees in her hometown, but they were all over California. These trees were new to her and could represent the east, but really and secretively they could symbolize her dedication to try to speak with Graciela. The tissues represented her tears, and that was good enough for the west. What about the south? Xochitl decided on a book, because reading and learning had always given her energy and power.

Xochitl gathered her sacred items and the journal and walked out of her room, across the hall, and into Nana's bedroom. Marina and Fern were waiting, sitting on the bed. A small card table covered with a white cloth stood prominently in the center of the room. Three small white bowls sat in the middle of the table. The words "east," "south," "west," and "north" were written in red marker on pieces of paper on the corners of the table.

"Xochitl, please give Fern the journal," Nana said.

Xochitl handed Fern the journal with some trepidation and sat down next to her.

Standing behind the table, Rogelia looked down at her apprentices. "It fills my heart with joy to guide you on this very sacred journey."

At that moment the door to Rogelia's room opened as if someone had pushed it from the other side. Xochitl, Fern, and Marina looked over Rogelia's shoulder, expecting to see someone come in. No one stood on the threshold, yet there was an electric charge in the air. It felt like someone or something was watching them.

Fern pointed to the door. "The door . . . it just opened." A shadow played against the wall.

Rogelia glanced over her shoulder. She smiled knowingly at Xochitl, Fern, and Marina. "That is simply the presence of Spirit."

"But—" Fern began to protest, obviously in need of further explanation.

Rogelia's eagle eyes bore into Fern. "There is nothing to fear. You want to have Spirit present when you do magic. That way, your actions will be guided toward the highest good of all concerned. Now, one at a time, I would like you to place your sacred items on the table. I have marked each of the directions to make it easier for you. Xochitl, please bring your items first and tell us why you have chosen them."

Xochitl slowly stood up and placed the oak leaves in the eastern corner of the table. "These leaves represent everything that is new to me here." *And my promise to reach Graciela no matter the cost,* Xochitl said to herself. "These crumpled tissues," Xochitl said aloud as she put them in the west, "contain the tears I cried for Graciela and are like water and the west."

"They also symbolize what you have released to make room for something new," Nana said gently. She smiled proudly, as if Xochitl had taken some brave steps.

Xochitl shuddered as a surge of sadness threatened to overcome her. She only meant the offering to represent water. She wasn't thinking of giving up anything; it was exactly the opposite. She wanted to swipe the tissues off the altar, but she knew she couldn't. Xochitl had done enough work with Nana to know that once magic was set in motion, it could not be reversed. She stared at the western corner of the table. Her fear that the guardians of the west had accepted her offering as a final, irrevocable statement of intention felt stronger than she would have thought possible.

Perhaps she still believed in magic more than she realized.

"Go on," Nana urged. "It'll be okay."

Xochitl's hand trembled as she looked at the picture of Graciela she had intended to place on the northern corner. "I didn't mean to say goodbye. I don't want to say . . ." Xochitl choked. "I want to talk to her so bad. I can't let her go. I just can't." Tears streamed down Xochitl's face. Her shoulders shook with emotion.

"That's why we're here with you, *mi amor*." Nana stroked Xochitl's long dark hair. "We're here to help each other."

Fern and Marina both reached out and touched Xochitl on her back. A fresh set of tears fell down Xochitl's cheeks. With a shaky hand, Xochitl placed the picture in the north without having to explain anything. Why was she being pushed to let go of Graciela? Xochitl couldn't help wanting to blame Fern and Marina for pressuring her. If it weren't for them, she wouldn't be doing this ritual right now. She had to fight to stay in her body and not disappear.

Xochitl held up her copy of *Don Quixote* and placed it in the south. "This represents knowledge and power," she said flatly and sat down, relieved to be done.

"Fern, please go next," Rogelia said.

Fern put her Colombian book bag on her lap. She dug out a silken pouch filled with sand, several coffee beans, and a seashell. She stood up and held out the pouch. "This sand is from the Bolsa Chica wetlands, and to me it represents the east because I hope that the near future will bring the total elimination of the construction there," she said passionately. "The seashell is for the west, and the coffee beans I'm putting on the northern corner because they remind me of my family in Colombia." Fern extracted the flower from her bag and stared at it for a moment before placing it on the southern corner. "This red flower is for the south because the color reminds me of heat," she said quickly, then blushed.

"What else does it remind you of?" Rogelia prompted.

Fern didn't answer at first but rolled her lips inward and pressed them together, as if that would keep her from ratting on herself.

"Fern," Marina encouraged her.

"Tristán gave me the flower," Fern admitted. "But I still don't know if I like him or not."

"Sure you don't," Marina said.

"Well, I'm not sure if I *should*," Fern said, sitting down on the bed.

"Time will tell," Rogelia advised. "And last but not least, Marina, please place your items on the altar."

On the eastern corner Marina placed dog-eared flash cards with Spanish words on one side and English translations on the other. She wrinkled her nose at Fern. "I'm learning Spanish."

"Good for you," Fern laughed.

Marina smiled and then placed a gray stone on the western corner. "This is my worry stone. I got it from the Rio Grande on a vacation to Santa Fe, New Mexico. So it's from water, and I'm giving up worrying about what other people think. Well, at least I'm going to try." She put a stack of gift cards on the northern point. "These are all my birthday cards

from my Grandpy since I was three, and this blue ribbon"—
she placed it on the southern corner—"is a first-place soccer
prize. Winning at soccer gives me lots of energy."

Rogelia surveyed the treasures on the altar table. "I'm
very proud of the effort you put into deciding which items to
bring to your *limpia*. Now we need to go out to the garden.
There will be no talking." Rogelia dipped her hand into a little bowl from one of her shelves and scooped something out
of it.

Rogelia, Xochitl, Fern, and Marina filed through the Garcia house and into the backyard. Like most of the homes in
this older part of Santa Ana, the house was small but had a
large backyard that extended wide and deep. The Garcias had
a huge grass area bordered by kumquat, orange, lemon,
grapefruit, peach, and avocado trees.

Corn grew in long rows five feet tall near the back of the
yard. Next to the corn, sweet peas clambered over each other
against a maple-colored wooden fence. Tomatoes and beans
twined themselves over bamboo stakes on the other side of
the corn. To the right of the vegetables, beautiful rows of
green herbs grew in all shapes and sizes.

Rogelia headed directly for the spiny rosemary plant.
"This is called rosemary in English and *romero* in Spanish,"
she said. She opened her hand and sprinkled yellowish grain
over the rosemary. "This is cornmeal, our offering to the
plant. Xochitl, please close your eyes and run your hand over
the top of the plant. When your hand feels the heat coming
from the plant, break off a sprig."

Xochitl closed her eyes and allowed her hand to skim the
air above the *romero*. She didn't expect anything to happen.
Yet when she moved her hand to the left, her hand felt cold,

like she had placed it in snow. But when she moved her hand to the right, it felt warm, like it was near a fire. Lessons with Nana had taught her that magical energy was often warm and tingly. *The difference in temperature could mean anything,* she told herself. *Maybe the sun had a good angle on this side of the plant.*

Still, Xochitl reached into the plant where it felt warmest and tried to bend and twist the twig, but it wouldn't break. A surge of unexpected disappointment came over her.

Why do I even bother? she thought.

"Now ask permission," Nana suggested.

"I forgot," Xochitl said. The first lesson Nana had ever taught her and Graciela was to respect the spirit in every living thing. "May I please have this twig?" She held her hand underneath the plant. Instantly, the twig fell off into her hand without her even touching it.

"Whoa," Fern whispered. "Did you see that?"

"I don't believe this," Xochitl muttered. Baffled, she stared at the *romero* twig in her palm. How was it that magic worked here and now with this little plant but did nothing when it came to bigger matters? A feeling of injustice began to spread through her.

"The branch just dropped into her hand," Marina said, astonished.

"I meant the eyes!" Fern exclaimed. "I saw eyes in the plant."

"Did you?" Rogelia inquired. "Can you still see *los ojos?*"

Fern studied the plant. "No. What was it?"

"You saw the plant's spirit," Rogelia said.

"The plant has a ghost?" Marina asked.

"No, in this case I mean *las hades. ¿Como se dice en Ingles?* Ah. Fairy. You saw the plant's fairy," Rogelia answered.

"Fairies!" Fern shouted. "You mean I just saw a real fairy?"

Who cares about fairies? Xochitl thought. *I want to see my sister.* It bugged her to think that Fern was so excited by seeing fairies, when she had much more important things going on.

Fern squeezed Xochitl's hand. "This is great," she whispered.

Once again, Xochitl wondered how Fern and Marina couldn't see what she was going through. And why was there always this intense focus on magic and so little time spent just talking and getting to know each other? Maybe they really were just taking advantage of her.

"Look at the center of this bush, Fern," Rogelia instructed. "Let your vision soften and blur."

Fern stared at the center of the plant. She bent so close to it, her nose brushed the tip of a leaf.

"Slowly letting your eyes become blurry, back away from the plant," Rogelia said.

"Oh my gosh!" Fern exclaimed. "I can see this fuzzy wavy line around the plant. Was that its aura?" She turned to look at Rogelia, her eyes flashing with excitement.

"Yes," Rogelia confirmed. "Try once more. Maybe you'll see the fairy again."

Fern stared at the plant for a while. "I can see the eyes— they're all purple. I mean it. The iris takes up the whole eyeball. She's got dark sea green hair tinted with bluish purple streaks. I can see her whole face," Fern squeaked in delight.

Xochitl looked at the *romero* plant and then back at Fern. She had to force herself to remain cynical and not get caught up in Fern's enthusiasm.

"Ask permission to take from the plant and look for the lines that vibrate the fastest. They will point out which sprig is for you."

Fern stared at the *romero* for a moment before she confidently reached for a sprig, which snapped off and fell into her hand. She beamed as she held it up for Xochitl and Marina to inspect. "The fairy handed this to me, I swear it."

"Marina," Rogelia said. "I want you to silently ask this dear little *romero* which twig she wants you to have, and the plant will answer."

Marina closed her eyes for a second as if in prayer. Then she opened her eyes and looked directly at a branch sticking out to the right of the bush, as if she knew it would be there. "It's this one," she said, pointing.

"Receive it," Rogelia said.

Marina reached out, and the sprig broke off and dropped into her palm.

"Just like magic," Rogelia laughed. "Okay, back inside."

Xochitl was the last to walk into the house. No matter how hard she tried to deny it, a rush of adrenaline overcame her. Deep down, there was a part of her that was excited to be learning from Nana again. She looked at the candles flickering under the altar to La Virgen de Guadalupe in the living room and felt the rising of a small belief in the miracles.

However, once Nana gave Xochitl, Marina, and Fern each a white candle when they were settled in her room, Xochitl couldn't help thinking of Graciela and how they used to learn from Nana together. Suddenly, the rush of anticipation was gone, and all she had was the sadness brought on by the realization that the happy times with her sister would be only memories from now on.

Rogelia lit the candles. "I want each of you to concentrate on your heart's greatest desire while you face each of the four directions."

Come on, Great Spirit, Xochitl pleaded silently as she turned to face each of the directions. *I'll give you a second chance. I'll even believe Fern and Marina truly want to be my friends if you make Graciela appear right here, right now.*

"Lie down on the bed," Rogelia said. "It'll be a tight squeeze, but you can do it."

Rogelia took an egg off her shelf and rubbed it over Fern's body.

Fern giggled. "It tickles. What's the egg for?"

Rogelia then cracked the egg on the edge of a white bowl in the center of the table and dumped in the contents. "The egg absorbs all the bad energy or sickness in your body." She turned the bowl from side to side, inspecting the bubbles and white of the broken egg. The healer repeated the process over both Xochitl and Marina. Then she took each of their rosemary sprigs and brushed the girls with the little plant.

Xochitl lay between Marina and Fern and shut her eyes. With each breath, she willed her sister to visit her. *Please, Graciela,* Xochitl begged. She pictured Graciela's face and remembered her voice. Xochitl heard a small bump. Her heart jumped to her throat. She looked around hopefully and noticed the branch of a tree brushing against the window. She hoped it was a sign from Graciela. But when Graciela failed to appear, Xochitl felt her heart take on the heaviness of a lead weight.

Seventeen

After the ceremony, Fern and Marina began their way home in a bit of a daze. Fern stepped aside for a gaggle of kids as they ran by with a long jump rope.

"That was unbelievable!" Fern shrieked. "Couldn't you just feel the room vibrating with magic? And when Rogelia looked at you? Remind me never to lie to her." She paused. "Not that I believe in lying."

Marina nodded in agreement, although she was happy just being around Rogelia. She liked her sense of humor, her kindness, and her strength. She wondered if Rogelia was anything like her own nana.

"And next time we'll hike to a waterfall," Fern prattled.

"Remember Xochitl said Rogelia can walk for a long time and we had better bring good shoes. This is just too cool."

"Walk me to the bus stop?" Marina asked.

"Of course," Fern said, giving Marina a questioning look. "Are you taking the bus all the way home?"

"Only to the mall, to Fashion Island. Mom is taking me and Monica shopping for Grandpy's birthday party a week from Sunday. She went through my closet last night and decided I had nothing fit to wear." Marina rolled her eyes. "Whatever, I'll get new clothes."

"She's really making a big deal out of this one," Fern observed.

"He'll be sixty," Marina said. "The family is coming in from all over. We'll be taking over a whole room at some fancy restaurant called the White House."

"How very *white* of your family," Fern joked.

Marina laughed uncomfortably.

"Hey, don't forget the Los Lobos concert is coming up," Fern said. "I got the tickets. Xochitl said she can't come, but we'll have fun."

Marina twirled her hair nervously. "I never . . . exactly . . . said I *could* go . . . ," she said haltingly. "I just said I'd *like* to go."

"Come on, Marina," Fern said. "You have to come."

"I don't think my mom would let me, much less the night before a family party," Marina said. *Not to mention the grief she'd dish out about the crowd Los Lobos will attract,* she thought dryly.

"But I've already bought the tickets," Fern persisted. She grabbed Marina's hand and gave her a pleading puppy-dog stare with her amber eyes.

"I'm sorry, I can't go." Marina pulled her hand free. She

had a hard time admitting even to Fern how deep her mother's harsh judgment of Mexican people ran.

"You can sneak out," Fern suggested.

Marina sighed heavily. Could she risk it? She had never sneaked out before. She was such a sucker for her friend's begging that she studied the narrow sidewalks of the neighborhood in order to avoid Fern's eyes. The cement squares were buckled by the roots of the huge, sprawling trees on either side. The city trimmed the trees on the Peraltas' street every week to maintain their resemblance to overgrown lollipops. But here in Santa Ana, everything had more life. It reminded Marina of how much more connected and alive she felt when she spent time at Rogelia's house.

Differences can do that, the woman's voice said in Marina's head.

Marina sighed as she inhaled the smell of pinto beans cooking and the clean scent of lime soap that floated over from a bright red house.

"Come on. It will be fun. Pilar won't tell," Fern insisted.

"Why don't you just ask Tristán to go with you?" Marina said playfully.

Fern frowned and put her hands on her hips. "I wanted it to be a girls' night, but you and Xochitl aren't getting with the program, *comprendes?*"

"Okay, okay," Marina relented as they reached the bus stop. "The last thing I want is for you to be all mad at me."

"Hooray! We'll have a blast." Fern brought Marina in for a quick bear hug. Marina leaned on the bus stop bench for support. "You're a regular bus rider now," Fern teased. "Maybe once you get your license, they'll let you drive the bus."

"Whatever," Marina replied.

"Why didn't you ask Pilar for a ride? Or have your mom pick you up?" Fern asked.

"I kind of like the excitement of public transportation," Marina joked. The real reason she didn't ask Fern's sister for a ride was because Pilar might let it slip and tell her mother that Marina had been in the old neighborhood. And no one in Fern's family knew about Mrs. Peralta's low opinion of Santa Ana. Naturally, Marina tried to keep all that to herself. "Besides, you know what a pain Friday traffic can be," she added to make sure Fern didn't catch on.

No está bien, the girl's voice said.

You're not being very honest with Fern, the woman's voice said.

Marina batted hair off her ear, as if she could shake off the voices.

"It was pretty cool for Xochitl to let us into her inner sanctum," Fern said abruptly.

"Why do you say that?" Marina asked.

Fern watched the rolling clouds for a moment before answering. "Well, I don't think it can be very easy for her to have us learning from her nana. Xochitl is pretty guarded," Fern said.

"Did you see another aura?" Marina asked, fascinated.

"No. It's just a feeling I have. Rogelia works for your family, too. That's got to be awkward," Fern said as she swung around the bus stop pole.

"It doesn't have to be," Marina objected.

Fern shrugged as the bus came to a stop in front of them.

"See ya," Marina said in an annoyed tone as she stepped onto the bus and expertly slid her dollar bill into the receptacle.

Fern had definitely touched a nerve. Marina hadn't thought about how their training with Rogelia might raise complications for Xochitl. But now that the subject was brought up, Marina wondered if Xochitl thought they were horning in on one of the only relatives Xochitl had living with her.

Marina's cell phone rang, jolting her out of her thoughts. She looked at the phone and winced before opening it. Just to be on the safe side, she held the phone several inches from her ear.

"You said you would be at Anthropologie at six. It's 6:03!" Marina's mother exclaimed.

Marina gazed through the large windshield of the bus. They were a few lights away from her stop. "Um, I got caught up at the music store." Marina quickly muffled the mouth-piece as the automatic recorder announced the major inter-section they were crossing.

"What was that?" Marina's mother asked.

"They announced the need for another checker at the checkout," Marina lied. "I'll be right there, Mom."

Marina snapped the phone shut and stood up, ready to spring off the bus at her stop.

The woman's voice said, *One of these days, you'll need to find the courage to speak your truth.*

Claro que sí. The girl's voice seemed to be affirming what the woman said.

Even though the voices were right, Marina couldn't help feeling a little indignation. Shouldn't voices in your head be helpful and supportive?

We are being supportive, my dear, insisted the woman. *We are trying to encourage the power within you that, so far, you have failed to recognize.*

Marina shook her head at the voices' confidence in her as she jumped off the bus and ran through Fashion Island's massive parking lot. They had no idea what she was up against. She slowed to a brisk walk as she neared the first group of kids loi-tering around the directory sign. Marina ran up the escalators and didn't even bother turning around to catch one of her favorite views of the ocean and Newport Beach. She raced past the Venetian carousel, a ton of high-end stores like BCBG Max Azria, an art gallery or two, and hip shops like Juicy Couture. She pulled open the gigantic wooden doors of Anthropologie and slipped inside. She found her mother shaking her head at the dresses on display.

Standing beside their mother, Monica looked at Marina's disheveled hair and mouthed, *Where were you?*

Xochitl's, Marina mimed.

Monica's hazel eyes widened in amazement as she quickly raked her fingers through the front of Marina's hair and patted down the flyaway strands on top, then nodded her approval.

"Hey, Mom," Marina said merrily.

Marina's mother turned. "There you are." She flicked her finger at the dress she had been scrutinizing. "None of these will do. These dresses are too strange. We should have gone to one of the department stores."

"So we can buy cookie-cutter outfits," Monica mumbled.

Marina giggled. Her mother glared menacingly at Monica. Marina sobered up and stepped in front of her sister as if to guard her. "Mom, we like these clothes."

See? You have power when you want it, the woman's voice said. Marina smiled inwardly at the encouragement.

"They aren't nice enough for Grandpy's party," Marina's mother complained.

"We'll find something," Marina said reassuringly.

Within fifteen minutes, Marina and Monica had selected a few dresses and skirts and were headed to the fitting rooms. Marina's mother beelined for the handicapped room.

"Mom, that room is for handicapped people," Marina protested.

"People with special needs," Monica interjected.

Marina's mother looked around arrogantly. "Well, I don't see anyone with special needs but us. We need the space."

Marina and Monica exchanged looks as if to say, *Sometimes there is no stopping her.*

Mrs. Peralta settled comfortably on a cushioned bench in the large fitting room. Marina closed the door and turned her back to her mother when she took off her shirt. Her mother watched her in the mirror.

"You need another bra," Marina's mother said brusquely. "That one is too small."

Marina whipped the shirt back over her head. She wanted to tell her mom off, but she couldn't think of a response in time to stop another devastating remark.

"Didn't we just buy you a bra?" her mother continued. "I didn't grow that fast. Maybe you've put on a few pounds. How much do you weigh?"

"Mom!" Monica and Marina objected together.

"I was only asking." Marina's mother balked, hands in the air as if she were innocently shielding off a brutal attack from her daughters.

"You know, Mom," Monica began carefully, "why don't you wait for us outside?"

Mrs. Peralta patted the cushion. "There's a bench in here. I'm tired."

Marina grabbed a dress and Monica's arm and yanked her sister out of the fitting room. Once they were safely secluded in another dressing room, Marina whispered, "*She's* the one with special needs."

Monica stifled a laugh. "Come on, hurry up before she hunts us down."

Marina tried on a white dress with a pink ribbon sash.

It wasn't exactly her style, but she figured her mom would like it and they could get out of here sooner. Marina looked at herself in the mirror before walking out. What was her style, anyway?

You have yet to find it, my dear, said the woman's voice.

Sí, the girl responded in agreement.

Marina sighed. *Fern and even the voices are right. I always buy whatever is in fashion. I don't have a color scheme, except for whatever appears the most in my magazines.* If the clothing was expensive, displayed on a mannequin, or with a popular label, she bought it. But that didn't mean she always liked it or felt comfortable wearing it. How many times had she gone into her jam-packed closet and still not been able to find anything she wanted to wear?

Marina opened the door to the handicapped room to model for her mother. Marina's mother lounged on the bench as if she were kicking back poolside at some fancy resort. All she needed was one cabana boy to feed her peeled grapes and another one to fan her with a palm frond.

Marina's mother sat up. "You look lumpy," she said.

"How can you say something so mean? You're my mother," Marina asked in a small and confused voice.

Keep calm, the woman's voice said.

Marina felt Monica walk up behind her. The extra support reminded Marina of how strong she felt around Rogelia, who would never say anything like that to her.

"I thought you would want me to be honest," Marina's mother said frostily.

Hable tu verdad, the girl's voice said.

Yes, just speak your truth, the woman said.

"There is a difference between honesty and cruelty," Marina stated.

Marina's mother gathered her purse and stood up. "Marina, I'm sorry, but I just don't know how to love you."

"What?" Marina asked.

"Not the way you want me to." Marina's mother pushed past Marina and stormed out of the fitting room.

A store clerk walked up at that opportune moment. Red-faced, she looked from Marina to the retreating form of her mother. "Um, do you need any other sizes?"

"No." Marina sniffed. "I think we're done here."

⌘ ⌘ ⌘

After the unfortunate shopping excursion, Marina waited in anticipation all weekend for Rogelia to come back to their house. She woke early Monday morning and listened to the birds chirping outside. Finally, she heard Rogelia opening the front door. Marina whipped off her bedcover.

Esperate, came the girl's voice.

Yes, wait until she gets her work done, said the woman.

Marina sighed and obeyed the voices, even though she didn't quite understand why she couldn't talk to Rogelia while she worked. But then, she guessed Rogelia would speak more openly with her if they had some privacy. Marina put on a baby-doll tank and a pair of light pink lounge pants and, with no electronic distractions in her room, as per Rogelia's instructions, she read magazines in her room for a few hours. Finally, Rogelia shuffled Samantha off on a playdate with one of her little buddies and took her lunch into her room. Marina knocked on the door.

"Come in," Rogelia called.

Marina opened the door and inhaled deeply, beginning to find comfort in the scent of copal. She handed Rogelia an embroidered handkerchief she had bought just for her.

"*Gracias.* Sit down here, Marina." Rogelia patted the bed. "What do you want to talk about?" Rogelia pulled up a chair so that she faced Marina.

Marina sat on the bed. "It's my mom," she said, looking into her teacher's tender gaze. She was beginning to trust those wrinkles of Rogelia's. "She gets so mad at me, and I don't know why I let it hurt me, but it does."

"There is something innate in most everyone that needs to have that connection with their mother," Rogelia said. "Have you been practicing your meditation work?"

"A little," Marina said, wondering why Rogelia was changing the subject.

"It will help you strengthen your will," Rogelia assured her. "And then you won't be bothered so much by other people's opinions or outbursts."

"So when I get good at hearing these voices, will I be able to read minds like you?" Marina asked.

"Maybe," Rogelia chuckled. "I knew you were going to need some privacy to talk with me today," she said.

"How did you know that?" Marina asked, gazing with admiration at Rogelia. She was just about the coolest person Marina had ever met. "I didn't even think that in your presence."

"Intuition, *mi amor.*" Rogelia smiled. "I keep telling you and Fern how important it is. I think you will understand this lesson better if we go outside."

Marina followed Rogelia through the house. Monica glanced at them curiously when they passed her bedroom. They walked outside and followed the path to the far end of the yard, near where Fern and Marina had buried the god's eyes.

"Watch those hummingbirds." Rogelia pointed to the small birds.

Marina peered at two ruby-throated birds diving in and

soaring out of the Australian bottlebrush tree, stopping on occasion to stick their long beaks into the mass of conelike red flowers.

"What are they saying?" Rogelia asked.

"I don't know," Marina said. How was she supposed to know that? Did Rogelia think she spoke bird language?

She'll explain, just give her a moment, the woman's voice said.

"Listen," Rogelia said. "And you will be able to understand."

Marina listened to the birds and clearly heard agitated buzzing and chirping as the birds zipped back and forth. "They're buzzing?" she said questioningly.

"Yes, but I believe you can understand what their voices are saying," Rogelia said as she watched the birds fly in and out of the tree. "You just need to trust your intuition, and no more second-guessing yourself. Tell me, when do you most often hear the voices in your head?"

"I hear them when I'm by myself, and once when I was really scared," Marina said. "But mostly as I'm waking up or just before I fall asleep."

"Sit down and close your eyes," Rogelia said.

Marina glanced once more at the birds, then found a smooth place on the ground to sit. She closed her eyes.

"Take three deep breaths," Rogelia said soothingly. "Pretend you are lying in your bed. You are enjoying a dream of floating on a cloud."

Marina imagined just that, and she could feel her body relaxing.

"Ever so slowly, the cloud drifts down from the heavens. You're still far above the earth, but getting closer all the time."

Marina felt the gentle sway of the cloud's descent.

"Now you've landed on the top of a mountain peak, where there sits a lone tree. What do you hear?" Rogelia asked.

"Get off my branch," Marina repeated. Her eyes flew open. "It's the birds!"

"Now, watch the birds," Rogelia instructed. "But hold on to the dreamy state you had during the visualization."

Marina gazed at the birds. They continued to chirp, but instead of indecipherable noise, she discovered that she understood them. She laughed. Instead of buzzing, she heard words. "They're fighting over the pollen," Marina reported. She pointed out the smaller of the two birds. "That one just told the other bird to get out of his tree." Marina laughed even harder as one of the birds zoomed off. "The one that left, he just said, 'I hope your beak gets stuck in a bees' nest.' "

"Hummingbirds are well known for being territorial little beasts," Rogelia said.

"I thought they were sweet. They're so pretty," Marina said.

"Not everything pretty is nice," Rogelia said. Nodding her approval, she added, "That's a good lesson for today."

Eighteen

The following Friday afternoon, Fern held the journal in one hand and swung a bag of black beans in the other as she walked to Xochitl's house. A bunch of kids ran through sprinklers. The sun shone bright overhead, warming Fern's back. Fern had been looking forward to her meeting with Rogelia.

Rogelia opened the door for Fern. *"Buenas tardes."*

"Good afternoon, Doña Rogelia. I brought you some beans." Fern held up the bag.

"Gracias." Rogelia smiled at Fern's formal respect. "This way," she said, making her way through the house to the kitchen.

Fern followed her, stealing glances on either side of her

for a sign of Xochitl. Rogelia passed through the house silently. "They are shopping for clothes at The Second."

"Clothes? Xochitl is getting new clothes?" Fern asked.

"Yes. After Mrs. Peralta gave me a bag of Marina and Monica's old clothes for Xochitl, my son realized that a young woman needs more than two pairs of pants." Rogelia snorted.

Fern smiled inwardly. The wish Xochitl had made during their magic ritual had come true! Rogelia ripped open the bag and poured the contents onto the peach tiled kitchen counter. "Would you please spread these out, Fern?" Rogelia asked while filling a pot with water. "Pick out the shriveled beans and any dirt."

Fern selected a few shriveled beans and threw them into a small wicker wastebasket.

"A few bad beans can spoil the whole pot of *frijoles*. But with a little attention and patience, you can make a good thing better." Rogelia scooped up the remaining beans, and put them into a pot of water to soak. She set the pot on an unlit burner on the back of the stove.

The *curandera* took a metal stool from a cupboard and put it in front of the stove. She stepped onto the stool, opened the liquor cabinet above the stove, and removed a container of condensed coconut oil and a small brown glass jar. She handed the container, the jar, and a spoon to Fern. "Spoon the coconut oil into the jar. The oil will melt once we are outside." Rogelia got off the stool, pulled open the screen door, and descended the few steps to the backyard.

Fern scooped the oil into the jar and quickly followed Rogelia. She noticed a worn hemp rope with a swing tied to one of the branches of the avocado tree that had grown over the house. Fern wondered if Mr. Garcia had put up the swing when he first got here, in hopes his family would arrive soon. A black cat lay in a bright patch of sunlight beside the tree. Rogelia bent down to pet the cat. Fern stared conspicuously at the blue shawl over Rogelia's thin shoulders despite the warmth of the day.

"Old age makes me cold," Rogelia answered without turning around.

"It's kind of freaky when you answer questions I haven't even asked."

Rogelia shrugged, hands raised up to the sky. "Bad habit of mine." She led Fern to a row of chili plants with orange, green, yellow, and red peppers of all sizes. *"Siéntate."*

Fern did as she was told and, hitching up her red vintage pedal pushers, sat down on the soft grass next to the plants. Ladybugs flew around her. She lifted her face to the sun and grinned. Rogelia watched Fern and waited for her to relax into the peace of the garden. Fern turned her gaze to Rogelia.

"Today I will help you sharpen your ability to sense the aura or energy field around people by working with plants," Rogelia said. "Sometimes it is easier to see an aura when the subject is still. The best part of seeing auras is that it gives you advance notice on how to best approach a situation or person. The trick," she said with her index finger in the air, "is figuring out what the auras mean, and that takes mostly time and practice."

Rogelia traced the whorls of small, hooded white flowers of the basil plant, then tapped underneath the oval leaves, releasing the herb's pungent smell. "Recognizing the aura is the first step to appreciating a plant's unique spirit. Once you see the aura, then the fairy may reveal himself or herself. Now look deep into the plant. Move slowly forward, then back up and let your gaze fall upon the perimeter of the plant. Think of yourself as meeting someone shy."

"Like Xochitl?" Fern asked.

"Yes," Rogelia laughed.

Fern dipped her face toward the plant until the broad basil leaves tickled her cheek. As she slowly backed away, Fern let her vision become blurry. She saw several wavy lines hugging the top of the herb. "There it is." Gradually, the smoky lines of energy moved together to form one thick band of vibrant green aura. "Ooh, what was that?" Fern leaned in closer to the plant and moved away again. "It's gone." She crossed her arms and furrowed her brow.

"What did you see?" Rogelia asked.

"A green color, very bright, like in a rainbow."

"*Muy bien.* Very good," Rogelia said. "Seeing colors is the next step after being able to detect the aura."

"I've seen colors before, but I don't see any now." Fern squinted at the plant.

"It will come and go," Rogelia said consolingly.

"I thought once you saw an aura, you could always see an aura," Fern said. She thought about telling Rogelia how she had seen the different colors around Tristán, but she didn't know how to bring up the subject without admitting that she kind of had a crush on him. Also, Fern wasn't sure she wanted to hear what Rogelia might say about a gray aura, especially if it was bad.

"It takes practice and trust in your instincts to see auras on a regular basis. My intuition and respect for the life force in each plant, or as you call it, the fairy, helps me understand how much water or sun they need. Then they become little friends that help me with my *remedios* whenever I need it."

"How do you know the difference between an instinct and something that you've just made up?" Fern asked. "Say, for example, you like someone, but you have a funny feeling about them at the same time. How do you know which side to choose?"

Rogelia gave Fern a kind look. "Stop chattering long enough for the silence to answer." Rogelia laughed at Fern's look of indignation. "Now that you've seen the basil's aura, why don't you work on seeing the fairy? Direct your attention to the center of the plant, not the shadow outside the plant."

Fern hadn't really gotten the answer she needed, but she figured the lessons were bound to help her figure out what auras meant. Then she could decide what to do about Tristán once and for all.

Fern softened her focus around the plant. Immediately, she saw the wavy lines move into the green aura that outlined the plant. She looked deep into the center of the basil. Grass green eyes stared back at her. Fern held her breath, hoping this fairy would reveal itself in its entirety. She smiled encouragingly at the fairy and waited. Ever so shyly, a wide face with a yellow-green complexion, long pointy ears, and a shock of white hair styled in a cute bob revealed itself. Fern felt goose bumps spring up all over her body. She forced herself to remain calm even though she was bursting with excitement. Fern moved back, away from the plant, to give the fairy some room.

The fairy, which was about the size of Fern's hand, fluttered out from its hiding place and flew to the top of the plant. The fairy wore a tiered dress, brown and green striped tights, and pointed shoes covered with white blossoms and iridescent fairy dust. She looked curiously, and a bit suspiciously, at Fern.

"Hello," Fern whispered.

The basil fairy laughed and covered her hand with her mouth. She pranced on top of the plant, swishing her skirt over her knees as she moved. After a few turns, she looked expectantly at Fern and fluttered her double set of green wings.

"You're very pretty," Fern said.

The fairy flew a loop around Fern, leaving behind the scent of basil. She flew back to the plant and floated cross-legged above it. She winked at Fern.

"Can I hold you?" Fern held out her hand.

The fairy gave a startled cry and sped back into the plant.

"Where did she go?" Fern asked, disappointed. She peered into the basil plant but saw nothing.

"You were too forceful for the fairy's comfort," Rogelia said. "I told you fairies are shy. Well, most. Some of them can be very bold, but I know basil to be secretive and timid. Come on, I want to show you more of the garden."

Fern looked reluctantly at the basil plant, then followed Rogelia. As she walked behind Rogelia to another section of the garden, she couldn't help feeling special and powerful. This was the second time she had seen a fairy!

Rogelia squatted down to point out a myriad of plants. "This is my poison garden, where I grow datura, digitalis, belladonna or deadly nightshade, and a few others." The healer pointed to a small, low wooden bridge. "Next to the bridge I grow very helpful weeds, such as stinging nettle and dandelion, as well as indigenous plants like white sage, yarrow, and yerba buena. And on the other side are thyme, rosemary, basil, and ginger. All these plants are helpful in some way or another."

"Even poisons?" Fern asked skeptically.

"Intuition can help you strike the right balance, and then even so-called poisons can restore health. That is why you must be clean as a panpipe when you are interpreting auras or doing *curandera* work. If your fear stands between you and your judgment, you will only see the fear. When you form a relationship with plants, your connection to the core of Mother Earth deepens. Once you connect to her, the real magic begins. But during the process you will make some mistakes."

"I don't like to make mistakes," Fern whispered, looking down to her tank top, which featured peacocks and flowers.

"Every practitioner will make mistakes," Rogelia said firmly. "I have made plenty of mistakes. It is part of learning. *El que la sigue la consigue.*"

That particular *dicho*, meaning "if at first you don't succeed, try again," was one Fern's mother repeated often to her. She didn't really like the idea of incessant attempts at success. She liked the notion of success as something that came naturally and intrinsically, not something she had to attempt repeatedly to get right.

"You have a rare gift, to be able to see auras and the fairies so quickly. I believe once you learn their ways, the fairies will ensure that any leaf you pluck for magical or healing purposes will carry the most powerful essence of the plant. Allow your intuition to guide you and choose three plants and place them in your jar of coconut oil for your first healing ointment," Rogelia said.

"A potion," Fern whispered reverently.

"What?" Rogelia asked.

"Nothing," Fern said quickly.

Fern strolled through the garden, observing the many different auras around the plants and trees. She selected yarrow leaves, orange blossoms, and a piece of ginger root to place in her coconut oil. Rogelia pulled the ginger plant for a new remedy she was making and helped Fern wipe the root clean of mud. After she made the remedy, Fern used colored pencils to write down her potion instructions in the journal. Next to her potion recipe she drew her favorite inlet at the Bolsa Chica wetlands. She fell into a trance while drawing. Fifteen minutes later she looked down to see she had drawn the likeness of Tristán right there in the journal she shared with Marina and Xochitl.

⌘ ⌘ ⌘

Later that day, as Fern approached her house, she noticed a large rectangular package propped against her cobalt blue front door. Fern knew it was the posters. She hesitated a minute, then slowly increased her pace before breaking into a run. She picked up the package and ripped it open.

She pulled out a single poster announcing the Hands Across the Wetlands, just two weeks from tomorrow, and carefully set the package down. Pride filled her heart as she stared at the glossy posters. The first thing she wanted to do was call Tristán. But even if she'd had his number, she wondered if she would have had the courage to use it.

Holding the poster in her left hand, Fern ran her right index finger over the top of the eucalyptus grove as if she were tracing the line of an aura above the cluster of trees. This was a sacred place, and she was helping to protect it. She admired her color choices: seafoam green, cornflower blue, sand, soft white, *cafe con leche*. But that was only a quarter of the colors the printer had picked up. She could almost hear the seagulls cry and smell the salty air.

"Hey, Fern," a voice called out.

Fern turned to see Tristán sauntering up her driveway. Before she could stop herself, Fern dropped the poster and ran to him. She gave him such a big hug, it nearly knocked him over. "Thank you so much for helping make this real," she exclaimed.

Tristán staggered in Fern's embrace. "What are you talking about?" he asked, bewildered.

"This! This!" Fern ran back to the porch. She carried the poster to Tristán and handed it to him. "You believed in my idea. You encouraged me to go for it, and I did. I've never done anything like this before."

Tristán looked at the poster and back at Fern. "Congratulations. It was a great idea," he said warily.

"It was just a pipe dream, you know. But you believed it could be real. And here it is," Fern continued to jabber.

Tristán shifted his feet uncertainly. "Fern, I can't thank you enough for helping protect Bolsa Chica wetlands. My ancestors are buried there, you know. My family means a lot to me."

Suddenly, Fern felt really foolish. Of course it wasn't *her* he believed in, as much as he believed in the cause. *Why can't I ever keep my mouth shut?* She smiled faintly at him. "So did you want something?"

"I just came by to see, um . . ." Tristán fumbled over his words. ". . . if you got the posters, and you have."

"Yeah, we should put them up soon," Fern said.

"I'm ready to go right now. But before we go anywhere, I need to tell you something. See this bear claw?" Tristán held up his necklace. "It's soapstone from Catalina Island. This carving has been passed down for so many generations, we've lost track. This land and my family are like one, and they are everything to me."

"I'm sorry I just thought it was my dream you were supporting," Fern replied glumly. "Of course it was your family's dream first." She stared at the huge pepper tree in her front yard. She couldn't bring herself to look Tristán in the eye.

Tristán reached for Fern's hand. "Fernanda, I also believe in you, if you would just let me show you." He touched one of Fern's ringlets. "I think you are really incredible."

Fern bit her lip and stared down at her pink toenails. She wanted to believe that Tristán cared for her this much and that it was safe to lend her heart to him. Impetuous though she was, something held her back from simply giving it away. As she glanced up, she saw a band of dark green light float over his body. The ring of light around him pulsated rapidly, like it was agitated. And the intense way Tristán was looking at her scared her; he was standing way too close.

"Let's go hang up some posters," Fern blurted out suddenly. She backed toward the door and picked up the posters.

Tristán looked hesitantly at Fern, as if he wondered whether or not she had understood him.

"We've got work to do," Fern insisted, forcing herself to sound light and cheery. "Where should we start?"

"All right," Tristán said. "Well, it's got to be places a lot of people visit."

"The malls," Fern said quickly. "Probably the ones closest to Bolsa Chica. That way it'll make it easier for them to get to our, I mean, *the* event. So, um, how are we going to get there?"

"I'll drive," Tristán offered.

"Okay," Fern said. "I'll go get some tape and stuff to hang them." Fern sprinted into the house. *Shake it off, girl,* she told herself. That was easier said than done, though.

Tristán was waiting for Fern with his passenger door open. She slid into the seat and squeezed the packet of posters to her chest. His car smelled like cherries. She wondered if she should scoot over the bench seat to be closer to him or just stay where she was. As he was opening his car door, Fern put the posters in the wheel well, and when she sat back up she scooted a little closer to Tristán. It might have passed for a smooth move, or maybe not.

It was market day at the Huntington Beach pier. Tristán parked on a side street, away from traffic jamming up Pacific Coast Highway. He plunked a few quarters in the meter and turned expectantly to Fern. "Where to?"

"Let's go to the Surf Museum," Fern suggested. "They'll want to keep the coastline pure."

"Good idea," Tristán agreed.

As they walked down Main Street through the swarms of people, Tristán's shoulder bumped into Fern, giving her the shivers. Emotions bubbled in her stomach, causing her to feel woozy. She started to feel warm all over. Fern tried to tell herself it was the heat of the blazing sun. But she knew it was because of the hot guy walking next to her.

The museum manager was happy to promote their cause and offered to send some people to their event. Inspired after such a great start, Fern and Tristán ran from beach shop to surf shop to sandwich shop along the downtown Huntington Beach scene. At lunchtime, they decided to take a break and check out the marketplace at the pier. More than twenty white pop-up tents shaded the artisans, fruit mongers, bakers, jewelers, and other vendors as they sold their wares. Throngs of beachwear-clad people moved lazily through the warm July weather. While Tristán bought them a bag of kettle corn, Fern shaded her eyes to look down the sandy beach and out at the vast Pacific Ocean. A group of skaters were ripping up the cement stairs that led to the boardwalk. At the end of the wooden-plank pier, sunshine glinted off the red roof of Ruby's restaurant. Tristán offered Fern the bag of kettle corn.

Fern dipped her hand in the bag. "I love this stuff," she mumbled through a mouthful.

Tristán laughed at Fern's childlike enthusiasm.

"It's good stuff, man," Fern said.

Tristán smiled at Fern. He took her hand. She really liked it when he did that. She smiled back, but Tristán continued to stare without saying anything for the longest time. It made her feel self-conscious. Finally, she couldn't take it anymore.

"What?" she asked. "Do I have something in my teeth?"

"Do you want to go out sometime?" Tristán asked.

"We are out," Fern laughed, throwing a piece of popcorn at him.

"No, I meant on a date," Tristán murmured, moving closer to Fern.

Fern gawked at Tristán without saying anything. His aura was a thick rosy pink that floated softly around him, like fluffy clouds. She was really beginning to dig that color. Yes, she wanted to go on a date. But she wasn't sure how she felt about him yet. She knew she liked him—she *really* liked him. That was what had her so confused. She had the weirdest feeling in her gut about that first aura she'd seen, and she just couldn't erase it no matter how hard she tried. The question hung in the air, unanswered for an awkward moment.

Just then, a pair of towheaded boys raced up at breakneck speed on their Heelys. "Watch out," one of the boys called as they broke Fern and Tristán apart.

The bag of popcorn flew high in the air and rained down on them. Fern giggled as she tried to catch the falling popcorn in her mouth. Tristán joined her fun and began throwing the few remaining pieces of popcorn in the air and trying to catch as many as he could. With the tension broken, Fern didn't have to answer the question, and Tristán didn't push for a response. Fern wasn't sure if she was relieved or annoyed with herself.

Afterward, they canvassed the small shopping centers

in Sunset Beach, Newport Beach, and Laguna Beach. Fern laughed as she watched Tristán use all kinds of tactics to gain permission from the store managers to plaster their windows with the posters. He seemed to quickly figure out whatever the manager needed to hear, whether that was information about how the wetlands affected tourism or just the environmental angle.

Wherever they went, Fern tried to catch a glimpse of Tristán's aura. She saw lots of colors. When it was just the two of them, his aura shone that romantic pink color. When he was talking to the store owners, the colors of light around his body shifted to green, blue, or even orange. But not once all day did she see anything like the gray aura she had seen before.

"We've got about a hundred posters left," Tristán said, looking at the stack of posters, which had dwindled since the beginning of their trek three hours earlier.

"Let's hit our hometown," Fern suggested. "There are some really forward-thinking businesses in the Santa Ana artists village. I bet we won't have any problem putting posters up there."

"Another great idea," Tristán said with a smile. "Your chariot awaits."

Fern hopped into Tristán's car. He roared off, and Fern shivered with delight as they sped down the freeway back home. She rolled down the window and put her head outside to feel the wind blowing on her face. The sun was nearing the horizon, but it was still warm out when they got back into Santa Ana.

After taping posters up in several of the stores, they decided to staple the remaining posters to community bulletin boards.

"My arms are getting so tired," Fern said as she held a poster above some postcards on the community board in the funky coffee shop the Gypsy Den.

"I'll hold it while you tape it," Tristán offered.

Tristán held up the poster and Fern ducked under his outstretched arms to tape it down.

"Fern," Tristán said softly.

She turned and found herself nose to nose with Tristán, who leaned in and kissed her.

It took Fern a couple of seconds to realize what was happening, but she lost herself in their kiss soon enough. Tristán's bottom lip was so soft, but his top lip pressed against her with just the right pressure. The kiss was sweet and lingering. She could smell the warmth of the sun and even some salty sea air lingering around him. He threaded his fingers through her hair at the nape of her neck.

Fern pulled away and looked dreamily at Tristán. To her shock, she saw that his aura pulsed bloodred with a very clear and very ominous border of steel gray pressing down like a vise. Tristán leaned forward to kiss her again. She pushed against him and backed up.

"Fern?" Tristán said.

"I gotta go," she mumbled.

Then she turned and ran all the way home.

Nineteen

A week later, Xochitl sat on her bed, watching the little alarm clock on her dresser tick closer and closer to three o'clock. How had she allowed herself to get roped into another *curanderismo* lesson with Fern and Marina? She could disappear, but her nana would just sniff her out like last time.

"Xochitl!" Nana called.

Reluctantly, Xochitl got out of her bed. She trudged down the hall to the kitchen. Marina and Fern stood there waiting for her. Both of them wore expensive-looking hiking boots and carried plastic bottles filled with ice water.

"Look, Mom bought these for me at REI," Marina said, stretching her legs to show off her new shoes.

Xochitl couldn't speak. She had told them to wear

sensible shoes, but she hadn't meant for them to go out and buy something expensive. Fern laughed at the look of incredulity on Xochitl's face.

"What?" Marina asked Xochitl. "You said to wear good shoes."

"I didn't mean you had to buy new ones," Xochitl said.

Both Fern and Nana laughed.

"I think they're cute," Marina said defensively, twisting her feet to admire her shoes from another angle.

"Fern, did you bring the journal?" Rogelia asked.

Fern held up the feather-covered book. "Here it is."

"Please give it to Marina," Rogelia instructed.

Fern handed the journal over to Marina with a little hesitation.

"It's okay," Rogelia said. "Remember, we're learning to trust and depend on each other. This journal is intended to bring you closer together."

Xochitl turned her head so Nana wouldn't see her look of disbelief. She wasn't sure that Nana's plan to use the journal as a way to get her to bond with Fern and Marina was really working on her.

⌘ ⌘ ⌘

The sun was directly overhead by the time they arrived at Silverado Canyon, a nature preserve that lay behind a funky little town of the same name. It was also located between two small mountain ranges of the Cleveland National Forest. Their goal was the hike to a waterfall called Holy Jim Falls, about one and a half miles inland. The pungent scent of pine filled the air as Xochitl plodded behind Fern, Marina, and Nana.

A raptor's high-pitched squeal resonated through the still

air as a red-tailed hawk dove into the tall grass. The predator plucked a gray squirrel off a sprawling live oak's branch and with a second swoop pinned his prey to the ground a mere twenty paces in front of Rogelia. The hawk turned his cold marauder's stare on her and her apprentices.

"What a wonderful hunter you are," Rogelia complimented him. The hawk picked up his prey and flew into the air. Rogelia turned to the girls. "There are fewer predators than prey in nature. It is a perfect balance. One hawk eats hundreds of rodents a year. One bat will devour three thousand mosquitoes in a night. Each system supports the next. It's important to remember how connected we all are."

"That's like our work at Bolsa Chica," Fern piped up. Rogelia waved her hand in encouragement, so Fern continued. "Ranchers planted tons of grass all over the wetlands a long time ago, but it doesn't feed the animals who live there. We've been ripping out the grass and replacing it with native plants. The cool part is, we only need to clear a five-foot space for the native plants to thrive. The native plants reach for each other under the root system of the nonnative plants, push out the intruders, and grow stronger through their connection."

The wind picked up and blew through the trees, sounding like the rushing of a train. "And yet," Rogelia began, "these connections constantly change their relationships and how they appear. Life is change. The wind that blows around us right now is continually shaping the earth. Nothing stays the same."

Xochitl dragged behind everyone as they crossed a small creek. The changes she was going through were too much for her. She watched Fern, Marina, and Nana with growing frustration. Graciela should have been with her and Nana, learning the lesson about how nature serves as a guide for life. Then they could break into family gossip afterward like they used to.

Rogelia plucked a few pine needles off a branch. "The first people of this land wove their baskets from these needles."

"Tristán's aunt teaches basket-weaving classes," Fern said. "He said the Native Americans from here used baskets in cooking and to store all their goods."

"Ooooh, Tristán." Marina laughed and poked Fern in the ribs.

Fern rolled her eyes.

"We're going to pick sage, also known as *chamiso,* for our next blessing ceremony," Rogelia continued. "Sage bushes can be large or small, depending on their age. I want you to look for a plant with oval, silver-green leaves."

Xochitl knew exactly what sage looked like, but she didn't feel like helping if no one was going to bother talking to her. Fern and Marina seemed so involved with her nana that Xochitl wondered why she was even there. She tried to distract herself by watching Baird's swallowtails, black butterflies with yellow-tipped wings, darting in and out of the trees, careful to avoid the cobwebs clinging to the branches. Iridescent violet, emerald green, and fuchsia flashed from the strands waving slightly in the breeze. It was enough to make Xochitl forget about her troubles.

"What are we going to do with the sage?" Marina asked.

"After we cut off some branches, we'll bind several sprigs together with string and then hang the sage upside down by the woody end. After three or four days, the sage will dry and we can burn the bundles, or smudge sticks, to cleanse just about anything of bad energy and seal in the white light of protection," Rogelia explained.

"Is that what you did the first night in your room?" Fern asked.

"Yes," Rogelia said.

"Is this sage?" Fern asked, bending down to inspect a plant.

"No, that's mugwort," Rogelia said.

Xochitl looked over at Fern, Marina, and her nana. They sat huddled over a mugwort plant, examining the five-pointed dark green leaves. Xochitl hid behind the thick trunk of a pine tree. She ran her fingers along the grooves of the chunky bark and aimlessly picked at the amber sap leaking out of the tree. She was thinking of vanishing and going someplace to be alone. It wasn't like her nana and "friends" would notice she was gone.

"You must develop a relationship with the creations of Mother Earth," Nana was saying. "Often mugwort is thrown on top of fires. The smoke of the herb brings on visions."

Jimsonweed also brought on visions. Halfheartedly, Xochitl looked around for the hallucinogenic weed. She thought if she could have a vision of Graciela or hear her voice, she could make sense of everything that had happened. But jimsonweed was only used in very sacred ceremonies by trained shamans and healers because of its highly toxic nature. It could kill you if you took too much, or worse, could paralyze you or put you into a coma. Nana had warned Xochitl about the dangers of jimsonweed when she had pointed the plant out in her garden. If you even brushed against it, you could get a horrible rash. Xochitl did want to see Graciela again, but was it worth that kind of risk?

"Is this sage?" Marina asked, reaching out to touch a spearlike leaf.

"Yes, that's it," Rogelia said.

"It's sticky." Marina brought her fingertips up to her nose. "And smells strong." She coughed.

"Bring out your water bottle, Fern," Rogelia said. "Please water the plant while I sing. Then, asking permission first, you can take some sage."

Rogelia began a chant. Fern poured water on the plant, and Marina began to trim sprigs. Rogelia's chanting grew stronger, and the feeling of magic draped itself like a cloak over everyone. Xochitl swayed with the repetitive, hypnotic singing. The more Xochitl allowed the music to carry and move her body, the more she felt a welcome trancelike feeling wash over her. Xochitl looked hazily at the sway of Saddleback Mountain. It reminded her of the mountain range that surrounded her home in Mexico and the times she and Graciela spent together.

Xochitl did not realize that as she thought of these things, she began to drift away. Her body began to grow pale and faint. Without even consciously trying, she became transparent, invisible.

"This reminds me of when we would harvest sage in Mexico." Rogelia turned around to look for her granddaughter. "Xochitl, where are you?"

Xochitl glared at her. *I'm right here,* she fumed silently. *About time Nana thought to include me in this lesson.*

Nana looked directly through Xochitl, who sulked about ten paces from her. "Xochitl!" Nana shouted. "Where are you?"

Xochitl was stunned. She looked incredulously at her hands and realized she had become invisible without intending it. She was overcome by a creepy, tingly sensation. Xochitl had spent months learning to suck in her energy to create the illusion of invisibility. She had always controlled her disappearing, and Nana could always sense her presence. This absolute disappearance from her nana was new.

Xochitl waited for Nana to look past her to the cattails on the side of the trail. She dug her heels into the dirt to drive the earth energy into her feet. She visualized waves of pulsating sensations race up her legs and arms, drawing the form back to her body. "Here I am."

"Oh, there you are," Nana said with a sigh of relief. "Don't do that again. You scared me."

"I didn't mean to," Xochitl said, pulling on her shirt.

Nana gazed inquisitively at Xochitl, as if she wasn't sure what to believe.

"Rogelia," Marina said, wavering back and forth, "I'm feeling funny."

"Stomp your feet, Marina. It will help you ground your energy," Rogelia said firmly. "You need to get your head out of the clouds. We don't want you to faint."

"I can't," Marina mumbled.

"We've picked enough sage," Rogelia said, taking Marina's hand and looking concernedly into her apprentice's face. "*Dios,* your hands are cold. You girls are really open to the spirits today."

Xochitl stared at her fingers and hands. Maybe that was why she had she disappeared without intending to. Could she stay this close to the Spirit World long enough to make contact with her sister? If so, she wanted to be away from everyone else. Xochitl forged ahead of the others through a green, grottolike tunnel made of low-hanging branches. The air smelled cool and earthy. When she made the last bend in the trail, she gasped at the beauty before her. They had reached the thirty-five-foot cascade of water known as Holy Jim Falls. Lush ferns grew out of the granite rock on either side of the waterfall. The water rushed hard and fast into a deep pool.

Rogelia held on to a wobbly Marina and guided her to where Xochitl stood before the waterfall. The *curandera* turned to Fern. "Practice more of what we did the other day."

Fern stared at the nearest plant until her eyes shifted out of focus.

"I can see the plant's aura." Fern beamed.

"Now slowly look around," Nana suggested.

"Oh wow! It's like a sparkling horizon hugging the tops of all the trees," Fern said.

"What can you see around us?" Nana asked.

"Your aura is green and wavy, Doña Rogelia. Marina's is orange and shooting out of the top of her head. That's pretty weird-looking. But ooh—Xochitl's aura is all zigzaggy. Like shards of light."

"What does that mean?" Xochitl asked while tugging on her wishing bracelet. Perhaps it represented her proximity to the spirits! If that was so, where was Graciela? Xochitl looked around but didn't see her sister. Angrily she pulled again at the bracelet that was supposed to represent the dream, the connection, she shared with Graciela. Graciela had left her. So why should she be holding on to this piece of her twin? She should just rip the bracelet off and leave it here.

Suddenly, a shocked expression appeared on Marina's face and she staggered away from Rogelia.

"What is it?" Rogelia asked.

Marina stared at Xochitl with her mouth gaping. Her big brown eyes were round with dread and anxiety.

"*¿Qué tal?*" Rogelia asked again.

Marina's hands went to her throat, then fluttered quickly over her lips, like she was trying to keep a tidal wave of words from pouring out of her mouth. "Oh, Xochitl."

"What?" Xochitl asked, her finger still curled between the bracelet and her wrist.

"She says, 'No, don't do it. Not yet,' " Marina whispered.

For no apparent reason, a bone-chilling cold flooded Xochitl. Why did she suddenly feel so scared?

"Who?" Fern asked.

"Graciela," Marina whispered. "I just heard Graciela tell me to stop Xochitl."

This is not happening, Xochitl thought. *Graciela would not talk to Marina before she spoke with me. She wouldn't let someone come between us.*

"I don't believe it," Xochitl replied tersely.

"Graciela spoke to me, I swear," Marina protested.

"Maybe it was one of the other voices in your head," Xochitl persisted.

"No, Xochitl, it was Graciela." Marina maintained her stance. "She called you '*mi hermana,*' and I know that means 'sister.' " Marina looked over at Rogelia for support, but even she seemed stunned. "Graciela said to tell you something about oranges, but I couldn't understand all of it. Do you know what that means?"

Xochitl felt an electric shock vibrate through her body. Her sister had always smelled like oranges because she ate three of them almost every day. It was the one thing Xochitl had teased her about. Despite the confirmation that Graciela was watching over her, Xochitl felt so jealous that her sister had revealed herself to Marina she couldn't help lashing out in anger.

"Why are you doing this to me?" Xochitl cried. "I have been trying to talk with her ever since the accident."

"I'm not trying to hurt you, Xochitl." Marina moved forward and reached for her hand.

Xochitl whipped it from her grasp and ran back through the grotto, down the narrow canyon, away from everyone.

As she neared the bottom of the hill, Xochitl looked on both sides of the trail, through the dense thicket of sycamore, willow, alder, and maple trees. *Marina is lying,* she told herself.

The woods remained silent except for Xochitl's panting. She traversed the thin trail at top speed for as long as she could. After sprinting for several minutes, Xochitl finally had to slow to a walk. Her side was beginning to ache. She came to a mountain stream that intersected the trail and had to tiptoe on the rocks to cross. Soon after, the narrow canyon opened up to a large field. She walked to a sycamore tree at the edge of the field, sat down, and leaned against its thick trunk.

"Xochitl!" Marina called as she entered the field of yellow and purple wildflowers. Once she saw Xochitl, she dashed over to her, out of breath. "Why did you take off like that?"

Xochitl turned her back to Marina and crossed her arms.

"Please talk to me," Marina pleaded, but Xochitl didn't respond. Marina reached out to touch Xochitl's shoulder.

"Go away, I don't want to talk to you," Xochitl said.

Marina stared at Xochitl, but didn't walk away until, a few moments later, Fern and Rogelia came down the hill. Marina walked over to join them. They stood a fair distance away, but Xochitl could hear every word they said.

"She won't talk to me," Marina murmured.

Rogelia looked sadly toward her granddaughter. "Just give her some time. She has been through so much."

"I think the girl's voice has been Graciela's all along," Marina said. "She always spoke in Spanish. That's part of why I wanted to learn the language, so I could understand what she was saying."

Xochitl couldn't believe what she'd heard. It was so painful to even think of Graciela talking to anyone but her, but to know that her sister had been speaking to Marina for weeks? It was enough to make Xochitl burst into tears.

Twenty

Pilar drove Fern and Marina to the Los Lobos concert later
that evening. Marina had told her mother she was sick and
gone to bed early. She pushed her dresser in front of her bedroom door, then snuck out her window. Now she stood next to
Fern in line at the will-call window. She stared at the lights
shining on the front of the House of Blues concert hall. People rushed by her with dizzying speed. The cars honked down
Sunset Boulevard. The sheer grandness of this famous theater
left her dumbstruck. She felt totally out of her element. She
had never left her safe suburb and gone into Los Angeles, except for the one time she'd gone to Olvera Street on a school
field trip.

Los Angeles had a wildness about it that made Marina anxious. Orange County, with its dos and don'ts of how to fit in, kept her very aware of where she stood in the social pecking order. But Los Angeles was like a feral cat, impulsive, volatile, and uninhibited. Everybody was somebody and nobody here, it was that big. Or at least it seemed that way to Marina.

You'll be okay, the woman's voice said in her ear.

Stay with me tonight, Marina silently prayed.

I always do. But you won't be able to hear me tonight because of the noise.

Marina sighed. Feeling so out of place in L.A. made her thoughts drift to Xochitl and how alone she must feel living without her family. She wondered what she could have done differently at the waterfall. Marina had tried in vain to talk with Xochitl on the ride home, but Xochitl had remained stone silent. It didn't seem fair to Marina. It wasn't her fault she was hearing Graciela's voice. And Marina wouldn't have been a good friend to Xochitl if she'd kept quiet about it. What else could she have done?

She wanted to help Xochitl feel more comfortable in her new environment, and she figured that hearing from Graciela in any way might do the trick. However, as Marina looked around at all the strange faces, she started to understand a bit more what Xochitl must be going through. There is no cure for loneliness.

Suddenly, movement on the ground caught Marina's attention. A trail of cockroaches marched in front of her feet. She squealed and jumped.

Laughter rang out from a group of Latino homeboys.

Marina held her purse closer to her body, feeling stupid and afraid. One of the *vatos,* a bald, tattoo-headed guy with a white shirt and baggy khaki pants, leered and said, "Hey, mama, you gonna dance for us tonight?"

"Back off, *pendejo*." Fern scowled, turning away from the ticket window. She grabbed Marina's arm and led her away before the guys could do any more than catcall. "Damn, that took a long time. They couldn't find our reservation. Stupid Ticketmaster. They charge you an arm and a leg and still can't get it right." Fern inspected Marina a little more closely and let out a chuckle. "I keep forgetting this is your first concert."

Fern took Marina's purse and handed it to the security guard for inspection. She held out her arms and the guard waved a metal detector over her body. Marina held out her arms like Fern and suspiciously waited while the guard with her plastic gloves patted her down. Then they showed their tickets and moved into the entrance of the theater.

Marina marveled at the large stage, the multicolored lights, and the slightly bizarre art on the dark red walls. The place hummed with excitement.

"You'll be fine once the music starts," Fern affirmed.

Marina shook the stardust from her eyes. This place was too cool. "I'm fine now."

"Sure you are." Fern led Marina close to the stage.

Marina gawked at the audience. People of all ages had come to this concert: families, middle-aged couples, some kids their age. Mostly, it was a mix of Latino people. She saw a man with short hair wearing a Reyn Spooner shirt, a guy with a black ponytail sporting a T-shirt with an Aztec warrior depicted on it, a man with a large mustache wearing a cowboy hat, and a smiling hoochie-mama so crammed into a sequined dress she looked like a sausage in too tight a casing. A group of kids around their age stood laughing and talking in Spanish.

"Hey, look, a Sacred Heart." Marina pointed to the red heart with flames projected onto the stage curtain. The tension drained from Marina's shoulders. Suddenly, she just felt like she belonged. "You know, I think I like it here," Marina called over the recorded Los Lobos music, warming the crowd for a night of rock, corridos, mariachi, and blues music.

"Told you," Fern shouted back.

Marina looked back at the Sacred Heart. It reminded her of Rogelia, and that brought her thoughts back to Xochitl. "Why do you think Xochitl is mad at me?"

"I have no idea. We'll work it out. I promise it will be all right." Fern scooted sideways to stand in the front row. "I'm glad you like it here. You just needed a little push to show you what you've been missing. You're learning Spanish, and look at you here. I'd say you're no longer a *pocha*."

Marina followed Fern through the crowd. "What's a *pocha*?"

"A *pocha* is someone who forgets their Mexican roots," Fern said.

Marina laughed. She stole a look behind her at the waves of people. She felt a rush of pride looking at the masses of brown, mocha, toffee, and beige faces. She was so happy to be part of such a group of laughing, passionate people.

"I wish Xochitl was here," Marina yelled. After all, it was because of Xochitl and her nana that Marina had begun to gain a little Latina pride.

"Me too."

With the strum of an electric guitar, Los Lobos walked onto the stage to a roar of applause. "Let me hear ya!" Cesar Rosas shouted with his hands held high, wearing his signature dark Ray-Ban sunglasses. "Yeah, uh-huh. Welcome, music lovers."

Marina clapped loudly with the rest of the crowd,

howling like a coyote at the full moon. She danced with a boy about twelve years old wearing a fedora and the woman wearing the sausage-tight dress until sweat streamed down the sides of their faces. Marina sang the songs they'd been playing since before she was born, like "La Bamba" and "Will the Wolf Survive," and newer ones like "Kiko and the Lavender Moon." She laughed at her attempts at Spanish and was impressed at her ability to keep up all the same. At the end of the night, she even caught a guitar pick from guitarist David Hidalgo.

"Gimme that," Fern insisted.

"Hell no," Marina retorted. There was no way Fern was going to pry that special token from her grip. Marina turned the tortoiseshell guitar pick over in her hand. The words LOS LOBOS were embossed on it in gold lettering.

Pilar drove them home and actually promised to not tell Marina's mother about the whole night. Marina couldn't wipe the silly grin from her face. But then she thought of Xochitl and how she had refused to speak to her. Why couldn't she get all the parts of her life to work in harmony at the same time?

When she got home, Marina pulled open the side gate and crept along the side of the house. She dragged a chair to the wall under the tiny bedroom window.

Andale, Graciela whispered.

Yes, hurry up. Your mother will want to check in on you soon, the woman's voice added.

Marina reached up and pushed the window open with her fingertips. She pulled herself up like she was doing a pull-up in gym class. Normally, she had no upper-arm strength.

Se puede, Graciela urged.

Marina's legs scrabbled against the stucco of the house,

scraping a long scratch on her right leg. She scrambled through the window and jumped down into her bedroom. She shut the window and rifled through her chest of drawers, pulled out a pair of purple pajamas, and got them on as quickly as possible.

Marina slipped into her bed but was too excited to sleep. She pulled out the journal and a flashlight from her end table drawer and wrote about how the Los Lobos concert had made her feel more welcome and, for the first time, like she truly belonged to the Mexican race—something her family had never made her feel. She closed the book and tucked it under her bed. She got up and stood in front of her closed bedroom door, contemplating whether or not she dared paste her Los Lobos guitar pick on her door with the other memorabilia.

A chill wind blew over her right shoulder. Marina looked around, expecting to see someone standing behind her.

Move the dresser, the woman's voice spoke in her head.

Marina immediately obeyed without thinking.

Instantly, the door opened. Her mother jumped back a little when she saw Marina, who hid the pick behind her back.

"You're up," her mother said curiously.

"I—I need a glass of water," Marina stammered.

"I wanted to be sure you'll be okay for your Grandpy's birthday party tomorrow," Marina's mother said.

"Yeah, I'll be okay," Marina assured her, feigning a weak voice. "The extra sleep helps."

"Good. Okay, brunch is at eleven," Marina's mother said. "You need to be ready by ten-thirty. They won't seat us until everyone is there." Marina's mother gave her daughter a once-over. "How did you get that scratch?" She pointed to Marina's leg.

"I—I got it earlier, when I was out with Fern and Xochitl," Marina spluttered.

"Not at the barrio, I hope," Marina's mother said pointedly.

"No, Mom, I wasn't in the barrio," Marina snarled. The impulse to say something nasty grew steadily in her gut.

Watchale, Graciela cautioned.

Marina forced her mouth into a smile.

Satisfied, Marina's mother turned and walked down the hall.

⌘ ⌘ ⌘

Wearing a preapproved dress, Marina walked into the White House restaurant behind her mother and stepfather the next morning. Perfectly pressed napkins sat propped up on gold plates that rested on perfectly pressed white linen tablecloths. White roses in simple glass vases adorned each table. A pianist played Bach on a white piano. The whole restaurant reeked of uptight, pompous attitude. Marina longed for the camaraderie she had felt the night before at the concert.

You need to find the balance between the two, the woman's voice said. *You can belong in two worlds.*

Well, she could try.

Marina hugged her aunt Carmen. "Don't squish my hair." Aunt Carmen fussed with her brown mass of curls. A few of Marina's younger cousins ran past her but were instantly scolded by the maitre d'.

Marina wove in and out of the white chairs to reach her Grandpy, who sat at the head of the table.

"Happy birthday, Grandpy." Marina sat down next to him and gave him a kiss on the cheek.

"How's my oldest granddaughter?" Grandpy asked with a wide grin. He had warm brown eyes and long ears, and his full head of black hair was perfectly combed with brilliantine.

"Fine," Marina replied lovingly.

Grandpy pinched her cheek. "Did I ever tell you I love you?"

"All the time," Marina said with a smile.

"Good." Grandpy patted her hand. Marina reached for a glass of water and took a sip.

"Hey, Marina."

Marina looked up to see her twenty-one-year-old cousin, Jordan, sitting down across the table from her. He was tall and broad-shouldered and had played football all four years of college.

"Hey, Jordan," Marina said, setting down the glass. "Glad you came."

"Wouldn't have missed it," Jordan said. "Happy birthday, Grandpy." Grandpy gave Jordan a wink.

Aunt Carmen pushed a bowl of calamari soup in front of Jordan. "Eat it," she insisted.

Jordan smiled his big wide grin and crinkled his nose. "No." He shook his head.

Aunt Carmen pushed the bowl in front of Jordan. "Just try it," she cajoled. "For me, your mother."

Jordan gently pushed the bowl back. "No thanks."

Marina would have blown a gasket by now, and Jordan was being so calm. Maybe patience came with age.

It is certainly an option, the woman's voice said.

Marina's mother leaned closer to Aunt Carmen. "Have you ever had your boys' astrological charts done?"

Marina rolled her eyes. She was so tired of these incessant personality definitions she would puke if she saw another one. Her mother was always putting people into little boxes so she could pretend she knew everything about them.

Pon atención, Graciela said.

Yes, pay attention. There's something for you to learn here, the woman said.

The waitress leaned between Aunt Carmen and Jordan to clear the soup bowl Jordan had pushed away.

Aunt Carmen gripped the waitress's forearm to stop her from taking the bowl. "No, he's not done yet." Aunt Carmen handed Jordan a spoon. "Just a little spoonful." She glanced at her sister. "No, Rebecca, you know I'm not really into that." Carmen turned her attention back to her son. "Please try it, Jordan."

Marina couldn't help staring at Jordan as he gingerly dipped his spoon into the bowl. He had traveled all over the world on a cruise ship with the Semester at Sea. He had been to Venezuela, China, Myanmar, and about six other countries. Marina watched, horrified, as Jordan chewed and chewed and chewed the soup.

Carmen's eyes glowed with happiness as she watched Jordan finally swallow. "Oh, I love it!" She clapped her hands like a giddy five-year-old.

Jordan looked across the table at Marina and shrugged. His face broke into a grin.

The woman spoke in Marina's head. *Even if his mother forces him to do something like eat disgusting squid soup, it doesn't mean he lost any of who he is.*

That was something to aspire to.

"I had Marina's astrological chart read the other day," her mother continued. "Since she was born on the cusp between Sagittarius and Capricorn, this was the only way to know for sure." She dropped her voice to a whisper, as if she were sharing a dirty little secret. "Marina is officially a Capricorn."

"But you always told me I was a Sagittarius," Marina said.

Her whole life, her mother had read the Sagittarius forecast, which explored the sign's fiery, philosophizing, free-spirited characteristics. Marina had never quite felt in her proper skin when her mother described her like a gypsy adventurer. She admired the Sag's qualities but had always been confused by the lack of any mention in the astrological clippings of her determination or her tendency to worry. Had her mother misled her on purpose to make her into the daughter she wanted?

Marina's mother went on, "I convinced myself that since she should have been born two weeks earlier, she could still be a fun-loving Sagittarius. Anything but the worrying, serious Capricorn. But I was wrong."

Capricorns are also determined, strong-willed, and reliable, the woman's voice added.

Marina leaned closer to her mother and asked in a fervent whisper. "Why are you talking about me like I'm not here?" She kept quiet because she didn't want Grandpy to sense any disharmony on his big day. Anger rose so that her breathing became slightly raspy.

Breathe, honey, the woman encouraged her. *Don't let her get to you.*

"It was all there in the chart you picked up a few weeks ago," Marina's mother replied with a sneer. "I had to know. And now I do. A Capricorn. Such a disappointment."

Something exploded inside Marina's head. Marina was so fed up with her mother's snide remarks and tendency to pigeonhole everyone and everything so rigidly.

"You're using my birthday against me now?" Marina asked incredulously, forgetting to keep her voice low.

"Rebecca," Grandpy growled.

"Dad, all I said was—" Marina's mom began.

"That's *enough*, Rebecca," Grandpy said, reaching out and covering Marina's shaking hand with his own.

Marina's mother crossed her arms and didn't say another word.

It has nothing to do with you, mi'jita, the woman said in her head.

Driven by the need for comfort food, Marina reached out for the bread basket and her mother recoiled as her hand brushed against her forearm. Marina knew this discussion was far from over.

Twenty-one

The morning of the gathering for Hands Across the Wetlands broke bright and sunny. Fern looked out her bedroom window and gave a yelp of delight. It was a perfect sunny California day. The sky was bright and the August sun radiated a warm glow. Fern dressed in her favorite Levi's, a cute purple tie-dyed tank top, and a pair of Rainbow sandals. She pulled aside the crinkled voile curtains over the mirrored closet doors. She really liked the change from having those mirrors exposed all the time to having them covered up. Not only was she not tempted to look at her image too often, but she also found her room more peaceful, as if a noisy crowd had been silenced.

As Fern inspected her reflection, her thoughts drifted to Tristán. How would she explain to Tristán why she had bailed on him right after he had kissed her? He had called a couple of times, but so far, she had managed to avoid the subject by talking about the details of today's event or simply not answering the phone. Now that they would be face to face, Fern didn't know if her escape would come up.

She had really enjoyed the kiss, but it bothered her that Tristán was the only person she had seen so far with so many different-colored auras around him. Did that make him neurotic or schizophrenic or something worse?

Rogelia had said that a big part of Fern's training was learning to trust her instincts. And her first impression of Tristán, without his being able to control or cover up his true nature, had made her wary because his aura had been gray, just like Ruben's. And who wanted to risk getting her heart broken? Fern liked life to be exciting but preferred to avoid painful situations whenever possible. And yet, she thought as she touched her lips, his kiss had made her feel so warm and alive.

A knock on the door interrupted Fern's ping-ponging thoughts. Fern checked her clock. It was a few minutes before eight—time to get going. Fern raced down the hall and pulled open the door to find Xochitl on the doorstep. "Come on in. We'll leave in a few minutes," Fern said.

Xochitl smiled without responding and stepped inside. Fern was used to Xochitl being quiet, but this felt different. She tried to read Xochitl's aura. It was a deep blue, and so close to her it almost looked like a second skin.

"*¿Qué pasó?*" Fern asked as she followed Xochitl to the living room and sat on the blue lounge chair nearby. The deep lavender of the walls made the room feel cool, but Xochitl's attitude was nearly frigid.

"Nothing," Xochitl said, staring at her hands resting in her lap.

"Are you still upset about Marina?" Fern asked bluntly.

Xochitl flinched and crossed her arms but didn't answer.

"Why don't you talk with her?" Fern leaned close to Xochitl.

"Not now, Fern." Xochitl looked away.

At that moment, Fern's mother walked into the living room. "Are you ready to stop corporate America from bull-dozing?"

"Yes, we are." Fern studied Xochitl's face, which remained impassive. Fern sighed. She hated when people fought, partic-ularly her two best friends. But there was nothing she could do to resolve their conflict now. She needed to reserve her energy for the protest at Bolsa Chica. But even more impor-tant than her environmental causes was getting to the bottom of her dilemma with Tristán. Her instincts told her today she would find out which way her heart would go.

❀ ❀ ❀

The Bolsa Chica wetlands looked spectacular with the morning sun shining down on the sand dunes, palm trees, marshland, and water. The Bolsa Chica Stewards and the Surfrider Foundation had set up tents and tables to display their brochures. Kim and her crew of stewards were passing out flyers about the restoration act. A couple of media vans were parked in the lot. About one hundred people had al-ready gathered to participate in the demonstration. Fern looked around for Tristán, but she didn't see him anywhere.

Fern and Xochitl walked over the bridge to join the throngs of people.

"Fern!" Marina called as she strode up to them. "Hey, Xochitl. I'm so glad you're here. I really wanted to talk to you. I've been calling you all week—"

"I'm not ready to talk with you." Xochitl turned on her heel and quickly disappeared in the crowd.

Marina looked longingly after Xochitl. "I wish she wasn't so mad at me. I don't even understand what I've done wrong."

Fern scratched the back of her neck. "Maybe she just needs time."

Marina glanced around at the parking lot, which was filling up fast. People were walking over across the beach and from the Jack in the Box and fire station parking lot across the street. Squawking mallards swam in the water under the walk bridge. "This is really exciting. How many people do you expect?"

"I don't know," Fern said. "Tristán and I put up about five hundred posters, so hopefully a few hundred people." She scanned the hordes of people, hoping to catch a glimpse of Tristán.

"How's it going with Tristán?" Marina asked.

"Not good," Fern said, shaking her head. "I've kinda been avoiding him."

"I thought you liked him," Marina said, stepping aside so a man with binoculars could get a better look at a cormorant.

"Well, I do, but you know, ever since I saw that gray aura around him, it just seems like a bad idea to go for it." Fern pursed her lips and took a big sigh. "He kissed me the other day."

"That's a good sign," Marina said.

Fern smiled weakly. "Yeah, well, I ran away, and I've been blowing him off ever since."

"Why?" Marina asked.

"I saw the gray aura right when he kissed me, and it really freaked me out."

"Why don't you ask Rogelia about the different colors in auras?" Marina asked.

"I know how colors make me feel," Fern said defensively. "Besides, Rogelia told me to trust my intuition."

Marina pointed into the crowd. "There's Tristán. Let's call him over."

"No," Fern objected. "Marina, don't."

"Tristán!" Marina called despite Fern's protests. She waved to catch his attention. "Tristán!"

Tristán turned and looked at Marina and Fern. He waved back at Marina but gave Fern a deadpan look before turning his back and falling into a conversation with a pretty girl with dark brown hair in a pixie cut.

"See, he doesn't want to talk to me," Fern grumbled.

"That's too bad." Marina frowned. "I thought you two would make a cute couple."

Remorsefully, Fern gazed at Tristán's back. Who was that girl? Then a happy thought occurred to Fern. Maybe she was his sister! No, wait, he said he only had brothers. Perhaps Marina was right and Fern should have asked Rogelia about the aura. Now Fern wasn't so sure she *should* trust her instincts anymore.

Kim called for everyone's attention through a bullhorn. "Okay, everyone, thank you for coming." The wind whipped her hair, and she pinned it back behind her ear. "Thanks to the Surfrider Foundation and all the media. I also want to extend a special thank you to Fern Fuego and Tristán Castillo for putting up posters all over Orange County. Fern, Tristán, please come up here."

Fern stepped up to where Kim was standing on a sandy berm looking over the crowd. She glanced over at Tristán, then around at the men and women in red shirts who were acting as security guards. Tristán had made sure everyone would be safe. Wasn't that a sign that he was a nice guy?

Tristán walked up to stand next to Kim but refused to acknowledge Fern as the crowd clapped for them.

Amid the noise, Fern whispered urgently, "Tristán."

But he didn't respond, because he didn't want to or because he couldn't hear her, Fern wasn't sure.

"Okay, now let's join hands and see how far across this beautiful wetlands we can reach," Kim called through the megaphone.

Everyone shuffled and Fern lost track of Tristán. Marina ran up and took Fern's hand. Xochitl reappeared and took Fern's other hand. More than two hundred people had come to stand in demonstration to keep the wetlands wild. There were surfers with their surfboards; nerdy scientist-type guys; deadheads; hippies; soccer moms; kids; a group of older people with surprisingly dewy, young-looking skin; and lots of creative folks Fern recognized from the artists village. It took a while to straighten out the line, but in the end, they managed to reach from the marshlands at the farthest northern point, close to Sunset Beach, to the walk bridge, near the Huntington Beach side.

As a news helicopter flew overhead, Marina shouted in Fern's ear, "You did it! You really made a successful day."

Almost, thought Fern as she glanced over at Tristán.

An hour or so later, the crowd began to disperse. Fern ran frantically up and down the trails looking for Tristán. She found him just as he was reaching his Grand Prix. Fern raced along the dirt path and through the parking lot.

"Hey, Tristán," Fern called.

Tristán turned around. His hand rested on the handle of his car door.

Fern trotted the rest of the way to his car. "I think we really got a lot of people's attention," she said nervously. "I bet we'll turn the tide on that vote next week."

"Uh-huh," he said noncommittally as he stared at a seagull flying over the wetlands.

"So, um, Tristán," Fern began. "I was just wondering who that girl was you were talking with earlier. I think I know her from somewhere." She hoped she sounded casual and not jealous.

"My cousin Jade," he answered.

Her face broke into a wide grin. "Oh, that's great."

Tristán looked at her questioningly. "Why would that be great?" he asked with a hint of irritation.

"N-n-no reason," Fern stuttered, taken aback by the wintry gaze in Tristán's eyes.

"I gotta go," Tristán said, and opened his car door.

"Wait. I was thinking maybe, well, if that offer still stands, maybe we could go out and, I don't know, catch a movie or something," she said.

"Fern, I've tried to get close to you, but you've done nothing but blow me off since we put up those posters. A guy can only take so much," he said as he got into his car.

Fern's stomach twisted in knots as Tristán zoomed off.

Her indifference had really hurt him, especially since he had tried so many times to show he liked her. Fern knew she had really messed up. Bad aura or not, she liked him way more than she'd thought she could like any boy. She would have to win him back; that was all there was to it.

Twenty-two

The next morning, there was a knock on Xochitl's front door. Xochitl approached it cautiously, wondering who could be on the other side. None of her dad's friends ever bothered to knock. They just came right in and took either food or beer out of the fridge without asking. Nana was in her room doing her Sunday meditations, which no one disturbed for any reason. Xochitl opened the door and stood frozen.

"Xochitl, I don't want you to be mad at me," Marina said quickly.

Xochitl stared at Marina with a blank expression. She had fully convinced herself that Marina had only been interested in getting close to her to learn about magic from her nana. How else could she be so callous as to tell her she spoke with Graciela without even thinking about how it might affect Xochitl?

Then again, if Marina only cared about Nana and magic, why had she come here when there was no lesson? Regardless of the reason, Xochitl didn't offer any words of reconciliation.

"I'm sorry," Marina said, opening the screen door and forcing a small jewelry box into Xochitl's hand. "I don't know why Graciela spoke to me and not to you, but I was only trying to help. I know how much you miss her. I thought I was doing the right thing."

"How can you think she really spoke to *you*?" Xochitl snarled. It was easier to believe that Marina had been confused rather than that Graciela had really chosen to speak to a stranger instead of her own sister.

Marina bit her lip and took a deep breath, as if she were reeling from being slapped across the face.

"You've been training with Nana for only a few weeks and you think you're hearing my sister, when I can't . . . I can't . . ." Xochitl was unable to finish the sentence. It was painful to admit she could not reach Graciela, no matter what she tried.

"I can't explain how it happened, but it just did," Marina muttered. "I would never hurt you on purpose. Please try and understand."

"How can I? We are *nothing* alike." Xochitl had meant to sound strong, but her voice cracked and gave away her emotions.

Marina took the window of opportunity with Xochitl's guard down and reached out to her. "Yes, we are," Marina said adamantly.

Xochitl pulled her hand out of Marina's reach and stepped back. "No, we are not!" she retorted, angrily wiping away a tear.

Marina's eyes were tearing up too. "Xochitl, you are one of my best friends."

"You have a funny idea of friendship. Your money can't buy mine." Xochitl thrust the jewelry box back at Marina.

Marina stared at the box, her lower lip trembling as tears streaked her cheeks. "I never . . . I only meant, you know . . . This is just a peace offering."

"I don't need your peace offering or your old clothes. I don't need *anything* from you!" Xochitl yelled. "You got what you wanted. My nana taught you magic, so now you can leave!"

When Xochitl slammed the door shut, her body shook from head to toe. She waited on her side of the door, listening for Marina's retreating steps. Instead, she heard Marina sniffling and crying. Xochitl reached for the doorknob but could not bring herself to turn it. Finally, the screen door slammed shut and Xochitl could hear Marina walking away.

Xochitl turned slowly from the door and flopped down on the couch in the living room. She stuffed her face into a small throw pillow and screamed. From a rip in the pillow, a small feather flew into her mouth. Xochitl spat out the feather in disgust and threw the pillow. She covered her face with her hands.

"Why won't you speak to me, Graciela?" Xochitl asked. "Marina is just a novice. She's not even part of our family. We always said we would be by each other forever. And then you left."

Nana's bedroom door creaked open. Xochitl hurriedly wiped the tears off her face. Had Nana heard her fight with Marina? If she had, Xochitl was most likely in for another lecture on the value of friendship, and that was the last thing she needed. She hardened herself for the speech, feeling a concrete ball of bitterness form in her stomach. But instead of her nana's preaching, Xochitl heard Nana scuttle down the carpeted hallway and across the kitchen's linoleum floor. When Nana heaved open the sliding glass door and stepped outside, Xochitl sighed with relief.

But soon enough, the back door opened again. Xochitl heard the chink of something metal being placed on the tiled kitchen counter. This time Nana did enter the living room, where Xochitl still lay on the couch. Xochitl rolled onto her side and looked up to see her·nana carrying a bunch of red roses she had clipped from the garden. Xochitl sat up lazily, a little curious. Nana handed her a single rose in full bloom.

"Come," Nana said reassuringly. She took Xochitl's other hand and pulled her off the couch. "Maybe I should have done this before, but I didn't think you were ready. I'm not sure if you're ready now."

Nana led Xochitl to the shrine dedicated to La Virgen de Guadalupe. Xochitl looked at the star-spangled blue cloak of the Madonna and glumly thought of heaven and her sister. Nana took the dying roses out of the small bud vase on the altar and dropped them in a wastebasket a few feet away. She arranged the fresher roses in the vase.

"You have been abusing the invisibility spell," Nana said flatly. She turned to look at Xochitl. "I taught you that charm because your connection to the magical world was so great you could not function properly. Your aura was shredded to pieces after visits to Guadalajara. You would be so feeble and need to sleep for hours. Now you are stronger than you think, and it is time for you to bloom."

"Five months is hardly enough time to grieve," Xochitl protested.

"I am not saying you need to stop missing Graciela,"

Nana replied serenely. "You will miss Graciela until the day you die."

Xochitl choked on her tears. "Sometimes I wish I had died too; then I'd be with her." Tears spilled down her face.

"No, *mi'jita*." Nana wiped Xochitl's tears with a delicate white handkerchief she'd pulled from her skirt pocket. "Life is a gift. You must never wish it away. There are souls waiting to be born here on earth. We live in a very magical place at a very magical time." Nana nodded toward La Virgen de Guadalupe. "Her people are waking to their power. You want to be here for that." Nana lifted Xochitl's chin and kissed her eyelids. "It will be like a million rainbows at once." Nana lit the tip of an incense stick. The fragrant smoke wafted around Xochitl.

Xochitl smiled and brushed away her tears.

"When I say you must bloom, I am speaking of developing your magical skills further." Rogelia lit a votive and placed it at the base of the La Virgen de Guadalupe statue.

Xochitl looked wary. Long ago—actually, it seemed like another lifetime—Nana had said that after Xochitl mastered the skill of invisibility, she would learn more about manipulating her energy. It had once been an exciting prospect. Now Xochitl wanted—no, *needed*—that something more.

"When you become invisible, you pull your energy into a tight space," Nana said.

"I also concentrate mostly on the space instead of feeling my body," Xochitl added eagerly.

"Yes. Now that you understand how to draw your energy in, I want you to practice sending your energy out. I have met with some healers, including the owner at Four Crows. They call it astral projection here." Nana lowered her voice, although no one was around. "It may be that if you concentrate hard enough, you can send your energy, your awareness, to Graciela and find her wherever she is."

Xochitl nearly fell over with excitement. This was exactly what she had been waiting for. She placed the rose on the altar.

"We will begin with something a little closer to earth than to heaven. Imagine anyplace that you can see, taste, hear, and feel."

"Home," Xochitl said quietly. "Mamá at home."

Nana smiled a little sadly. "Breathe deeply. In through your nose and out through your mouth. With each breath, visualize your energy field puffing out larger and larger. If you get scared, look down at your hands. That will help you feel connected with something you understand."

Xochitl concentrated on her breath and sent her energy out in waves. Flashing colors sparkled before her closed eyes. She thought of her village in Mexico, and with a swoosh of wind, she was there in an instant, watching her mother bustle around the kitchen. "I see Mamá. She's stirring the mole. Oh, I can smell the chili powder and the chocolate. José is chasing Pepito. Oops, Pepito knocked a bag of flour off the table. Tano is doing homework. Of course, Amelia is brushing her hair."

"Let's try something different," Nana suggested. "Where are Fern and Marina?"

Xochitl let her attention linger on her family for a while. Then she thought of Fern, and immediately Xochitl hovered above Fern's house. "Fern is in her bedroom staring at her phone." Xochitl sent her awareness to Marina and watched her pay her bus fare. "Marina is riding the bus," she said dully. Now that Xochitl was experiencing a rush from learning this new piece of magic from Nana, she could understand Fern and Marina's excitement.

"And now, Graciela," Nana said.

Xochitl went immediately to the accident scene. She felt the jerky bouncing of the truck, the launching over the embankment, and then she shot into space. Darkness surrounded her, and she felt weightless. She wheeled backward through a star-strewn universe, completely against the natural clockwise direction of the planets. Xochitl tumbled over and over. She could feel herself everywhere and nowhere at once. There was no end to her expansion. Her awareness encompassed everything. It felt as if she had previously seen life through a pinhole and now her vision took in all directions at the same time. She floated light-years away, watching the stars streaking and planets coming in and out of view.

Somewhere in the recesses of her mind, Xochitl began to feel a slight tug back to her body. She could hear the distant call of "Xochitl!" very far away. She looked around, and no matter where she reached out, she passed through everything she saw, as if she were a ghost. The lack of boundaries and depth perception frightened her. She tried to recall where her body lay. She vaguely remembered last seeing Nana's face in the living room. She mustered all her concentration on her nana, and in a flash she zoomed back to her house.

Xochitl hovered above the altar dedicated to La Virgen de Guadalupe, watching Nana shake her body. Xochitl saw her own glazed expression and drooping limbs hanging lifelessly by her side. She tried to lift an arm or a leg, but she couldn't. Her awareness, her consciousness, seemed to be locked out of her body. Xochitl watched helplessly as her body collapsed.

Nana fell to her knees by Xochitl and bent her head closer

to Xochitl's mouth. When she couldn't detect breath, Nana placed her fingers on Xochitl's neck behind her ears to check for her pulse. Nana pumped on her chest and breathed into her mouth, performing CPR.

Nana turned a pleading look at La Virgen de Guadalupe. "Please, Mother. Please help me. Help bring my baby back. I can't lose them both."

Xochitl tried to send her energy like a bullet to her heart. She felt a whoosh of energy and then nothing. She disappeared instantly. There was no warning. No floating sensation telling her that her body had begun to turn invisible.

Nana grasped at the thin air where Xochitl had been lying. Nana looked around in wild desperation. She obviously could not see Xochitl. Nana patted the ground, searching. Finding nothing, her eyes grew wild with worry and fear.

Xochitl tried to force her energy back to her body, but she had completely lost the handle of her energy. She had swung from one end of the pendulum to the other, from deep space outside her body to the deep space within her body.

Nana struggled to her feet. "Xochitl!" she called, stumbling from the living room to the kitchen. "Xochitl!" Nana screamed repeatedly as she ran from room to room.

Xochitl followed her nana as a misty waif in spirit form. "I'm here. I'm right here!" she cried silently.

Nana pulled open the sliding back door. "Xochitl!" she yelled. Nana clutched the doorjamb with her right hand and gripped her chest with her other hand. She stumbled down the back steps. With purposeful determination, Nana marched toward her herb garden. She veered toward the poisonous plants. Nana looked back at the house. "Xochitl, where have you gone?" Nana whispered imploringly.

Xochitl trailed behind Nana, frantically wishing she could force the wind to blow or a bird to chirp to let Nana know she was okay.

Nana began to pant and reached out to the tall, flowering foxglove. With a trembling hand she pinched off a bright purple petal, tore the petal in half, and popped one half into her mouth.

Xochitl watched Nana suspiciously, nervously wondering why she had eaten that particular plant. It was part of her poison garden. And that worried her to no end.

Nana whispered a prayer to the plant. Her posture drooped as if a large weight had been placed upon her shoulders. She trembled, and her left arm shook.

Xochitl had never seen Nana look so weak before. *Nana, what's wrong? What's going on?* she cried silently. But no words reached Nana's ears.

Then, without warning, Nana swayed and fainted, her body crumpling to the ground in a heap.

The shock of seeing her formidable nana lying unconscious on the ground drove Xochitl back into her body. She twitched violently, like someone waking from a bad dream. Xochitl opened her eyes and found she was still in the living room. She stood up, and though she felt weak, she ran outside, hurtled down the dirt path, and dropped beside her fallen nana. Xochitl shook Rogelia, trying to rouse her, but her nana would not awaken.

Twenty-three

On the bus ride home, Marina felt like her insides had been torn to shreds. She hadn't meant to appear condescending with her peace offering, as though she thought she could buy friendship or she was better than Xochitl.

She'll come around, the woman's voice said comfortingly in her ear.

Marina wasn't sure. Xochitl still seemed so upset with her, and nothing she said made a difference. She bounced along from the backseat for a while; then another concern descended upon her when she stepped off the bus: *I should have been home for dinner an hour ago.*

Marina picked up her pace and ran up the hill to her

house. It would be just her luck if this was the night her mother chose to break out the Pampered Chef stone casserole dish and make enchiladas. If sauce or rice simmered in the heavy black and white speckled cast-iron skillet of her great-grandmother, then Marina would really be in for it.

Once in the house, Marina caught her reflection in the mirror of the hall tree directly in front of the door. She ran her fingers through her thick caramel-colored hair until it lay perfectly smooth. She glanced to her left. Samantha sat cross-legged in front of the television, watching cartoons. Thankfully, the smell of dinner didn't fill the air. Marina inched down the short passageway to the kitchen. No pots or pans littered the counters. Monica sat on a high wooden stool, scooping spoonfuls of Shredded Wheat into her mouth with loud slurping noises.

"Where's Mom?" Marina asked.

"Dunno," Monica said, revealing bits of cereal stuck in her teeth.

Marina relaxed with a deep sigh. At least she didn't have to deal with a demented mother in addition to her guilty feelings about hurting Xochitl. Marina turned and headed down the hallway to her bedroom. She would go and relax, listen to Los Lobos, or check her e-mails. Or maybe she'd write in their journal about how much Xochitl meant to her. That way if Xochitl ever read the journal, she would see how much Marina truly valued their friendship.

Marina opened her bedroom door. Her mother was sitting on the edge of her bed, reading the journal. She glanced up. For a fleeting second Marina thought she saw an expression of terror flicker across her mother's face—the exact kind of look one should have if caught invading another's privacy.

"What are you doing?" Marina roared. She marched to her mother and lunged for the journal.

Marina's mother swung the journal out of her reach. "What is this?"

"None of your business," Marina yelled. "Give it back!" She leaned heavily on her mother and leveraged the book out of her grip. A couple of crow feathers fell off and fluttered to the carpet. "How could you read this?" she asked angrily.

"I have to see what you're up to," her mother said. "Who you're talking to, where you are. I don't know what you're up to with these girls."

"Mom, you've know Fern for—"

"I saw what you wrote about me," Marina's mother interrupted. "And you went to a concert without telling me? Los Lobos," she added in disgust. "I can't imagine what kind of people were there."

"No, I . . . ," Marina began, but stopped. What was the point in lying? She was being backed into a corner. The truth was the only way out. "Los Lobos's music and their crowd made me happy."

Marina's mother shook her head. "You simply don't get it. You don't understand what it's like to be Mexican."

"I *am* Mexican," Marina shot back.

"You're only *half* Mexican," her mother said dismissively. "A true Mexican daughter would never be so unkind to her mother."

"So now you're blaming me for being only half Mexican?" All her life her mother had been keeping her from her Mexican roots, and now she was giving Marina a hard time for not being Mexican enough. It was too much. "What next? Do you blame me for your mother's death, the fact that my deadbeat dad left you all alone?" Marina looked all over her room and lifted her hands as if she were a preacher talking to her congregation. "Why not blame me for your hideous taste in decorating?"

"How dare you!" Marina's mother barked.

"You call our old neighborhood the barrio, and yet you grew up there. Why are you so embarrassed to be Mexican? You know what, Mom—as far as I'm concerned I'm not Mexican *enough*." Marina's voice had begun to shake. "Or didn't you read that?" she added scathingly.

"Don't you speak to me in that ungrateful tone. I am your mother!"

"As if I could forget," Marina shot back.

Marina's mother moved to slap Marina. She refrained, her hand trembling in midair. Marina looked boldly into her mother's eyes. Her mother lowered her hand but seemed to grow a couple of menacing inches as her posture straightened.

"At least you have a mother," Marina's mother said. "I wish I had my mother with me every day of my life. And look at you. Look at the way you treat me. I never treated my mother like this."

Time has a way of making us look better, the woman's voice said. *Be loving.* The voice seemed to echo through the room.

Marina's hold on her journal loosened.

Love each other. I beg you. The woman's voice, which sounded so sad, drifted through the room, and with it, a slight breeze.

Marina's mother faltered for a split second, as though she heard something, but regained her composure quickly. She charged forward and grabbed the journal, wheeled around, and stormed out of Marina's bedroom.

Marina felt numb. She wanted to cry, but it seemed like there were no tears left.

Calm down, Marina, Graciela said in English. Either that or Marina was beginning to translate Spanish so quickly in her head, she didn't recognize the difference.

Marina paced back and forth across her room. She couldn't calm down. She had to get out of the house. Where would she go? Neither Grandpy nor Aunt Carmen would harbor her. She could stay at Fern's. Mr. and Mrs. Fuego wouldn't notice. She could be gone for a week or so, maybe more, before she would call home. That would give her mother a big scare. Then maybe for once she would think about how horrible it would be to lose a daughter.

Just go get the journal, the woman's voice said.

We won't let you get caught, Graciela said.

Yes. She needed the journal. Marina felt a shield of protection like a golden, glowing shell surround her. She silently pulled the door open and tiptoed down the hall.

You look like you're up to something, Graciela said. *Just pretend you're getting a glass of water.*

Marina stood straight and tried to act as if she weren't planning on escaping. Her heart thumped against her chest as she stepped into the kitchen. She walked to the pantry and pulled out two black garbage bags to put some clothes into. She stuffed the bags behind her in the waistband of her jeans. Marina checked the pantry shelves in case her mother had hidden the journal there. Her gaze slid across the kitchen countertops. Could her mother have taken the journal to her bedroom?

Marina jumped when she heard the turning of a page. She peeked around the corner. Her mother was reading in the den.

The book is in the cabinet, the woman's voice said.

Marina noticed one of the doors of the china cabinet ajar. She crept to the cabinet and pulled it open. The feather-covered book had been shoved to the back. Marina lifted the journal, careful not to make any noise. She closed the door. It creaked and Marina froze. She waited. Evidently her mother hadn't heard.

Marina tucked the book under her shirt and fairly raced back to her bedroom, closing the door behind her. She rifled through her closet and chest of drawers for pants, skirts, socks, and underwear, and stuffed them all into the two bags. Marina pushed the end table below the window next to her bed. She stood on the table, poked her head through the window, and looked around to make sure the coast was clear. Then she gritted her teeth and shoved the first bag of clothes through the window.

Marina jumped off the table to collect the other bag when her cell phone rang. She kicked the second bag toward the wall behind the bed. "Wild Thing," Fern's signature song, blared from Marina's phone.

Marina hesitated for a moment. She didn't want to lose her nerve to run away. Then she decided it would probably be a good idea to give Fern a heads-up that she would be spending the next several days with her. Marina scooped the phone off her bed and flicked it open. "Hey, Fern, I—"

"Marina," Fern interrupted, her voice panicky. "Rogelia's collapsed. She's been taken to St. Joseph's Hospital."

"What happened?" Marina asked, her gaze falling on the feather-encrusted journal, which lay on her bed. Tightness began to constrict her chest and throat.

"I don't know. Xochitl was crying so hard when she called

I could barely understand her. But it doesn't sound good. My mom and I are leaving now. Can you meet us there?"

"Of course," Marina said.

"Okay, see you soon."

"Bye." Marina snapped the phone closed. She stuffed the journal into one of her bigger purses.

Rogelia is going to be okay, she tried to convince herself as she thundered down the hallway while fearful thoughts flooded her head. She ran through the kitchen to the den, where she found her mother still reading on the couch. "Mom, I need you to take me to the hospital. Rogelia's sick."

Mrs. Peralta glanced up from her book. "Can't this wait until the morning?"

"No! We need to go right away!" Marina screamed. She was so scared she started shaking. Her breathing was short and shallow.

"Well, okay, if it means that much to you." Marina's mother put her book on the glass coffee table and stretched. "Let me put on some makeup first."

"Mom, Fern said it's urgent. We need to go *now!*"

Twenty-four

On the drive to St. Joseph's, Mrs. Fuego noticed Fern's trembling hands. "You really care for Rogelia?" she inquired.

"Yes," Fern said. "She's been very helpful lately." *And reliable and available.*

Fern's mother looked remorsefully at her daughter. She reached out and squeezed Fern's hand. "Rogelia will be okay."

"Uh-huh," Fern agreed, although she didn't sound convinced.

As the looming structure of the hospital complex came into sight, Fern felt her heart race. She had developed a dislike for hospitals and a distrust of doctors after they misdiagnosed her appendicitis when she was nine. From that moment forward, Fern only used naturopathic and alternative remedies if she became ill. She hadn't even been able to bring herself to visit Pilar in the hospital when she'd given birth to Danny or Miguel.

Since it was after business hours, the parking lot was nearly empty. Fern's mother drove under the raised arm of the gate and found a spot. Fern opened the door before her mother's car had come to a complete stop.

"Uno momento, mi amor," Fern's mother said.

Fern jumped out and waited for her mother to emerge from the car. Together they raced under the long and winding outdoor corridors to the hospital entrance. Fern glanced around the waiting room but didn't see Marina or Xochitl sitting on any of the steel-blue chairs.

Fern's mother approached the woman sitting behind the reception counter. "Is Rogelia Garcia registered here?"

The woman scanned the computer on her desk. "She's just left the ER. Are you family?"

"Yes," Fern's mother answered immediately, staring the woman directly in the eye.

The woman nodded and peeled off two orange visitor passes. Mrs. Fuego glanced sideways at her daughter and gave her a sly wink.

The woman looked up and handed the stickers to Fern's mother. "Go straight down the hall, turn right, up the elevator one floor, left, then right again. She'll be in room two-twenty-nine."

"Thank you," Mrs. Fuego said, taking the passes. She handed one to Fern, who stuck the pass on her shirt. Mrs. Fuego led Fern down the hall. "If she's no longer in the emergency room, then they must have her stabilized."

They passed pictures of donors and members of the

hospital's board of directors. Several passages from the Bible were painted in calligraphy on the walls, and the gift shop was filled with balloons, flowers, and little get-well bears. Fern screeched to a halt.

"I need to get something for Rogelia," she said to her mom.

"I'll wait for you out here," Mrs. Fuego said. "And I'll keep an eye out for anyone from the neighborhood."

A bell tinkled as Fern entered the gift shop. She dazedly scanned the aisles. *What happened to Rogelia? How will Xochitl handle another death?* she wondered.

Fern selected a small ceramic angel and paid for it, almost forgetting to wait for her change. When she came out of the gift store, she felt disoriented and couldn't find her mother anywhere. She wandered the halls, trying to block out the medicinal smell and the urgent calls over the intercom.

Clutching the ceramic angel tightly, Fern located the elevator, stepped inside, and allowed it to take her up two flights. Her mind flooded with memories: Tristán's kiss, the first spell she and Marina cast, the day when she'd had aura overload and Xochitl had taken her to see Rogelia. Fern hadn't known Rogelia long, yet the *curandera* had not only healed her but had also helped her uncover a talent that made her feel totally empowered. Fern felt that she and Marina, and maybe even Xochitl, owed Rogelia for their new spiritual lives.

The elevator doors opened, and Fern stepped out onto the third floor. She wandered down the stark halls until she reached a sign that read THE CANCER INSTITUTE AT ST. JOSEPH'S HOSPITAL. Without knowing why, she didn't immediately return to the elevator, even though she was obviously on the wrong floor. Fern stopped outside the first door in the ward. She looked inside and saw an older woman with short salt-and-pepper hair holding the hand of a young man in his late twenties who lay propped up in a bed. The thin skin on his face stretched over his skull, giving him a skeletal appearance. The woman patted his hand. "We'll be okay. You've been a good son, Jeff."

Jeff smiled at his mother, then sat bolt upright and reached out like he was taking somebody's hand. In that moment, Fern saw his spirit separate from his body, which fell limp. Jeff's spirit floated in a circle around his mother, gave Fern a wink, then soared out of the window.

Fern gasped and quickly scurried from the door. The mother's wail pierced her ears. A buzzer went off. A nurse sprinted past her to Jeff's room. Just then, a gray light very similar to the aura she had seen over Tristán cloaked every visitor pacing the halls, vibrating slowly.

A terrified Fern turned back and ran to the elevator. She frantically pushed the fourth button and felt the car ascend. Why was she seeing auras and spirits everywhere?

When the doors opened, Fern felt the distinct change of energy on this floor. The vibration was buoyant and happy. Fern stepped out of the elevator and realized she was in the maternity ward. Fascinated, she watched the spirit of an unborn child float beside his pregnant mother as she waddled up the hall. The auras around the visitors and parents were pastel yellow and pink, much happier colors than she had seen downstairs.

Then an idea dawned on her. Hospitals are pretty much a breeding ground for emotions. Most everyone is experiencing some raw, intense feeling right out in the open for a clairvoyant to see. What if colors in an aura reflected the *mood or state of mind* you were in, not the kind of person you were? *What if auras are like crayons?* Fern thought. *I choose which colors to draw with based on my feelings. When I'm happy, I choose joyful colors. When I'm sad, I pick dreary ones. And since there are such strong emotions in the hospital, that's why I can see so many different auras.*

Fern raced back to the elevator and got out at the second floor, where her mother was waiting for her in the hallway.

"There you are," Mrs. Fuego said.

She and her mother found room number two-twenty-nine, but the door was closed. Marina and her mother came sprinting down the hall. Through the long window on the side of the door, Fern saw Xochitl and Mr. Garcia standing on either side of the bed, holding Rogelia's hands. Tubes lined Rogelia's wan face. A machine was monitoring her slow heartbeat. At that moment, Xochitl looked up and upon seeing Fern, waved her inside.

Fern opened the door, and Xochitl melted into her arms. "Xochitl, I'm so sorry."

The doctor, a tall man with thinning hair and glasses, came in. "Mr. Garcia, may I see you for a moment?" Mr. Garcia nervously stroked his mustache as he followed the doctor into the hall. Fern, Marina, and their mothers entered Rogelia's room. Fern strained to listen to the conversation in the hallway.

The doctor began tentatively. "We don't know exactly what is the matter with your mother. There are a few additional tests to run, but frankly, right now, we're baffled."

"I didn't realize doctors could confess to not knowing something," Fern whispered to Marina.

Marina just shrugged and cast an anxious glance at Xochitl, then at Rogelia.

Fern looked up, and for the first time, she saw an aura around Marina. The light emanating from her friend was not a happy color but a bleak gray light that was pressed against her. It looked exactly like the gray light Fern had seen around Tristán on the first day they had met, around Ruben, and around all those people in the cancer ward.

"How are you feeling, Marina?" Fern asked.

"Really frightened," she mumbled. "I'm scared for Rogelia."

Marina was feeling frightened right now. What if fear was associated with the color gray? That would explain the gray auras she saw in the cancer ward, but why had Tristán felt fearful on the day they'd met?

Fern instantly recalled the screeching tires, the powerful jolt in her stomach, and the crushing metal of the fence. It had been pretty scary. And when Tristán had first seen Fern, she was slumped over, as if she'd been knocked out.

He was probably scared when he saw me at the accident scene, and that's the aura I saw, Fern thought. *And the other day when we kissed, he was probably nervous. I know I was. So Tristán isn't a bad guy after all. Oh, I so owe him an apology.*

However, with one glance at Rogelia, Fern knew there were more pressing matters to tend to. Tristán would have to wait.

"Mom, I want to stay until Rogelia wakes up." Fern placed the ceramic angel on the table next to Rogelia's bed.

"Honey, that could take hours, maybe days," Fern's mother said.

"Well, I'm staying here," Fern said stubbornly.

"Me too," Marina said.

"It will be good company for Xochitl," Mr. Garcia said gruffly, returning from his conversation with the doctor.

After a few more minutes of debating, both Marina's and Fern's mothers relented. Marina's mother would return at eight p.m. to take the girls home. After the mothers left, Mr. Garcia went to the hospital cafeteria to grab a bite to eat. Xochitl sat down and took Rogelia's hand.

Fern looked at Xochitl, whose aura was not only gray but also had silver-blue lines swirling sluggishly through it. It was the saddest aura Fern had ever seen.

Twenty-five

Xochitl held tight to her nana's hand. She rubbed her thumb over the wrinkles. In light of the horrible truth that she could lose another person she loved dearly, it didn't seem so important that Graciela had spoken with Marina. Xochitl looked at Marina, whose concern for Nana was evident in her worried brown eyes. What was most important was that they had each other. Xochitl needed to make sure they stayed together.

Xochitl slowly let go of her nana's hand and turned to face Marina. "I'm sorry I got mad at you."

Relief softened Marina's worried expression. She scurried around the hospital bed and embraced Xochitl. "I am so sorry I hurt you."

Xochitl hugged Marina tightly. "I felt like you had come between my sister and me. No one had ever done that before. I tried for so long to talk to Graciela." Xochitl pulled back to look into her friend's face. "It seemed impossible that you could do it after such a short time."

"It doesn't feel like anything I've accomplished," Marina said with a shrug. "It's more like a radio that suddenly gets turned on inside my head. I barely understand how to adjust the volume, much less how to figure out how to change the channel and purposely talk to one person over another."

Fern laughed. "Next thing you know, you'll be doing commercials."

"Nah, it's not like that." Marina took Xochitl's hand. "Do you forgive me?"

"Yes, if you'll forgive me," Xochitl replied, smiling.

Marina looked at Rogelia. "Is there anything we can do to help your nana?"

"If there is, then I don't know what it could be," Xochitl muttered.

"What about making a potion or something?" Fern suggested.

"Shouldn't we know what the potion is for?" Marina asked. "We don't even know what we're trying to fix."

"Did you see what happened, Xochitl?" Fern asked.

"She ate a flower, then collapsed," Xochitl said.

All three girls turned their attention to their mentor. Xochitl felt the prickles of magic race down her forearm. At that moment, Rogelia's eyelashes fluttered and she opened her eyes. She seemed disoriented and didn't say anything at first.

Xochitl held her breath.

Rogelia looked around at her protégées. *"Mi'jitas,"* she said hoarsely.

"Don't try to talk," Xochitl said.

"I must." Rogelia cleared her throat and clasped her fingers around her granddaughter's hand. "I need your help." She smiled wanly. "Sometimes *curanderas* take on so much fear, pain, and sickness, it sticks to our insides and we can't heal ourselves, or anyone else."

"How can we help?" Xochitl asked.

"Work together, stay connected. Use the tools I have given you. I'm counting on you." Rogelia closed her eyes and lapsed back into unconsciousness. Xochitl, Fern, and Marina exchanged looks before each returned her gaze to Rogelia, as if waiting for a better explanation.

"We need to get outside," Xochitl said, suddenly confident.

"Why?" Marina asked. "I don't think we should leave her." She picked up Rogelia's hand and caressed it.

"I'm listening to my intuition, just like Nana said we should." Xochitl marched out the door, and without another moment's hesitation Fern and Marina followed close behind.

Xochitl watched the elevator doors close and felt the car lurch as it descended. She scanned her brain for a memory of a healing ritual Nana might have taught her. All the work she and her nana ever did required herbs and prayers under a wide-open sky. They needed to be outdoors if they were going to help her nana. After that, though, she had no clue what to do.

Xochitl shook her clammy hands, trying to work up a breeze that would dry them off. She could not handle another death, especially not Nana's. But Xochitl didn't feel ready to lead a ceremony as important as one to restore her nana to health; she didn't feel as if her faith was strong enough, and faith was the core that gave magic its power. Still, Xochitl had to find a way to believe in herself. She had to try.

"We've got to do something," Fern insisted. "A ritual for healing."

"Another ritual?" Marina asked. "What if we do it wrong and Rogelia gets worse? I don't know if I want to do magic anymore."

"You can't turn off your connection to the supernatural like a switch," Fern said as the elevator doors opened.

"But—" Marina began to protest.

"This isn't a game you can just quit," Fern insisted as she strode out of the elevator and down the hall. They passed a carved statue of St. Joseph standing in an alcove in the wall. Several votive candles sat at his feet.

"We went down the wrong path once. Why should we try it again?" Marina asked as they hurried through the lobby and out the door.

"Con amor todo se puede," Xochitl said automatically, remembering how nana had proclaimed that *dicho* to her and Graciela all the time in Mexico.

"With love you can do anything?" Marina translated. "Is that right?"

"That's right. We can't back out now," Fern said as they reached the end of the outdoor corridor. The blue of the early-evening sky was just beginning to deepen. A lone star winked at them. "Walking around the hospital tonight, I saw a spirit for the first time. Seeing beyond the physical is part of me now. I can't walk away from this. No matter how scared I get."

Marina looked around nervously, like a child lost in a department store. "What are we doing, anyway?"

"We'll start with the elements." Xochitl took Fern and Marina by the hand and led them to a white gazebo. "Magic always begins with the elements."

"How?" Marina asked in a panicky voice.

"I don't know!" Xochitl cried.

"I'm sorry," Marina said quickly. "I want your nana to get well. I'm just so scared."

Xochitl sat down on the bench in the gazebo, and Marina and Fern did the same. She held her friends' hands. "The answer will come. We just need to be quiet and sit still."

An elegant woman wearing heavy perfume and a tailored suit walked to a garden next to the gazebo. She stopped before a three-foot-tall wooden carving of Mother Mary that was surrounded by rosebushes. The woman reached up, held the hands of Mary, and looked imploringly into her eyes. After a few minutes of prayer, she bent over and smelled the flowers at Mary's feet.

Once the woman had stepped away, Xochitl stood up and walked to the statue of Mary. She bent down to look at the flowers and examined a tight rosebud. She could almost hear Graciela tease her about how her name meant "where the flowers bloom" and how Xochitl remained as closed off as this flower. She had refused to open herself and trust life, always using Graciela as a crutch and bodyguard until she arrived in America without her. Recently, she had been forced to welcome many changes and push way past her comfort zone.

For the first time, the meaning of her name felt more like a compliment than a burden or imposition to Xochitl. It was an invitation to grow, not an obligation.

"They find comfort where the flowers bloom," Xochitl whispered.

"What?" Marina asked.

Xochitl looked at Marina and Fern, who obviously thought of Rogelia as more than just a teacher. Maybe all their love would help her nana get better. Together they were that much stronger. Suddenly, Xochitl knew what they had to do.

"The journal. We need the journal."

"I've got it with me," Marina said. "Graciela told me to grab it, so I stuffed it in my purse. Here it is."

Xochitl took the journal and gave Marina an uneasy smile. Now was not the time to obsess over her sister. "Did you ever notice the sealed envelope in the back of the journal?"

"I thought you put that there," Marina replied.

"No, it was there before I got it," Xochitl said.

"It must be a letter from Rogelia," Fern said with conviction.

"You think so?" Marina asked.

"She's right," Xochitl said. "I'm sure of it."

Xochitl pulled out the envelope and began to read.

> *If you're reading this, something has happened to me. Opening this letter means you have accepted responsibility for your ability to heal and do real magic seriously. Share your journal entries with each other. When you do this, light a candle for each of you and one to represent me,* por favor. *As you share with each other, you will break down walls that keep you isolated. By being connected, we will all receive a healing.*
>
> *Con cariño,*
> *Rogelia Garcia*

"I hadn't even thought to read what you guys wrote when I had the journal," Marina said. "I just focused on my own thoughts."

"I read Xochitl's poem," Fern admitted. "But I didn't really get it."

"Yeah, well," Xochitl said shyly.

"So who's going to read their entry first?" Fern asked.

"We need candles, though," Marina said.

"I saw some inside," Fern said. "I'll go get them." She jumped up and sprinted toward the hospital entrance.

"Isn't that stealing?" Marina called after her.

"No, it's *borrowing*," Fern yelled back.

Marina looked at Xochitl anxiously. "Do you think this will work?"

"I hope so," Xochitl said.

Fern returned with four votive candles and a stick of incense. "It's a good thing we're at a Catholic hospital." One of the candles was already lit. "I didn't have matches."

Xochitl arranged the candles in a square on the floor of the gazebo. She held the incense stick to the candle and, when it caught the flame, blew it out. She placed the stick in the dirt of a nearby planter. Xochitl took the book from Marina and placed it in the middle of the candles. "Who is going to start?"

"I'll read my entry since you two had to write in it first," Marina said.

"Which way is east?" Fern asked.

"The mountains are that way." Marina pointed behind Fern. "So that's north."

Xochitl turned to the right of the mountains and faced east. She held up the burning candle. "I welcome the Guardians of the East."

She smiled when the wick caught the flame and flared up. Then she held the flame to the wick of the votive directly opposite the north.

"I welcome the Guardians of the South." Xochitl lit the next candle in a clockwise direction. "I welcome the Guardians of the West." When she lit the last candle and said, "I welcome the Guardians of the North," it was almost as if Graciela was by her side, encouraging her to embrace the spirits and the true magic of friendship.

So Xochitl grinned at Marina without an ounce of anger in her heart and signaled with a nod of her head that it was time to proceed.

Twenty-six

Marina sat up straight and held the journal out in front of her. Despite the fact that they were doing magic in public, Marina didn't care one bit what passersby might think. She felt proud and empowered to be doing a spell to help Rogelia. She had a passion for magic she had never felt for anything before.

Marina opened the journal. She read through her entry and hesitated. All too quickly, her newfound confidence faltered.

You can do it, Marina, Graciela said in her ear. *Xochitl needs to feel your honesty.*

Just speak from your heart, the woman said.

Marina took a deep breath and read:

Fern and I went to see Los Lobos tonight. She said I'm not a pocha *anymore, and that really feels good.* :) *When I looked into the faces of the concertgoers, I felt like I belonged to the Latino family. I wish it wasn't so difficult to even be Mexican in my own house. My mom calls the old neighborhood a barrio, like that's a bad word and no one would ever want to live there. I wish I didn't care what she says. She's so mean sometimes, I'm not even sure she deserves my love. Rogelia would never make me feel so bad. She makes me feel good about myself. She's taught me to trust the voices I hear.*

Marina looked up from the journal. "I'm sorry about the barrio part," she said apologetically.

"It's not as if we never noticed, Marina," Fern said pointedly.

Marina stared at Fern in wide-eyed astonishment. "I thought I had done such a great job of hiding it."

"Really?" Fern asked with a mix of shock and pity.

Marina glanced uncomfortably at Xochitl, wondering if she dared to go on. She had to. "I didn't think my mom's arrogance had the slightest effect on me until you and your nana came into my life." Marina looked down at her jeans and plucked at the hem of her pocket. "I never bothered to learn anything about being Mexican before. I mean, I ate the food and all, and was pretty happy to be able to tan better than most, but that was it." She chewed her fingernails and when she next spoke, her voice shook with emotion. "I feel like such a self-centered snob."

"For your family, being Mexican has been a choice," Xochitl said matter-of-factly.

"I can't help wondering if my nana would have kept the family closer or further away from our Mexican culture. I mean, who started this refusal to accept our Mexican side?" Marina listened intently for an answer from the voices, but none came. "I guess it doesn't matter. But I don't like how my mom keeps me from it. It's not right."

"You know what, Marina, I feel sorry for your mom," Fern said. "She has no pride in where she is from."

"She makes me feel so small," Marina said. "I hate that she can affect me so much. She tries to dictate my identity, choosing my clothes and how my room is decorated."

"But look at you, breaking away," Fern said soothingly, leaning around the candles to give Marina a hug.

"Yeah," Marina conceded.

"I think you're really brave." Xochitl jumped in on the hug and they all three fell over. Fern and Xochitl rolled off and resumed sitting cross-legged in front of their candles. "You might just have to accept your mother the way she is," Xochitl told Marina. "Kind of like I have to accept that Graciela is no longer with me."

"Her personality defects don't have to mean anything about you. We all choose our identity by what we choose to focus on," Fern said, shaking her head thoughtfully.

"You sound like Nana," Xochitl quipped.

"Well, that's kind of my lesson here," Fern admitted.

"Good, let's get me off the hot seat," Marina urged with a sigh.

"Marina, you should try to talk to your mom," Fern insisted. "Promise?"

"Promise." Marina smiled.

Fern nodded, took the journal, and opened it to the picture she had drawn of Tristán. She showed the book to Marina and Xochitl. "I really like Tristán."

"This is new information?" Marina asked playfully.

"Well, to me it is," Fern said, giggling. "I've been stopping myself from liking him because of that gray aura I saw around him on the first day we met."

"You're not supposed to judge a book by its cover," Marina teased.

"Yeah, well, I thought gray meant really bad news," Fern replied. "What I didn't understand was that auras are like paintings of our feelings. I didn't realize that until I saw a gray aura around you in the hospital, Marina, and you told me you were feeling fearful. Before, I thought the color was about the type of person you are, like your identity. I saw the same gray aura around Ruben Gomez when he was talking with Analisa. And you know the rumors about Ruben."

"Those are just rumors," Marina said with a dismissive wave.

"Analisa and Ruben are dating," Xochitl pointed out. "Even I know that."

"See?" Marina said.

"Then I saw Tristán talking with all sorts of girls whenever he was at Bolsa Chica," Fern said. "But at least one of them turned out to be his cousin."

Marina laughed. "Wouldn't it have been easier to ask Rogelia about the auras?"

"I think she wanted me to find out on my own," Fern said.

"She doesn't exactly hand out answers," Xochitl said.

"So what's the problem?" Marina asked. "You've figured out Tristán isn't a shady guy, so now you can go for him."

"Except for the fact that I've totally dissed him and now he doesn't want to speak to me," Fern moaned with her head in her hands.

"How hard did you try?" Xochitl asked. "How many times?"

"Once," Fern replied.

"You've gotta try more than that," Marina encouraged, putting her hand on Fern's shoulder.

"What if he rejects me again?" Fern wailed.

"You never know," Marina said. "He's a really nice guy. Did I ever tell you he gave me a lift that night after Rogelia healed us?"

"No!" Fern said, stunned. "That would have been helpful information."

"You're so hard-headed, it would have only confused you more," Marina said. "Plus, it wasn't exactly a stellar experience to be stranded, then picked up by some guy because your mom won't drive to come get you."

"He helped me, too," Xochitl confessed.

Fern whipped around to face Xochitl. *"What?"*

"Yeah," Xochitl said. "I'll tell you about it, if you promise to tell Tristán you really like him."

"Okay," Fern said, smiling. "But *you* have to promise to bring me a box of tissues if he says to bug off or something."

"Deal," Xochitl agreed.

Fern handed the journal to Xochitl. Gingerly Xochitl took the book and opened it to her poem. She handed the journal to Marina to read.

"I've been holding back from you both," Xochitl began slowly. She glanced around the gazebo as if waiting for more courage. Her gaze rested on a rose in full bloom. "When you guys first asked to learn about magic, I told myself it was Nana you were really interested in."

"Xochitl, that's not true," Fern protested, reaching out to touch Xochitl's arm.

"Give her a moment," Marina insisted.

Xochitl looked gratefully at Marina. "I missed Graciela so much. I just had to see her, talk to her if I could. I went to Four Crows by myself to get supplies to have a ceremony to summon Graciela's spirit. I wasn't sure if it would work. I'd lost a lot of faith in magic after the accident, but I was desperate. Tristán was at the store. I think he figured out what I was up to by the ingredients I bought, but he kept my secret. Never breathed a word of it to anyone."

Xochitl looked up to the sky before continuing. Marina thought she might begin to cry, her face looked so sad. "Only, the ritual didn't work," Xochitl whispered. "Which is why I was so angry at you, Marina. I had tried so hard to connect with her, and you made it seem so easy."

"I can't imagine what it must be like to lose a sister," Marina said, looking at her friend with compassion. "I guess it would make you feel all kinds of crazy things. Because I can tell you this: I care a heck of a lot more for our friendship than I do for hearing voices." Marina took Xochitl's hand and squeezed it.

"And I'd give up seeing dancing lights everywhere if I had to, to keep from losing you," Fern said, reaching out to hold Xochitl's other hand.

"I guess I have been holding on to Gracie so hard that I couldn't bear the idea of moving on and making new friends," Xochitl said.

"Well, we are your friends, and we'll be here for you, even if you just want to spend hours talking about her," Fern said.

"You don't have to let Graciela go so completely, either," Marina said. "She's still here, watching over you."

"Yeah, that's true," Xochitl admitted. She smiled at her friends. "I feel a lot better telling you what I was thinking. And I'm really glad I was wrong."

Fern grabbed Marina's and Xochitl's hands. "Its funny how our magical talents play into these confessions," she said mischievously. "Xochitl disappears in life in more than one way. Marina, you hear voices, and look at how you need to find a solid strength that has nothing to do with what others say."

Marina squeezed Fern's hand. "And you need to stop jumping to rash and dramatic conclusions just because of what you see."

"Yeah, I guess you're right," Fern said.

Marina looked from Xochitl to Fern and smiled widely. Rogelia had been right. Marina felt more connected to Fern and Xochitl than she had ever felt to anyone.

"So is that it?" Fern asked.

"No, I think we should do a *limpia* for Nana," Xochitl said. "First thing tomorrow morning, we'll perform it in Nana's room. Tonight we can each gather whatever we need."

"Using our intuition," Fern added with a wink.

"Then we'll take the bus back here so no one has to know," Marina concluded. "It's time to rely on ourselves."

❀ ❀ ❀

Bright and early the next day, Marina, Xochitl, and Fern returned to the hospital. Tiptoeing as fast as they could, they rushed down the hall toward Rogelia's room. Fern opened the door, and the three of them sneaked inside. Rogelia lay unconscious on her hospital bed with a peaceful expression on her wrinkled face. The monitors beeped in time with the *drip, drip* of her IV.

Marina took a moment to muster up her nerve. Rogelia looked so weak, laying there unconscious. The healer's normally vibrant complexion was pasty, drained of all energy without her warm smile.

You can do this, Graciela said.

You are more ready than you realize, said the woman's voice.

Marina took a deep breath, walked over to Rogelia's bed, and leaned over Rogelia to kiss her forehead. "You are going to wake up and be just fine. We're going to help."

Fern took a white advent candle, a long bundle of dried sage leaves, a small black cauldron, and a pack of matches from her wool bag. She struck the match and lit the candle. "We welcome the four directions to this healing ceremony." Fern lit the smudge stick and quickly extinguished the match flame with her fingertips.

"Doesn't that hurt?" Marina whispered.

"No," Fern said as she handed the sage to Xochitl. "You smudge Rogelia while I read her aura. I can already see she has some funky yellow spots over her heart."

Xochitl blew out the fire burning the sage leaves and walked to the four corners of the room, then slowly passed the smoke over Rogelia, paying close attention to her chest area. When Xochitl had covered Rogelia's body with the sage smoke three times, she smudged Fern, Marina, and lastly herself before smashing the sage stick in the cauldron.

Fern took a Tupperware container and sprigs of rosemary out of her bag and handed them to Marina. "Here," she said.

Marina popped open the Tupperware and took out an egg. She held on to the egg and imagined that it was a strong sponge, ready and able to extract all the negativity and sickness from Rogelia's body and spirit. She would be the one to wipe Rogelia clean.

That's the way, Graciela said.

Keep believing in yourself, honey, said the woman's voice. *You are more powerful than you give yourself credit for.*

Marina rolled the egg all over Rogelia while Xochitl chanted quietly. Marina cracked the egg into the cauldron. She examined the yolk and white of the egg. At first the white was filled with bubbles and seemed a little cloudy. But as Xochitl continued to chant, one by one the bubbles popped and the white of the egg became clear. "I think it's working," Marina whispered. She swooped up the rosemary with a shaking hand.

Take your time, the woman's voice said.

Fern leaned over the rosemary and whispered, "Come on, little fairies. Help us make Rogelia better."

I'm not ready for you to join me just yet, Nana, Graciela said.

Marina brushed Rogelia with the rosemary. "Graciela says she wants you to get better," Marina whispered in Rogelia's ear.

Xochitl took a piece of chalk out of her pocket and drew an equilateral cross on the floor beside Rogelia. She placed their journal in the east. "There's a lot more work to do here, Nana." She pulled Marina and Fern close to her and gave them a big hug. "Look, I'm trusting my new friends."

Fern smiled at Xochitl as she placed in the west a painting of a gray cloud with the word "fear" written on it. "All of us have agreed to let go of our fears, Doña Rogelia. Just like you told us to do in the beginning."

In the north Marina set a photograph of Xochitl, Fern, and herself with their arms around each other. "We're a family, but we need you. Nanas are the links who make us who we are."

Together, Xochitl, Fern, and Marina placed an empty glass candleholder with an image of San Miguel in the south. It was the same holder that had burned with the flame of their initiation. Now it was filled with water and three different kinds of flowers: a rose, a daisy, and a sunflower. The three friends held hands.

"This represents our energy," they said in unison. They took deep breaths simultaneously and chanted:

"We became stronger when we trusted each other.
You have taught us to love the earth as our Mother.
By the magic of three, and our deep love for you,
Rogelia Garcia, it is time to come to.
By our will you will rise from this bed well and whole
And be healthy and strong in mind, body, and soul."

The girls held their breath, waiting. Marina looked over at Fern and Xochitl. This was it. They had given Rogelia all they had. Marina closed her eyes and sent Rogelia all the love she had. She remembered Rogelia's lessons of courage and the power of having faith in yourself, the lunches she had made, the knitting and Spanish lessons, and her squishy hugs. She recalled Rogelia's laughter and her firmness. She loved everything about her.

Rogelia began to moan a little. The monitor at her side came alive. Marina's eyes flew open. She almost screamed with delight. Fern did scream. Xochitl began crying, and Marina had to catch hold of her so she wouldn't fall to pieces. The *limpia* had worked! They really were magical.

Rogelia opened her eyes and smiled at her three apprentices. *"Gracias,"* she said lovingly.

A nurse rushed in. She picked up Rogelia's hand and checked her pulse. She looked intently into the old healer's face and smiled. "This is wonderful. Looks like your grandmother will be better soon." The nurse looked around confusedly. "What is all this?"

"Magic," Marina said. "The best there is."

Yes, said Graciela. *It's called love.*

⌘ ⌘ ⌘

On the bus ride home from the hospital, Marina smiled broadly at the fact that Rogelia was better. Really her happiness was twofold: Rogelia was on the mend, and she had bona fide proof that she had some kicking magical powers.

I'm so very proud of you today, honey, the woman's voice said.

Marina's smile broadened. The bus stopped at a red signal. Marina stared out the window and noticed bright balloons swaying in the wind over the El Ranchito Restaurant sign.

I love that restaurant, the woman's voice said. *I used to take your mother there all the time.*

"What?" Marina asked.

Haven't you guessed it? the woman said. *I am your nana.*

The past couple of months she had been listening to her nana and hadn't even known it. "This whole time," Marina whispered. "Why didn't you tell me who you were?"

Timing is everything, darling, Nana said. *I was vicariously living through your bonding with Rogelia. But I need you to do something for me now.*

"There's so much I want to ask you," Marina said quietly so no one would hear her. "You're my namesake, and the family only speaks about you like you're some flawless saint or something."

Well, Mexican people often speak about their dead relations like that, regardless of whether we deserve it. Listen, honey, I want you to invite your mother to lunch at El Ranchito. You ask her questions about me first. You two need to work this out together.

"But—" Marina began to protest.

Whatever she doesn't answer, I will, Nana said.

Marina pulled on the cord to stop the bus. She flipped open her cell phone and dialed her mother's number. "Mom, can you meet me at El Ranchito? The one on First Street. It's really important."

⌘ ⌘ ⌘

El Ranchito was packed with people. A vibrantly colored mural of a rain forest was painted over the fireplace mantel in the first room. Marina passed a buffet of chafing dishes piled with beans, rice, chorizo, eggs, and potatoes.

Mmm, Nana said. *I miss eating.*

Marina hustled past a large pot bubbling with what she suspected was *menudo*. Gross. There were just some things about Mexican culture she didn't think she would ever understand.

Marina could hear the laughter of her nana ringing in her ear. *Maybe not.*

The hostess seated Marina in a large room with a rush and bamboo ceiling. Colorful *talavera* plates depicting cacti in various forms, shapes, and sizes; wrought iron decorations; and paintings of horses and beautiful women adorned the walls. Marina was on cloud nine. She not only had Rogelia back, but she also had her very own nana now.

Fifteen minutes later, Marina's mother walked into the restaurant. She whipped off her dark shades and imperiously looked around. Marina began chomping on her fingernail. Her mother spied her and walked over to her table.

Don't let her intimidate you, Nana said.

Marina pulled her finger out of her mouth and straightened up.

"What's this about, Marina?" her mother asked as she sat down. She jumped when the mariachis moved to stand next to their table and began playing "De Colores," a folk song about spring.

Oh, my favorite song, Nana crooned.

"I wanted to tell you. Rogelia is better. She's gonna be okay."

Marina's mother smiled. "Oh, that is great news."

A waitress dressed in a puffy white blouse and red skirt approached the table and took their drink requests.

Marina waited until the waitress left. "You know, Mom, I really need you to tell me something about my nana," Marina said. "A real story. I, um, I really need to connect with her." Marina paused. "Especially with everything that happened with Rogelia and seeing her and Xochitl together."

Marina's mother dipped a chip into the salsa and just shook her head no.

It's okay, Marina, Nana said. *Move slowly with her. You know how stubborn she is.*

Marina looked around the room. Fires in two fireplaces burned brightly in the large room. Ceramic clay containers and pitchers sat upon the mantels. Dim lighting from metal sconces warmed the casaba-colored walls. The waitress returned with their iced teas and took their food orders. Marina stared down at the square wooden table inlaid with brightly colored ceramic tiles. Maybe she should try another tactic to get her mother to open up. "What do you have against me going to Santa Ana?"

"There's nothing of value in the barrio," Marina's mother answered sharply. "No one has any ambition or makes the slightest effort to improve their situation. I don't want you anywhere near their negative influence."

She's forgotten the good times we had, Nana said quietly. *Tell her.*

"Remember the time Nana took you to the community center where you learned how to sing?" Marina asked. "Or the Cinco de Mayo parades, or the corner store where you got your first ice cream cone, but then you dropped it all over your new blouse and Mr. Muñoz gave you another one, no charge?"

"How do you know all that?" Marina's mother whispered. "I haven't thought about that in years." Her eyes began to water.

Marina just smiled. "Mom, please don't make me choose between you and who I'm destined to be. I feel as if whenever I make the slightest move on my own, I not only disappoint you, I get punished for just being myself."

"Maybe I have been a little too strict with you—you're my firstborn," Marina's mother conceded, still a little begrudgingly. "I thought if I could predict your behavior, you couldn't leave me like they did."

Marina knew "they" meant her nana and her biological father, who had left a few months after Monica was born.

Life just happens and change is inevitable, Nana said.

It was just like Rogelia said. "You can't control life or keep it the same forever," Marina said. "And you can't keep me in a bubble, Mom. I like our history, our roots. Santa Ana is where I was little and you grew up," Marina said.

"Santa Ana brings back too many painful memories," Marina's mom said with a tremulous voice. "And I guess it's easier to cover sadness with anger."

"Mom, I accept that you don't want to go back to the old neighborhood, but I feel really comfortable there," Marina said. "Can I please visit my friends without getting in trouble?" Marina pressed on.

"I can't answer that now," Marina's mother said. "We can talk about this later."

Marina's shoulders dropped. That wasn't exactly the answer she wanted.

The waitress brought their food. Marina and her mother ate in silence for a while.

"Your nana always fought for the underdog," Marina's mother said suddenly. "That is why I gave you her name, Catherine, as a middle name—so that you would always have a guardian angel to look after you."

"She does," Marina said. For a moment she considered telling her mother about hearing Nana's spirit, but she was interrupted by her nana's words.

Not now, mi'jita, Nana said. *Give her time to digest this. You've given her a lot to think about.*

Marina had wanted more of a promise that her mother would let her go to Santa Ana without a hassle, but she had to admit, their conversation today was a start.

"You're really growing up fast, you know," Marina's mother said. "You seem more mature and self-assured lately."

Marina smiled. It was true. Marina had felt much stronger in the past few weeks than she had ever felt in her life. She knew without a doubt that her newfound confidence was because of everything she had learned in Rogelia's house of magic.

Twenty-seven

Fern lived in a giddy state of bliss for the next few days. She was so excited that they had been able to heal Rogelia. Talk about a bonding experience! The doctors were baffled at Rogelia's immediate recovery, but Fern wasn't surprised. They had created one heck of a ritual, and she knew from the bottom of her heart that they had healed Rogelia completely on their own. A few days ago Rogelia had come home from the hospital and was now as good as new. They were taking a little break from their lessons, but Rogelia promised they would get together soon.

During the traumatic experience of Rogelia's illness, Fern hadn't given too much thought to Tristán, but now that all the drama was over, she could direct her attention back to him. She stayed up late night after night writing e-mails that she never sent. She had no idea what to say to smooth things over or how to explain her actions.

She rose groggily on the morning the verdict on Bolsa Chica would be announced. The Bolsa Chica Stewards were planning to gather at Kim Bradfield's house that afternoon. She only had an hour to get ready. The lawyer would call at noon to announce the decision on the Bolsa Chica Restoration Project, which would protect the entire wetlands. Everybody involved in the fight wanted to be together for emotional support, whichever way the vote went. Fern walked to the kitchen and made herself a cup of strong black tea. As she sipped it, she thought about Tristán and hoped he would be there.

Fern lumbered back down the hall to her bedroom and, holding her tea in both hands, stared at the clothes stuffed in her closet. She set the cup on a nightstand and began pulling out skirts and matching shirts. Fern dressed in colors and styles that matched her mood. How strange that she had never noticed how colors and moods were associated. She had also come to the conclusion that colors could mean different things to different people—just like her intuition was unique to her. Right now she was nervous and intent on getting Tristán to fall for her again. So did she wear her favorite pair of cutoff jean shorts or a yellow sundress cut to impress? She wanted to be herself but at the same time felt she needed to concentrate a little more on her appearance than she normally did, if only to show Tristán she meant business.

She rifled through her cherrywood chest of drawers for shorts and tank tops. During the next half hour, Fern tried on more than fifteen outfits. A pile of discarded clothes lay at her feet while she twirled and examined each ensemble in front of the mirror. Finally, Fern decided on a violet tank dress that she felt comfy in and she knew complemented her amber eyes so perfectly they nearly popped out at people. She tied on a beaded anklet, slipped into her Rainbow sandals, and dabbed nag champa oil on her wrists. She hardly ever wore makeup but decided if she was going for it, she might as well go all the way. So she put gold sparkles on her eyelids and rose glitter gel on her lips. A little mascara and she was ready to go.

Fern walked nervously to Kim's house. She was counting on the fact that Tristán would be there. But what if he had other ways of finding out how the vote went? Would he talk to her if he was there? What would she say to him? She could say what a great team they made. But she should start with how much she liked him and what a fool she had been.

Fern opened Kim's front door and saw most of the stewards she saw every planting day at the Bolsa Chica. Kim's house was kind of like a jungle. She had ivy plants hanging from the ceilings, a verdant money tree with a braided trunk in the far corner, and pictures of wildlife on every wall. Kim's three kids ran past like wild animals themselves. Fern looked in the living room, but she couldn't see Tristán anywhere.

"Fern!" Kim called as she approached with a platter of spanakopita and a stack of dessert napkins with CONGRATULATIONS printed on them.

Fern pointed to the napkins. "Do you know something I don't?"

Kim shrugged. "Not yet, but you know me—I'm a firm believer in the power of positive thinking." She hugged Fern even with her arms full. "I've been trying to call you. You did such a great job getting the word out on the event."

"Thanks," Fern said, peering over Kim's shoulder at the people who had come, hoping to catch a glimpse of Tristán.

"They ran the story in all the local papers, and even the Associated Press covered it, so it appeared in a couple of big papers out of the area," Kim continued.

"That's so great!" Fern exclaimed, looking back at Kim. "I didn't get a chance to check. A friend got sick, and I was pre-occupied."

"I'm so sorry," Kim said. "I hope it's not your friend Tristán."

"No, it wasn't Tristán," Fern said. Then catching on, she added, "He's not here?"

"No, I thought he would have come with you," Kim said. "By the way, honey, you look fantastic." Kim kissed her cheek before walking into the living room to offer the appetizers to the rest of the guests.

Fern followed Kim and slumped into a chair by the door so she could watch it for any sign of Tristán. There was no reason to believe that he wasn't coming, she told herself. A few of the stewards came by and congratulated Fern on her efforts to get the event together. Most of them asked about Tristán, which was getting insufferable.

While she waited for the phone call, Fern busied herself looking at the auras of the different people in the room. She tried to discern the meaning of the colors in the auras by matching them with people's facial expressions. Kim's aura glowed yellow, which Fern had begun to associate with hope. Mr. Diedrich, their avid bird-watcher, had a blue glow around him, which she had begun to connect with determination. Kim's children all had bright green auras, which Fern now linked with happiness.

Ten minutes later the phone rang and the room became silent. Fern left her post to stand in the crowd around Kim's kitchen phone.

"Uh-huh, I see," said Kim in flat tones. "Well, it's something, actually something pretty good." Kim hung up the phone. She turned to address everyone. "We saved the entire lower bench of the wetlands."

Whoops of joy rippled around the room.

Kim held up her hand. "But they found a loophole and we'll have to cede the upper bench."

Groans resounded. Fern felt sorely disappointed. She'd wanted to save everything.

"They're going to build about three hundred fifty homes there over the next three years. The eucalyptus grove will be saved, and they've agreed we can do some research to discover what value it has as a Native American astro-archeological site, and then it will have some serious protection."

"That's a victory in my book," a familiar voice said somewhere behind Fern.

Fern spun around to find Tristán standing a few feet behind her. "Tristán!" Fern dashed over to him. "I'm so glad you came."

"It was important to me, Fern," Tristán said. "Like I said before, I fight for the things I believe in."

"I know," Fern began, "and I really like that about you. As a matter of fact, there's a lot that I like about you. Tristán, I'm so sorry I've been such an ass. I should have been more trusting, but I don't know. I was just scared. Please believe me that I won't let anything like that happen ever again." Fern studied Tristán's aura, which moved close around him in a dark shade of blue.

Tristán smiled wryly. "I'd have to see it to believe it."

"I'll show you if you'll give me a second chance," Fern coaxed with her best smile.

She noticed Tristán's aura lighten to a shade close to teal and move a bit away from his body. Even though he didn't answer her, she took his aura as a sign that he was opening up. She took a deep breath and jumped right in. "I've been learning from a *curandera* who is also a *mamá*—that's what they call women who have the spiritual abilities of a shaman. And I came to an impulsive conclusion about you. And, well, I really messed up." Fern paused and bit her lip slightly. Could she tell him everything? Would he think it was weird? She had to tell him if she wanted to gain his trust again. "I see energy lines and colors around people and stuff. I misinterpreted your, your . . ."

"You mean you see auras?" Tristán offered.

"Yeah," Fern said, relieved. "How do you know about that?"

"Someone taught a class at Four Crows," Tristán said simply.

"Oh, did you take the class? Can you see auras?" Fern asked anxiously.

"Once I saw waving lines between my fingers, but that's it," Tristán said. "So do you see them all the time?"

"Not all the time. Mostly I see auras around you," Fern admitted. "The first aura I ever saw was around you, and it was gray."

"Ugh." Tristán frowned.

"I know," Fern laughed. "You looked like Eeyore with that storm cloud that always follows him around." Fern held up her hands as if she were holding on to a cloud. She dropped her hands and shrugged. "I thought the grayness meant you were just shady, because I saw the same color aura around a guy with a bad rep, and then you were talking to those girls."

"My cousins," Tristán said dryly.

"Yeah. I'm a bit of a hothead and can be kinda impulsive that way. But the point is, I finally figured out that auras have more to do with my perception of colors and emotions, and that first time you had just seen me get into an accident."

"I thought you were knocked unconscious and everyone had ignored you. They were all yelling at each other. I didn't know if you would be bleeding or really hurt in some way." Tristán paused as if he were seeing the accident all over again. "I've been at an accident scene like that before, when I had to pull someone out of a wrecked car." Tristán looked into Fern's eyes. "I'm really glad you were okay."

"Yeah, it was kind of a silly accident," Fern said.

"But it's how we met," Tristán said. "And that's no accident." Tristán took Fern's hand. "So would you go on a date with me?" Tristán smiled sheepishly.

"Anytime," Fern said, finding it hard not to bounce on her toes.

Tristán looked deep into Fern's eyes. "How about right now?"

Fern nodded. "Sounds good to me."

Tristán jerked his head in the direction of the front door. He and Fern jostled through the hordes of people celebrating their victory. Fern felt as if she were riding a wave of bubbles. Kim intercepted them before they reached the door. "Where are you two off to?"

"We're going on a date!" Fern exclaimed as she squeezed Tristán's hand.

He pulled Fern in close. "Yeah, I'm taking my girl out."

Fern gazed at Tristán. His aura pulsed that rosy, I'm-falling-in-love color, and suddenly he leaned over and kissed Fern tenderly. His soft lips pressed against hers for one perfect, magical moment, and then they walked out into the sunshine, holding hands.

She was by far the happiest girl in the world.

Twenty-eight

Xochitl gripped the handlebars of her bike, turning it away from the side of the garage, where it had rested unused for several days. A fountain of morning glory vine had grown ivylike leaves and soft purple flowers around her bike. She ripped at a vine that had twined itself around the spokes of the bike's front wheel and tossed the tendrils to the ground.

Xochitl swung her leg over the bike and began pedaling toward the Santa Ana River with the intention of following it to the ocean. As she rode through the neighborhood, the heat rose in undulating waves off the asphalt streets. The warm wind dried the back of her throat. She squeezed the grips, guiding the bike over the sandy and rocky path preceding the bike trail. Tall eucalyptus, sycamores, cottonwoods, and drooping willows grew on the left side of the two-lane paved trail. To her right, boulders made up the embankment that led down to the Santa Ana River.

Ever since Nana had come home from the hospital a few days ago, Xochitl had felt a strong urge to get to the ocean. But she couldn't leave her nana at first. She was so relieved that Nana was well. And on top of Nana's recovery, Xochitl felt ecstatic to realize the truth about her new friends. She just wanted to stay put at home and not do anything that would shatter her newfound security. But Nana would never let Xochitl play it that safe. And, to be honest, Xochitl didn't want to anymore. After Nana had begun to see some of her clients again, Xochitl knew the time had come to make this trek to the sea.

Xochitl could smell the ocean's salty air floating down the watery corridor. She didn't know what she would do when she got there, but she knew she was heading in the right direction. Xochitl smiled when she saw a big brown pelican dive-bomb a silver fish that had flopped out of the river. The closer she rode to the ocean, the higher the river rose. Swimming—or in this case, flying—fish must mean she was very close.

The bike trail dipped underneath the Victoria Street Bridge. When the trail rose, Xochitl could see the palm trees swaying in rows on either side of the river mouth, and the white line of crashing surf. She pedaled harder. A snowy egret stood on spindly legs in dark blue water that snaked through tall marsh grasses on her left. She squinted against the setting sun, which was about a hand's width from the horizon.

At the end of the trail, Xochitl hopped off her bike and walked it over the top of the rocky embankment. She crouched over her bike as she pushed it through the soft sand under the cement bridge. Cars roared above her as they sped along Pacific Coast Highway. She pushed the bike up the sand dune onto the northernmost point of Newport Beach. In front of her was a brown lifeguard tower, and across the river she could see the fire rings of Huntington Beach.

Xochitl propped her bike against a NO DOGS sign and kicked the stand into place. She locked the rusty bike, laughing to herself and wondering who would ever steal it. She took her towel out of a metal basket and began marching through the sand, taking in gulps of sea air.

A short hike later she stood on the sand shelf above the booming waves pounding hard onto packed sand. With eyes glued to the blue-green faces of the breaking waves, Xochitl dropped her towel and peeled off her shorts. She watched a sandpiper poke its long beak into the sand, seeking edible creatures.

"Hope you find what you're looking for," Xochitl said to the bird.

Xochitl pulled her shirt over her head. Adjusting her triangle bathing-suit top, she walked directly into the ocean. Wearing this bathing suit was almost more daring than anything she had done since arriving in America. Xochitl spun to face the shore when the first wave hit, allowing the cold spray to splash her back. She turned and trudged against the swirling water. The ocean stretched out in front of her for miles. In the distance, she could see the jagged outline of Catalina Island. Last week she might have debated whether or not she should keep walking into the ocean until she couldn't go any farther. But that wasn't what she had come for today.

For the past few months, Xochitl had been visiting the river because it had reminded her of the times she swam with her sister. But it was never the same. In Orange County the river was too low and too dirty to swim in. Today Xochitl had come to the ocean instead, where she *could* swim.

Xochitl dove under a looming wave. She pushed through the current, reaching for the sparkling sun low on the horizon. Xochitl broke the surface of the water with her black hair plastered against her back. As the next wave approached, she turned toward the shore and started swimming. The wave caught Xochitl, lifted her, and gave her a ride.

Xochitl gave out a holler, in love with the freedom she felt because she could trust this wave long enough to let it carry her along. Then, out of the corner of her eye, Xochitl saw something or someone riding the wave with her. She turned and her breath caught in her throat. There, beside her on the wave, was Graciela. Tears welled in Xochitl's eyes. Was it possible? Scared that it was just a dream but more hopeful than she had been in months, Xochitl reached her hand toward Graciela.

Her sister firmly clasped her hand, interlocking their fingers once more. Tears fell freely down Xochitl's cheeks, and she laughed out loud. Chills raced each other down to her toes. Xochitl took in all of Graciela's features, from her pug nose and heart-shaped face, identical to her own, to the smile that reached her eyes.

"I can't believe I've finally found you," Xochitl said joyously.

I have never left you, Graciela said. *And I never will.*

"How come you're revealing yourself to me now, after all the times I tried to talk to you?" Xochitl asked.

You were so focused on the fact that you didn't have me in a physical form that you couldn't see what we did have, Graciela laughed. *Not until you remembered your faith in the most precious thing we shared.*

"Magic," Xochitl said wistfully. "I guess that's why you talked to Marina first."

It is, Graciela said. *But from now on, I will be only talking to you, Xochitl.*

The wave subsided and, with it, the image of Graciela.

Xochitl scanned the ocean in vain. "Where are you? Graciela?"

I'm right here, spoke Graciela's voice.

A gray-flanked dolphin flipped in the water only ten feet from Xochitl. The dolphin swam in a circle around her. Xochitl watched the dorsal fin divide the water. She felt a rush of joy as the dolphin's entire side undulated through the wave. In the ocean mist, Xochitl saw the outline of her sister's smiling face.

Xochitl watched the dolphin join another dolphin, then another. Xochitl spun around and found herself in the middle of a dolphin pod with more than twenty members. A dolphin flipped backward, its tail catching the sun as it hit the horizon, the last light of the day. And as it sometimes does when it sets over the ocean, the sun ended the day with a green flash of light shooting across the horizon.

You are mi hermana, Graciela's voice echoed all around her. *I will never leave you.*

The music of the ocean filled Xochitl's ears. The seagulls squawked. The dolphins chirped and squeaked their songs. The waves collided with each other and the sand. The ocean was singing. Xochitl floated on her back with her arms outstretched and her bracelet tight around her wrist. Above her, tangerine, raspberry, and golden yellow veins streaked against a cornflower-blue sky. Xochitl closed her eyes and imagined she and Graciela flew with the seagulls toward the eastern horizon, where the stars began to shine.

Twenty-nine

On the last day of summer vacation, Mr. Garcia and Xochitl decided to throw a huge party to celebrate Rogelia's recovery. The mariachi band donned their white and gold outfits and played in the corner of the Garcia's backyard, next to the vegetable patch. Brightly colored banners were strung from the avocado tree to the frame of the house. Rogelia sat at the small table next to her garden and watched the party guests mingle.

The rich smell of carne asada cooking on the barbeque wafted toward Rogelia, causing her to turn and look around. Xochitl animatedly flipped her hands in the air as she spoke to her father and helped him place the cooked meat on a platter. Rogelia had not seen her first grandbaby this happy in a very long time. A light shone from Xochitl's eyes. The brightness that had faded the day of the accident was back.

Movement caught Rogelia's attention. Tristán was pushing Fern on the swing that hung from the avocado tree. Fern giggled as he caught her and the swing and gave her a kiss. Danny and Miguel ran by and teased her. Fern jumped off the swing to chase them. Fern's mother caught hold of her and gave her a quick squeeze before heading out to dance. Mrs. Fuego had cut down on her nighttime partying to spend more time at home. Just because Fern was strong and able to put on a happy face, it wasn't right for her optimism to be taken for granted.

Marina and her mother also danced together on the grass in front of the band. It was good to see Mrs. Peralta in Santa Ana without that scowl upon her face. She looked a little out of place in her navy Chanel dress, but she was clearly enjoying her daughter's happiness. Nearby, Monica, Samantha, and their father waltzed to a Mexican polka led by the accordion player.

Rogelia sighed happily. Her students had learned that a spell works only if the outcome benefits the highest good and if they speak from their hearts. And working together, they had healed her, possibly even saved her life. What more could anyone ask of their apprentices? She couldn't have been prouder of them.

Rogelia stood up and felt the creak in her bones. She glanced meaningfully at her apprentices. As if on cue, Marina, Fern, and Xochitl turned to look at their mentor. Rogelia beckoned them to her. Without hesitation, the girls dropped whatever they were doing and joined each other at Rogelia's side.

"*Mi'jitas*, how can I begin to thank you for healing me?"

Rogelia asked, beaming at the three of them. "I'm so proud of you, so grateful for your love. But you know, we're coming to the end of summer, and your commitment to me is just about over," Rogelia said, grinning widely. "I want to give you a hug before this party takes you all away from me."

They wrapped their arms around each other and gave a tight four-person hug.

"This doesn't have to be the end," Fern whimpered.

Rogelia pulled away and looked at each of the girls in turn. "Does this mean you want to return to your lessons?"

Fern, Xochitl, and Marina looked at each other and smiled. "Yes!" they all answered simultaneously.

"I get the first *plácita*!" Xochitl exclaimed. "And not just because I've been with you the longest, Nana, but because I want to. I'm going to need it with school starting on Monday."

"I'll be there for you, Xochitl," Fern reminded her, and she gave her friend a squeeze on the shoulder.

"And I'll be starting a MECHA group at my school," Marina said.

"MECHA?" Rogelia asked.

"Movimiento Estudiantil Chicano de Aztlán," Marina said with a perfect Spanish accent. "The Chicano Student Movement of Aztlán. Won't that be great?"

"Yes, it will." Rogelia smiled secretively, knowing what adventures lay ahead for her girls.

Magical Spells and Incantations for Beginners and Believers

Before performing any spell or incantation, make sure you follow the guidelines used in *Rogelia's House of Magic:*

1. Be responsible. Try to get your wish without magic first. And only ask for one wish at a time.
2. Be clear. The surest way to get what you want is to have clear and precise wishes.
3. Be honest. Make sure no one could be harmed by your wish coming true.
4. Be open. Keep an open mind so that you will recognize all the different ways your magical wish can show up in your life.

Charging a Crystal Wand

Wands are special instruments of magic that help you direct your intention. Wands made of crystal or with a crystal point carry with them all the power of the earth and the ability to make dreams real and tangible. Charging a magical object makes this tool specifically yours and gives it an extra boost. Charging a crystal wand begins with erasing and clearing your wand of all negativity or former energy. Dip your wand into a bowl of seawater or salt water three times. As you do this, say:

> *I release energies of old and impure,*
> *Imprints of others cannot endure.*
> *I seal this wand with my own intent*
> *To create a life of empowerment.*

Next, you want to fill your wand with your energy. Hold on to your wand, close your eyes, and imagine a fire in your belly that travels up your arms and into your wand. Place the crystal wand where it can be bathed in moonlight for several hours. Your wand will soak up your intent and the moon's energy of dreams and be ready for more spellwork.

Confidence Incantation

On the night of the full moon, surround yourself with the things that make you feel good—including wearing a favorite color, perfume or oil, clothes, etc. Prepare a comfort food or drink. At moonrise, rub a dime-sized amount of olive oil or an essential oil of your favorite scent on a candle. As you do this, keep a straight back and imagine yourself to be confident, self-assured, and poised. Light the candle. If you have any doubts or insecurities, send your fears to the candle and imagine that the flames will transform any uncertainty into trust and conviction. Repeat this incantation three times every hour until you go to sleep.

> *I am the place that Confidence shines through.*
> *I believe in myself to do what I must do.*
> *Rising to the greatness that lives within me,*
> *This I will find when I remain relaxed and free.*

Silky Smooth Skin Spell

INGREDIENTS:
$1/2$ cup organic white sugar
$1/3$ cup avocado oil
1 teaspoon aloe vera gel
1 teaspoon cocoa butter
6 drops lavender essential oil

Mix together the sugar, oil, and aloe vera gel. Place the cocoa butter in a container in a bowl of hot water to soften it. Add the cocoa butter to the first ingredients using a hand mixer on high speed for 3 to 5 minutes. Add the essential oil. Use the sugar scrub in the shower or bath for two continuous nights. Repeat the following incantation three times:

> My dream of [fill in the blank] is coming to me,
> Fast as flying horses doth it flee
> To rest on my lap as sure as can be.

Be sure to rinse out the tub after use, before the ants come marching in.

Creating a Magical Altar

An altar is any place where you go to make a special wish or to feel comfort. Begin by placing symbols that represent the four directions of east, south, west, and north. Symbols can be photos, images, or objects. East can have symbols of wind, air, yellow, animals that fly, or beginnings. South can have symbols of fire, orange, red, a candle, or courage. West can have symbols of water, blue, animals of the sea, or feelings. North can have symbols of earth, green, brown, trees, or family. Add something that represents you. Repeat the incantation:

Magic is true and I believe, too,
That what I wish will come true.
When I honor the directions four,
I will open a magical door.